DEATH ON THE RIO CHIQUITO

A New Mexican Homefront Mystery

DEATH ON THE RIO CHIQUITO

A New Mexican Homefront Mystery

SUSAN McDUFFIE

Cover Design, Interior Design, and Formatting by

www.e.m.tippettsbookdesigns.com

Published by Liafinn Press
ISBN Trade Paperback: 978-0-9997682-8-0

OTHER BOOKS BY
SUSAN MCDUFFIE

The Muirteach MacPhee Mysteries
A MASS FOR THE DEAD
THE FAERIE HILLS
THE WATERGATE: A Muirteach MacPhee Nobelette
THE STUDY OF MURDER
THE DEATH OF A FALCON

THE SUICIDE SKULL

For Salvador, with all my love

Cast of Characters

In San Antonito Pueblo:

Emily Wilson Schwarz: Anglo schoolteacher at the San Antonito Day School

Atencio Montoya: Alcalde or governor of the pueblo

      His wife, Juliana

      Children: Juan, 19, Gilbert, 9, young daughter

Gregorio Cruz, fiscal or sheriff of San Antonito

      His mother, Florencita

Paulina

      Her son Charley

Arturo

Ben

Hilario Mondragon

Demetria Gonzales

      Her mother, Agapita

Minguita

Albertina

Delia and Lorenzo Montoya, a young married couple

Señor Romero: Runs the San Antonito store but lives in La Cañada

      Consuela Romero, his niece

Father Simon, priest for both San Antonito and La Cañada

Professor Bateson, an anthropologist

Here and There:

Mr. Shepherd
Sheriff Wilcox, Sandoval County Sheriff
Sergeant O'Toole, from Albuquerque
Deputy Duran

At La Cañada:

Mavis Miller and her husband, who live in Peña Blanca
Señora and Señor Gallegos
Another Señor Romero
Pedro, Carlos, and Tony: Locals

Glossary

Keres and Zuni:
alcalde: governor, from Spanish (Keres)
beríina: small brown salamander (Keres)
cacique: medicine man or chief, from Spanish (Keres)
ch'úpe: eat (Keres)
fiscal: sheriff, also in charge of the church, from Spanish (Keres)
guw'aadzi: hello (Keres)
manta: traditional dress (Keres)
meleca: an Anglo (Zuni)
p'ákuri: large black and yellow salamander (Keres)
sabana: shawl, from Spanish for bedsheet (Keres)

Spanish:
acequia: irrigation ditch
atole: drink made from roasted blue corn meal
baile: dance
biscochito: cookie, like a sugar cookie typically flavored with anise
bultos: carved and painted wooden statues of saints common in Hispanic New Mexico
camposanto: graveyard
chica: young girl
chicos: in New Mexico, steamed and roasted dried corn

kernels, used in stews (also means boys)

chongo: traditional Native hairstyle, a bun at the back of the head tied with yarn

curandera: medicine woman

hijo: son

hija: daughter

horno: round adobe oven

jueros: white people

osha: root of Ligusticum porteri, traditionally used for coughs and lung trouble

primo: cousin

puta: whore

ristras: chiles, strung together and hung to dry

salón de baile: dance hall

tio: uncle

vigas: beams

vieja: old woman

yerba buena: spearmint

CHAPTER ONE

Emily Wilson Schwarz closed the door of the school building behind her. She took a deep breath of the hot dry afternoon air, smelling the sweet vanilla scent of the ponderosa pines on the mesa that mingled with the pungent scent of horses from the village corrals. Eager to stretch her legs, Emily left the brick San Antonito Pueblo Day School and headed away from the village, toward the fields that bordered the Rio Chiquito, a tiny tributary of the Rio Grande.

A large cottonwood stood close to the river. Emily headed towards it, striding along the border of the alfalfa field, her eyes hungry for anything green, her ears thirsty for the sound of water. It had been a dry year so far. Overhead some buzzards circled, their large wings black against the deep blue sky. Emily shrugged, wondering what they had found.

Nearby she saw Hilario Mondragon hard at work, lifting the gate on one of the *acequias*, the irrigation ditches that led to the fields and provided water for the crops. Hilario's corn looked almost ready to harvest. Above, reddish black cliffs towered up to the mesa tops on either side of the narrow valley.

Emily waved at Hilario, who gestured back. Emily taught three of Hilario's children at the day school. One older daughter was at the boarding school in Santa Fe; the oldest son, Nasario, had enlisted and was serving someplace in the Pacific, fighting.

Emily had been at San Antonito three years now, long enough to settle into teaching at the day school, run by the Federal United Pueblo Association in Albuquerque. Since her arrival, at age twenty-nine, war had broken out. The attack on Pearl Harbor, nearly two years ago now, had changed everything. Emily's brother Tom fought in the Pacific theater, and she constantly worried for him. She wondered if Tom and Nasario were stationed in the same unit, over there on the other side of the world.

Aside from the village boys in the service, and rationing cards for groceries and gas, life in the little Indian pueblo of San Antonito seemed remarkably unchanged by the war. Not like Racine. On her last visit home earlier in the summer, her mother had been sick with worry over Tom, and every night her dad drank far too many bourbons as he listened to the war news on the radio. It had been a relief to leave them both and come back to her job in New Mexico, teaching the five-to-twelve-year-olds during the day, and leading some adult education classes in health and home economics in the evenings. Canning and sewing classes proved popular with the ladies.

DEATH ON THE RIO CHIQUITO

The women of San Antonito did their part for the war effort, knitting wool socks for the troops. People took them up to the Red Cross in Santa Fe when they went into town for supplies. Emily had also helped the tribal officials organize a scrap drive, and folks had ransacked their barns and sheds for old tires and metal; they had managed to get over five hundred pounds of material.

San Antonito didn't yet have any electricity, so copies of the *Santa Fe New Mexican* folks bought from Romero's grocery in the village provided the only war news. Creased and wrinkled copies of the newspaper got passed around from house to house. Although the fighting sometimes seemed very far away, the community had been touched by it. Mothers worried for their sons everywhere, Emily thought, in Racine, and in little San Antonito.

The buzzards still circled, and Emily watched them swoop down on something near the big cottonwood. Probably a rabbit, she thought, but decided to go take a closer look. She could do with a little more exercise. There weren't any adult classes later on, and she was looking forward to a quiet evening, a sandwich, a cup of coffee, and maybe a novel. She had Daphne du Maurier's latest, *Hungry Hill*, which she had picked up while in Racine.

As Emily approached the tree the buzzards flew back into the sky with a rush, but kept on circling. Emily felt their eyes on her, watching from above. She shuddered and took a deep breath, catching a whiff of something on the breeze. Something dead. More than a rabbit. Coyote? A dog?

The ancient cottonwood grew next to the Rio Chiquito, its massive roots emerging from the undergrowth of salt cedar and Russian olive trees to seek water from the riverbed. Emily pushed her way through the scrub, down to the bank of the stream, not seeing any sign of a rabbit or coyote. Then she stopped short.

A body lay sprawled amid the roots of the cottonwood, partly in the river. Almost as though whoever it was had tripped and fallen into the water.

Emily went over and knelt, her heart racing, and gently touched the body. As soon as she felt the young man's cold, inert form she knew there was no chance.

Beneath the brown skin she saw the bluish pallor of death. A splash of dark red stained the man's chest, oddly displaced against the white shirt like some young child's angry watercolor. The clotted blood seeped from the wound and mixed with the waters of the Rio Chiquito, a red trail flowing down the current towards the Rio Grande.

Her gaze went to the dead man's face, and Emily belatedly recognized the corpse. It was Juan, the older son of Atencio Montoya, the governor of the pueblo.

CHAPTER TWO

EMILY STARED, UNBELIEVING. Juan. What could have happened? She suddenly felt icy cold and strangely clammy, and her heart refused to slow to a reasonable pace. She stood up and looked towards Hilario's field but saw no sign of the farmer; he must have headed for home. The canyon sat quietly, peaceful in the afternoon sunlight despite the dead youth at her feet, the slight breeze rustling the leaves of the cottonwood the only sound in the immense silence.

Nothing could be done for Juan. There was little chance of the corpse being washed away or moved by the Rio Chiquito, which honestly wasn't much larger than a small Wisconsin creek. She would have to leave him here, go up to the pueblo, and get some help.

Her decision made, Emily stood and turned towards the

village. She hurried back through the field and walked quickly up the dirt road that led into the settlement itself, towards the plaza.

She passed the schoolhouse, on the outskirts of the small village. Breathless, she approached the adobe houses surrounding the plaza. She saw few people about, not unusual for this time of day. A few dogs slept in the dusty earth, and the afternoon sun cast long shadows across the empty square. At first she walked towards the Montoyas' house, then she stopped. How could she knock on the *alcalde's* door and tell him his own son lay dead in an alfalfa field? The *fiscal,* Gregorio Cruz, functioned as the sheriff, the tribal official second in command to the alcalde. Perhaps it would be better to tell Gregorio, rather than bring the heartbreaking news of Juan's death to Mr. Montoya and his wife.

A couple of men lounged outside the small grocery store, owned by a Mr. Romero from the nearby town of La Cañada. They were speaking with a short woman in a traditional calico cotton dress, her *sabana,* or fringed shawl, pulled over her head. Emily recognized Paulina.

"*Guw'aadzi,*" Emily greeted them in their native language, and then switched to English. She was far from fluent in Keres, even after living at San Antonito for three years. She encouraged her students to speak English at school, although most families still spoke the tribal language at home.

"*Guw'aadzi,* Miss Schwarz," Paulina replied. "Have you seen Charley? My son? He said he was going into Albuquerque yesterday but he didn't come home."

"Don't worry, Paulina," Arturo interjected. "He'll be back when he sobers up."

"My son doesn't drink anymore," Paulina protested. "He's a good boy. You shouldn't talk like that about him."

"I haven't seen him, Paulina," Emily put in, anxious to speak with the *fiscal*. She didn't know Charley and Paulina well. "Is Gregorio around?"

Paulina walked away, looking annoyed by the set of her back. Arturo took a long smoke on his cigarette before he answered Emily.

"I think he went off chasing that horse of his. She ran away again. Kind of like Charley, maybe. I might bolt too, if my mother was always on my case like Paulina."

"Where is Gregorio? I need to speak with him."

"Like I said, Miss Schwarz, he's off chasing his fool horse. Of course," Arturo continued with a chuckle, "Gregorio's stubborn too. He's too pig-headed to tie her up."

Emily smiled, despite the grave nature of her errand. Gregorio's horse was a joke in the village. "Well, I need him," she said, her smile vanishing as the full import of why she was here hit her again. "It's urgent."

Arturo finally realized Emily was serious. "Come on," he said, nodding in the direction of a ramshackle truck that was parked behind the store. "I'll give you a ride up there."

"Thank you." Emily followed Arturo over to the truck, a battered old Ford. "So it's still running?"

"As long as my gas ration holds out. But I don't think Gregorio's too far away. That horse probably just wandered up the canyon, towards that back trail, the one that leads across the mesa to the mines. We'll find him all right." They got in. Arturo started the engine and pulled out. He took another look at Emily, who sat nervously twisting her skirt in her hands. Arturo didn't say anything else for a minute. "Is it bad?" he finally asked tentatively, as they headed north up the narrowing canyon on a rutted, dusty one-lane dirt road that followed the river into the hills.

"Yes, Arturo, I'm afraid it is. Bad news."

"Atencio's closer."

"No," she snapped. "I can't tell Mr. Montoya about this. Not yet."

Arturo didn't ask anything else. The canyon narrowed and the sun disappeared behind the cliffs. Emily shivered. The air was thin here in northern New Mexico, and once the sun went down it got cold quickly. Or maybe that wasn't the reason she was shaking.

"Hey, there's Gregorio now," Arturo said, bringing the truck to shuddering stop.

Emily saw Gregorio, lean and lanky, leading an equally lean old piebald horse down the dusty road near the river. His expression turned to a puzzled smile as he saw Emily climb down from the truck, followed by Arturo.

"*Guw'aadzi*, Miss Schwarz. What brings you to these parts?" Gregorio asked, still smiling. "Did you just come by to admire Flossie?" He patted the horse, who stood placidly next to him, not looking at all like a renegade.

"Sheriff Cruz, someone's been killed." The words tumbled from her mouth, like the rushing current of the Rio Chiquito. "Juan. The alcalde's son. I couldn't go and tell him—I . . . I just couldn't." Emily's voice was trembling. Behind her she heard Arturo's shocked breath as he took in the news.

"What happened? Where did you find him?"

"He's lying in the river, over by Hilario Mondragon's field. I went for a walk after the children were dismissed, and I found him. Over by that big cottonwood tree, caught in the roots. I'm sure it's Juan.

"Damn kids, playing in the creek," Gregorio said.

"No, it wasn't that. He didn't drown, Sheriff. He'd been shot."

Gregorio's gaze darkened, and he said something in Keres to Arturo. Emily only understood a few words of the language. She had no idea what Gregorio had said, but it didn't sound good. How could it?

"Arturo will take you back to the school," Gregorio said to her after a moment. "Wait for me there, I'll get some men and we'll go take a look." He paused, eyes narrowed in thought. "I guess you'll have to show us where. You'll be OK with that?"

Emily nodded. She could manage to do what was necessary.

"And Arturo," Cruz continued, "when you're done, drive up to Cañada and ask Señor Romero to use the phone at the mercantile; we'd better call the UPA office in Albuquerque and the sheriff in Bernalillo." There were no phones in San Antonito.

Arturo and Emily climbed back into the truck and drove the short mile to the village. The shadows from the cliffs had grown longer, and the air chill. Emily couldn't stop trembling. "You OK, Miss Schwarz?" Arturo inquired, concerned. Emily nodded tightly, not trusting herself to speak. They passed the plaza and the church, left the main part of the village, and reached the schoolhouse, where Arturo stopped the truck and let her out. The sun had dropped behind the western hills and the light was quickly fading.

"You'll be all right, Miss Schwarz?"

Emily nodded again, and watched Arturo's truck drive off and disappear down the road to Cañada in a cloud of dust before she went inside. While she waited for Gregorio, she went upstairs to the teacher's quarters and put on her plaid jacket. She couldn't get warm, and kept shivering. She found a couple of flashlights and checked to make sure the batteries worked. As she headed back to the schoolroom, a sharp knock at the door made her jump. Then she realized it must be Gregorio. She hurried to open up, and saw him standing there along with a few other men. Some of them held old kerosene lanterns. She recognized Hilario among the group.

"Let's go see what's what," Gregorio said, nodding when he saw the flashlights in her hands. They didn't need them just yet, there was still a little light, but it would be full dark on the way back. Emily stepped out and shut the door. Gregorio had tied his mare to the iron picket fence that surrounded the schoolyard, and left her there as the party set out walking. The evening breeze blew down the canyon, and Emily was glad she'd put on the jacket.

As Emily led the little procession over towards the river and the cottonwood, Gregorio said, "I thought Juan was working for that big construction firm.

"That's right," Hilario replied.

Emily had heard that several of the men from the pueblo had found jobs with a Texas construction company. "Where are they working?" she asked. "I hear the bus every morning. They pick up the men at five-thirty, just down the road where it heads up toward Cañada."

"I don't know. Nobody's said. The money's good, though," Gregorio replied. "McKee," he muttered reflectively. "That's the name, I think."

They approached the cottonwood. The dusk had strengthened, and at first Emily had trouble seeing the body. She hoped for a moment she had dreamed it, and adjusted her spectacles. No, there was the white of the shirt, a gleaming light patch in the growing shadows.

"Here. He's over here." Emily gestured, then hesitated, and Gregorio led the men the rest of the way to the riverbank. She pointed out the corpse and looked away while the men gathered around it. She didn't think she could face seeing it again. She heard the group speaking quietly among themselves in Keres.

"It's Juan, all right," Gregorio finally said to her in English. "What was he doing out here to get himself shot? Maybe he was hunting? Had an accident?"

Hilario shook his head. "I don't see any gun, Gregorio. Did you, Miss Schwarz, when you found him?"

Emily shook her head. "No. No, I didn't. He was just lying there." Her eyes filled with tears and she blinked them away. "I touched him. He was already cold." She bit her lip, reluctant to say more, afraid she might break down.

Gregorio sighed. "I'd better go tell Atencio and Juliana. Looks to me like he's been in the water for a while. I don't think he went to work today. Hilario, can you and Santiago stay here with the body? I guess we'd better not move it. Arturo should be back soon, with news from Bernalillo. Hope he got ahold of the sheriff."

The men nodded, and they waited while the darkness strengthened. Emily shuddered, thinking of the corpse. Finally, they saw headlights on the road by the fields and heard the unmistakable rattle of Arturo's truck. Emily sighed with relief.

"Once Arturo gets here, we'll take you back to the school," Gregorio said. "You must want some rest."

"I'm OK," she insisted, determined.

Gregorio nodded, and waved his lantern in the direction of the road. They heard Arturo get out of the truck and start across the field towards them, his footsteps rustling the alfalfa.

"I spoke with the United Pueblo Agency in Albuquerque," Arturo said when he reached them. "Someone was there working late. They're sending somebody up from the Bernalillo sheriff's office, along with one of the UPA men. Should be here in an hour or so, as soon as they can drive up. They asked us not to move him." He looked closer. "Jesus. Poor kid. Who could have done this?"

"I don't know," Gregorio said. Emily saw his fingers tighten around the handle of the lantern he held.

"Maybe he was fooling around, him and some other kids," Hilario said. "Somebody had a gun, they got some beers from the mercantile up in Cañada, maybe got drunk and had an accident, and the others got scared and left him."

"Damn kids," Gregorio muttered. "I should go tell Atencio. Here, Miss Schwarz, I'll get you back to the school."

"I'd like to see the Montoyas," Emily protested. "I found him, after all. I feel responsible."

Gregorio looked at her a moment, then nodded grimly. "Suit yourself."

They stopped at the school long enough for Gregorio to retrieve his horse, and walked the rest of the way into the village, Flossie plodding alongside. The Montoyas' house was a large one right off the plaza, built, as all the houses were, of mud-plastered adobe bricks. A long portal shaded the porch and front door from the sun during the day. Now, in darkness, the yellow light of a kerosene lamp spilled out through the screen door and the windows. Emily could smell beans and chile and coffee, and the scent of the wood-burning range as they approached the house.

"*Guw'aadzi*," Gregorio called.

"Come on in," Atencio replied. Gregorio pushed the door open.

Inside, the family was just finishing supper. A long table stood against one wall and Atencio and his wife, Juliana, sat on a bench at the table, along with their six-year-old daughter and nine-year-old younger son. Emily taught both children at the day school. They smiled shyly at their teacher, but Emily couldn't smile back.

Along the wall, brightly colored Pendleton blankets, as well as articles of traditional clothing—men's dance kilts and women's black *mantas*—were draped over a wooden pole that hung suspended from the ceiling. The old-fashioned lamp sat on the table, the soft glow of the flame illuminating the faces of the children and their father. Juliana rose from the bench when she saw the visitors and went to get two bowls from a shelf near the stove, which stood in the kitchen off the main room.

"Miss Schwarz. You must eat," Juliana said.

"Sorry, Juliana, we can't," Gregorio said. "We have bad news, I'm afraid."

At Gregorio's grim tone and expression, Juliana moved back toward the dining table. "What is it?" she said, her voice suddenly serious. "Is it Juan? What's happened?"

Gregorio spoke quietly to her and Atencio in Keres. Emily heard her own name amid the unfamiliar words. Juliana gave a shriek, and one of the bowls fell to the floor and shattered. The children watched, eyes wide with fright, while Juliana collapsed into tears. Atencio went to his wife and held her, trying to calm her a little. Emily dragged a chair over and got Juliana to sit, then brought her a glass of water. Atencio sank down on the bench near his wife, an ashen cast to his dark skin.

"You saw him?" Juliana asked Emily, before dissolving into tears again. Emily reluctantly nodded. Juliana gulped water and fought for composure. "I thought he'd gone into Albuquerque yesterday," she said shakily. "With some friends, he said they had gas coupons. But he didn't say goodbye. He just disappeared yesterday afternoon."

The day before had been Sunday, Emily thought. The body could have been there that long, she guessed. She wasn't all that familiar with dead bodies. "So he wasn't home last night?" she asked.

Juliana shook her head. "I just thought they were late coming back from Albuquerque. You know what boys are like. Oh, my Juanito, my son—" She started sobbing again, the sounds deep and ragged. The children started crying too.

Atencio spoke to his wife, his tone gentle, and she quieted a little, biting her lip. Emily was afraid Juliana would draw blood.

Gregorio said something to Atencio in Keres. Atencio nodded and got up, looking suddenly years older. "I'm going with Gregorio," he said to his wife in English, then glanced at Emily. "Maybe you could stay here with her, Miss Schwarz, at least until someone else can come? I'll stop at Demetria's house, and ask her. She'll be over soon."

Emily nodded. "Of course."

As the men left, Emily tried to smile at the children, but they kept crying, scared. Juliana had stopped sobbing and sat, staring woodenly ahead, ignoring her daughter and younger son. Emily heard the door open and a neighbor woman entered quietly, then another. Word had gotten out. Within a few minutes the room was full of people coming to help.

She told the women what had happened, and where Atencio and Gregorio had gone. "They have to wait for the UPA, and the Sandoval County sheriff," Emily said. "They may not be able to bring him back tonight." At those words Juliana's tears started flowing again. One of the women slipped an arm around her and led her into the bedroom to rest.

Emily busied herself with the children, trying to make conversation and get their minds off things. Another of the women had brought her own children along, and eventually all the kids sat together on the bench, talking and watching the grownups. Someone made a fresh pot of coffee, and Emily sipped at a cup thankfully while they waited for the men to return. The women talked among themselves, quietly, not wanting to disturb Juliana.

"You found him?" Demetria Gonzales asked her.

Emily nodded, and took another sip of coffee, glad of the sugar in it. She had always liked Demetria, who regularly came to the home economics classes Emily taught most Wednesday evenings. She guessed Demetria was about her own age, but married to Joe for several years. The couple had no children. Now Joe was off fighting. Demetria had told Emily he was a tail gunner.

Of medium height and build, with sharp brown eyes, Demetria wore her black hair in a traditional cut, with bangs and a bun at the back, but she had on a flowered modern style shirtwaist dress she had sewn herself. A fine seamstress, Demetria really didn't need to come to any sewing classes, but Emily guessed she liked the socializing.

"What happened?" Demetria asked again.

"It looked like he'd been shot. We'll know more when the men get back."

"With a rifle?"

"I don't know," Emily said. "Just one big bloody wound in his chest."

"Not a shotgun, then," Demetria said. "Most men around here have shotguns, but there are some rifles too. Small caliber. But who would want to shoot Juanito? He's just a kid."

"Old enough to work, though." Gregorio had mentioned Juan's employment, and Emily wondered how the family would fare without his income. Finding his body made her feel responsible, somehow, for his death. Involved. "Do you know what his job was?"

"He worked with that McKee Construction. Juliana said he made good money there. My Joe was thinking of seeing if they needed more men, but then he enlisted. I'm not sure where they're working, they can't say. Some kind of war work. Hush-hush."

Emily nodded. "Who were Juan's friends? Did he have a girlfriend?" *Maybe somebody got jealous*, she thought, but didn't say it.

Demetria lowered her voice. "He used to go with a girl from La Cañada. A Spanish girl. But Atencio and Juliana didn't

16

approve and I guess her folks didn't much like it either. They broke up; at least I think they did. Since then I don't think he's dated anybody much, at least not that Juliana knew of. She never said anything about it. In high school he and Delia were close, but she married Lorenzo Montoya, Juan's cousin. Juan sure was a handsome boy, though. Here," Demetria said, taking Emily's coffee cup and heading over to the washbasin. Emily followed her, and dried the cups as Demetria washed them.

"I'll finish up," Emily offered.

Demetria nodded. "I'll try and get the little ones to bed." She left Emily with the dishpan and flour sack towel, and collected the two Montoya children, leading them to the other room with one arm around each child.

It seemed an age before a noise at the front door woke Emily, who was dozing in a chair. Most of the women had gone back to their own families; only Demetria remained. Juliana, Demetria had said, was asleep, but at the faint creak of the door Emily saw Juliana enter the main room, her face ashen and her eyes red.

Atencio stood in the doorway, and Emily could just see other faces behind him in the darkness. She glanced at her watch. It was close to one o'clock. She glimpsed two men in uniform—from the sheriff's office and the UPA, she guessed. Atencio looked at his wife and shook his head grimly, saying something to her in Keres, and Juliana's eyes filled with tears again.

The men shuffled in. The two newcomers took off

their hats, and the large room suddenly felt crowded. "Mrs. Montoya, I'm very sorry for your loss," said one man, wearing a sheriff's badge, and Juliana began wailing. Demetria put her arms around her friend, speaking gently to her in Keres, and led her to sit down next to Atencio on the bench.

Demetria offered fresh coffee to the sheriff and his deputy. Gregorio took another cup as well and sat down next to Emily.

"What's going on?" she asked him.

"Juan was shot, but it sure wasn't a shotgun. Most likely a handgun. Since it's a homicide, the sheriff wants to take the body back to the morgue in Bernalillo before he releases it for burial."

Juliana overheard this and began crying again. Atencio spoke to her in Keres, probably urging her to calm down, and after a moment, her wails gave way to quiet tears.

"That's terrible," Emily said to Gregorio. The sheriff approached, and Emily turned towards him.

"Miss Schwarz? You're the teacher here at the day school?" he said.

"Yes, sir," Emily replied.

"I'm Thomas Wilcox, sheriff of Sandoval County. You found the body?"

Emily nodded and told him how she had discovered Juan that afternoon. It seemed a lifetime ago. Now the lives of the Montoya family would never be the same.

"We'll want to speak with you some more. Did you see anything else on your walk that seemed suspicious?"

Emily glanced at her watch, trying to marshal her thoughts. Her pupils would show up for school in just a few hours, and she hadn't gotten much sleep. Sheriff Wilcox noticed the glance. "You must be tired, ma'am."

"Yes, and there's school today. I have to be there, I'm the only teacher."

"Why don't you head on back to your place now, ma'am. I can get Deputy Duran here to give you a lift back. I'll come by and speak with you after school hours. Will that suit?"

Emily nodded gratefully. She said goodnight to Demetria; Atencio and his wife had retreated to the back room. She nodded to Gregorio and then left with Deputy Duran.

The deputy, a skinny man with wiry auburn hair, ushered her outside and opened the passenger door of the sheriff's car for her. "You live at the day school, right, ma'am?" he asked as he turned the key in the ignition.

"Yes, upstairs, in the teacher's quarters there."

"I'm Gerald Duran, ma'am. My family's from Cañada, actually, but I'm married now and live in Bernalillo. Guess Sheriff Wilcox thought I'd be a good man for this job, since I know the area."

Emily nodded, trying to keep her eyes open. Now that she'd left the alcalde's house, she realized how the day's events had drained her.

"Schwarz. That sounds like a German name."

Emily sighed inwardly. It was late and she didn't really feel like explaining. "My father's parents were from Austria. My mother's family came over on the Mayflower."

"My family came up here with the Spaniard Oñate in 1598," Deputy Duran countered. "My family's lived at Cañada since the 1700s when it was founded." He pulled up to the dark brick school building. "Well, here we are. Goodnight, Miss Schwarz. Sheriff Wilcox will be by to speak with you some more in the afternoon. Say around four o'clock? Will that suit?"

Emily nodded, thanked the deputy, and left the car. She made her way into the school building and turned on her flashlight, wishing there was electricity in San Antonito as she climbed the wooden stairs to her bedroom on the second floor. Too tired to light the kerosene lamp, she relied on the flashlight as she readied herself for bed and lay down. Despite her exhaustion, she didn't fall asleep immediately. Every time she closed her eyes, she saw Juan's face and bloody chest, his body lying tangled in the roots of the big cottonwood tree.

CHAPTER
THREE

Somehow Emily managed to teach that next school day. The students seemed quiet, unusually subdued in class, but she heard them chattering during recess. Atencio's children did not attend, of course. Emily sighed, relieved, as she rang the final bell, dismissed her students, and went to the kitchen to get a cup of coffee before the sheriff arrived. She had just drained the last of it, sweet with evaporated milk and sugar, when she heard a car pull up outside. She went and opened the door to the school building to see Sheriff Wilcox striding up the path to the front steps. Tall and lanky, the sheriff seemed at ease as he approached.

"Miss Schwarz?"

"Hello, Sheriff Wilcox. Will you come in? I've just made some coffee. We can talk in the classroom, or the school kitchen, if you prefer.

The sheriff nodded acceptance and followed Emily inside. They seated themselves at the large table in the kitchen and Emily poured the coffee. "This is a nice building," he observed as he spooned sugar into his cup and stirred. "I'm surprised San Antonito has its own school building. It's not a big pueblo. I'd think the kids would go down to the Cochiti Day School."

"The United Pueblo Agency built this place around ten years ago, after the mission school closed. I think it might have been in conjunction with the WPA. People don't feel that good about sending their children eight miles down the road to school, especially the little ones. They might just keep them home. It's good to have the school here, I think." Emily finished stirring evaporated milk into her coffee and looked directly at her visitor. "Now, how can I help you, Sheriff?"

"Why don't you just tell me what happened yesterday when you found Atencio's son."

Emily proceeded to tell Sheriff Wilcox for a second time about her walk the day before. She described the buzzards, and how the birds had led her to the body. "I hadn't taught Juan," she explained to the sheriff. "He'd gone off to boarding school in Santa Fe before I arrived here, and he graduated last year. But I recognized him. San Antonito is pretty small."

Sheriff Wilcox took out a worn bandana and mopped his face. The late August afternoon was sweltering; although there were some clouds further up in the Jemez, they hadn't yet brought much shade or coolness to San Antonito.

"Have you found out what happened?" Emily ventured to ask.

"Somebody shot the kid," Wilcox replied. "But you knew that, didn't you." He took a sip of his coffee. "Some days I hate

22

this job. Looks like it wasn't a shotgun. Which would've made the most sense, since most people hereabouts have a shotgun for hunting. It doesn't look like it could've been a rifle either, although I guess plenty of folks have those."

"The *fiscal*—Sheriff Cruz—said the body was being sent to Bernalillo. Will there be an autopsy?"

The sheriff grunted, possibly in disapproval of Gregorio's loose lips, or maybe it was just fatigue. "The medical examiner's doing it today, that should tell us more." He shook his head. "Nineteen years old. He's just a kid, for Christ's sake. Excuse me, ma'am. Sorry for the bad language, I didn't mean it. But this case vexes me."

Emily nodded and sipped her coffee. The case vexed her too. She thought about Juan, so young to die. But plenty of nineteen-year-olds had enlisted and were off fighting, kids doing a man's job.

"One of the women last night said Juan had been seeing a Spanish girl from La Cañada," Emily offered. "Neither of the families approved and they split up. That was a while ago, before he got this construction job."

"Hmm." Sheriff Wilcox mopped his face again. "Don't seem like a reason for murder, but God knows it don't always take much. I'll ask Gerald, he grew up there, and he might know something. Everybody's kin over there, seems like."

"Or else could Juan have been horsing around with his friends, and the gun went off?"

Sheriff Wilcox looked skeptical. "Maybe," he said, and put down his coffee cup. "Thanks for your time, Miss Schwarz. And for the coffee, it hit the spot. We'll be in touch again if we need you."

After he left, Emily sat awhile, thinking while she finished her second cup of coffee. She still felt exhausted and realized she hadn't really recovered from yesterday. But the strong coffee helped. Somewhat revived, she decided to walk up to the store in the village. Some canned peaches might taste good for dessert after supper, and it would give her a chance to check up on Juliana and Atencio.

Although a few dark clouds had built up over the Jemez Mountains, it didn't look like any rain was coming. It hadn't been much of monsoon season. The plaza drowsed in the late August heat and even the dogs just blinked and kept sleeping in the dust as Emily walked past them up to the little shop near the plaza, run by a Spanish man from La Cañada.

"Hello, Mr. Romero," Emily greeted the storekeeper when she walked in.

"Señorita Schwarz. What can I do for you today?"

"Just a tin of peaches, please. And a paper, if you've got it."

"We're out of today's *New Mexican*, but I've got yesterday's. There's a letter for you, too."

"I'll pass on the paper, thank you."

Mr. Romero took Emily's cash, and a few stamps from her ration book and handed them back to her along with an envelope and her canned fruit. "So you found the body?" he asked, his tone curious. "That's what they were saying."

"Yes. Are you related to Gerald Duran? The deputy sheriff?"

"He's my nephew. Moved off to Bernalillo just when the war started. He was 4F on account of his eyes, you know, but the county ain't as picky as the army. Plus he's married. Has a couple of kids."

24

Emily nodded. "I heard Atencio's son tried to date one of the Cañada girls. Do you have any idea who it was?"

Mr. Romero's gaze shifted away for a moment. "I think he was making eyes for a while at Consuela. She's Gerald's cousin, and her mother's my cousin too. She's a pretty girl. But Consuela's family put a stop to it, and they moved down to Bernalillo. Atencio didn't like it either, for that matter, so both families tried to break it up. That was back last winter, before Juan got his construction job."

"What does McKee work on? War work, I heard, but no details."

"I don't know. Nobody talks about it. But it's a job, *que no*? There's a few guys from home that work for McKee too. The bus picks them up every morning, early, and drops them off in the evening."

"Yes, I've heard the bus. Such a shame about it all," Emily murmured. "Thank you, Mr. Romero. Good evening."

Outside, she saw Gregorio standing next to a new car parked near the tribal office, and waved. He greeted her in turn. "How are you doing today, Miss Schwarz?"

Emily said she was fine, thank you very much, and asked after Atencio and Juliana.

Gregorio shrugged. "It's hard. They're strong people. They'll pull through, I guess." He nodded back toward the school. "Did Sheriff Wilcox find you?"

"Yes. He said they've taken Juan's body to Bernalillo. For an autopsy."

"Once they release the body, we can start the doings here. Father Simon from Cañada will come over, maybe Thursday morning if they've finished, to say Mass."

Emily glanced over at the small adobe church that sat a little away from the plaza. Franciscan missionaries had built it in the 1700s. Further to the north was the cemetery, or *camposanto*, with mounds of earth topped by simple wooden crosses, some decorated with artificial flowers. She thought of young Juan lying there, and shuddered.

"Who would shoot Juan?" she asked in a quiet voice.

Gregorio shook his head. "I don't know. He's just a kid."

"But old enough to be working on some mysterious construction job. Do you know what he did there?"

Gregorio shrugged. "Nobody will say. You know, with this damned war, nobody says anything. I guess it's something for the government. But McKee pays well. Atencio said Juan never talked about it with them. More interested in eating his mom's chile and tortillas when he came home, and hanging out with his buddies."

"Who else works for that company?" Emily asked. Maybe she was being too nosy, but she had found Juan. She wanted to know why the boy had died.

Gregorio thought a minute, his brown eyes shifting upwards. "Well, there's Charley, and Ben. I'll talk to them when they get back, see if they can tell me anything. I think the bus drops them off around nine most evenings. Late. The murder probably didn't have anything to do with that job, though. If somebody there wanted to shoot him, they could do it at work."

"I guess," Emily said, though she didn't think that was likely. She doubted people took their guns to a construction site, and why would any of Juan's co-workers want to shoot him, anyway? She sighed and glanced around the plaza, suddenly feeling like a stranger in the village despite having lived here three years. Or maybe she was just tired.

"Where's Professor Bateson?" she asked. An anthropologist who'd been living in San Antonito for years, the professor was the only other Anglo resident. She wondered where he could be, why he hadn't surfaced in the wake of what had happened. He might have some perspective on the murder.

"Oh, off looking at ruins I expect. Guess he knows every ruin from Rio de Frijoles down to Santa Ana. He's been gone since Saturday; at least my mother's been feeding that dog of his since then. Anasazi." Gregorio chuckled. "Why he'd give his poor dog a Navajo name like that, I don't know. Everybody knows that dog's from right here in San Antonito and speaks our language."

Emily smiled at the joke. Professor Bateson spent most of his time out in the back country, or doing small-scale excavations. He was affiliated, Emily knew, with a university in Chicago, and spent at least one semester of the academic year there teaching, but he lived the rest of his time at San Antonito and spoke the local language fluently. Emily had only managed to learn a few words since her arrival three years ago.

She knew Professor Bateson slightly, but found him a somewhat crusty academic, so the two of them didn't spend much time together. Today, though, his view of recent events might have been comforting.

"I wish they'd hurry with what they're doing in Bernalillo," Gregorio said, interrupting Emily's rambling thoughts. "We need to bring that boy home, and put this behind us."

"But how can that happen, when we don't know who killed him?"

"The sheriff's talking to the high school boys now. The ones that were around last weekend from the school up in Santa Fe. I imagine they were hanging out with Juanito, just fooling around with a gun, and they panicked."

"And that's how he got shot in the chest?" Emily felt her jaw tense. "Just goofing around?"

Gregorio shrugged. "Stranger things have happened."

"Juliana said Juan told her he was going to Albuquerque with some friends on Sunday. Didn't Paulina say her son went to Albuquerque?"

"Yeah, I think so." He looked at Emily, his eyes giving nothing away. "You must be tired, ma'am. You were up late last night. Just let Sheriff Wilcox do his job."

Emily nodded, her lips tight as she fought back annoyance. A meddling outsider, not to be trusted. Was that how the *fiscal* saw her? "Yes, and tomorrow's another school day. So you'll excuse me, won't you." She turned and walked away, across the plaza, back towards the brick school building down the road.

Back home, Emily looked at the envelope she had tucked into her pocket at Romero's. Not from home, or her brother. One note, postmarked Peña Blanca. She recognized the Spencerian handwriting of Mrs. Miller, the schoolteacher in the little Spanish town of La Cañada. The two women seldom saw each other, despite the relative closeness of their jobs.

Emily had been hired by the Federal United Pueblo Agency, who ran the reservation schools, while the Sandoval County School System employed Mavis Miller to teach at La Cañada. Still, Mrs. Miller had been friendly that first year

Emily had been at San Antonito, homesick, and the two women occasionally got together. Mavis and her husband lived a bit further down the highway in the slightly larger Spanish town of Peña Blanca, and she commuted up to La Cañada daily, although since the start of the war and gas rationing she typically boarded during the week with a family in the little Hispanic settlement to save on gas. Mr. Miller raised sheep and cattle, and ran a small apple orchard in Peña Blanca, about twelve miles away. The *acequia* that brought water to the fields from the nearby Rio Grande made for good grazing and farming.

Emily surveyed the note, addressed in Mrs. Miller's careful handwriting to Miss Emily Schwarz, General Delivery, San Antonito. There was no official post office at San Antonito; mail was left at Romero's Mercantile for folks to pick up, and word usually got around the pueblo quickly if someone received a letter.

Emily opened the envelope and unfolded the note. She read:

Dear Emily,

It has been so long since we've seen each other. The summer passed too quickly; there is always a lot to do helping Charles with the livestock but now I'm back at work teaching, as are you. I trust you had a good visit with your family in Racine.

Emily nodded. Her visit home, earlier in the summer, had proved strained. The three weeks she'd spent there had felt much longer, and she had not been sorry to board the westbound train back to New Mexico. She returned to Mrs. Miller's note.

As you may know, I've been rooming with the Gallegos family in La Cañada during the week. Mr. Gallegos is a fine musician. He plays guitar—all the old folksongs of the area—and his brother plays the fiddle. I believe there is an accordionist in the village also. The Gallegos's sons are also reported to be fine musicians, but all three of the boys have enlisted. However, despite the dearth of younger folks, the little town is holding a baile, a dance, in the dancehall right on the plaza. It is to be this Saturday. I thought you might enjoy the chance to see a little of life from the Spanish side; it's something you might not otherwise get a chance to observe. I'm not sure if any of the residents of San Antonito attend or not, but thought you might appreciate the opportunity. Charles will attend, as well, so we will be well chaperoned!

We could come and fetch you late on Saturday afternoon, and drop you back at the schoolhouse on Sunday. With all their boys off fighting, Señor and Señora Gallegos don't mind putting you, as well as Charles and myself, up for the night.

I do hope you'll agree to come. It has been too long since we've seen each other, and I look forward to hearing about your trip home and how your school year progresses.

Yours sincerely, Mavis Miller

Emily put the note down on the kitchen table, thinking. She wondered if Mavis had heard about the shooting death in San Antonito and that Emily had found the body. News tended to travel quickly and a murdered man definitely qualified as news. But Mavis was a kindly soul, not given to gossip, and it might be fun to get out of San Antonito for a night—even if it was only two miles up the road, well within walking distance. Away from murders, funerals, corpses.

Emily got out her Parker fountain pen and some notepaper. She quickly penned an acceptance before she could change her mind.

CHAPTER FOUR

THE NEXT DAY Emily's students, far less subdued than on the previous day, seemed almost back to normal. The older children, at least, were well aware that their teacher was the person who had found the dead body, and Emily heard a couple of fifth-grade boys whispering at recess when they thought she couldn't hear. She ignored the chatter but gave the fifth graders extra homework that night, due the next morning. Two pages of long division problems.

After school was dismissed and the students had left for home, Emily settled herself in the kitchen with an afternoon cup of coffee and a sheet of lined paper. She had a couple of hours' break before the home economics class that she taught every Wednesday evening. Tonight they were sewing. Many of the women had Singer treadle machines at home, and Emily enjoyed the activity; it was something she had in common with the mothers of her students.

She heard a car drive by and looked out the window to see a hearse driving up towards the main village. Emily crossed herself, her mood suddenly more somber. Juan Montoya was returning home.

Early that evening the ladies arrived for class. The adult classroom had five treadle sewing machines; usually the ladies had to take turns with their projects but this Wednesday evening only three women attended. Albertina and Minguita came in handmade cotton dresses, tied with colorful woven belts, and wore the *sabanas*, or traditional shawls, over the dresses. A few of the younger girls had taken to wearing more mainstream shirtwaist dresses, skirts, and blouses, and permed their hair, but most of the San Antonito women still wore traditional clothing and hairstyles. Emily supposed that most of her usual attendees were over at Atencio and Juliana's, helping to lay out their oldest son's body, but she was glad to see the friendly face of Demetria among the trio that did show up for class.

Emily smiled at her friend. "Have you seen Juliana?" she asked.

Demetria nodded, her face sad. "There's a wake tonight at the house, and the Marian ladies from Cañada are coming over to say the Rosary," Demetria told her. "Father Simon will come up tomorrow morning to say Mass at the church."

Emily nodded. She wondered what the autopsy had showed, but none of the women volunteered any information. Perhaps they didn't know anything, or didn't want to speak of it.

She got on with the class, showing the women the evening's sewing project, an apron with a gathered skirt and rickrack trim, and helped them pin the pattern pieces on the calico she supplied. They had just about finished that step when she heard the outer door open and Delia Montoya entered the classroom. The ladies turned to stare a moment before going back to their projects, and for a moment the friendly chatter died down.

Emily remembered Demetria saying that Delia was close with Juan in high school, but the nineteen-year-old had later married Atencio's nephew, Lorenzo. Slim and pretty, Delia wore an Anglo-style shirtwaist dress and her thick dark hair was cut and curled above her angular face. As she got the latecomer settled at the last vacant sewing machine, Emily noticed the girl's eyes looked puffy.

"I'm sorry to be late, Miss Schwarz," Delia said. "I was over at Auntie Juliana's."

Emily nodded. "Don't worry about it," she said. Delia started to thread the machine, biting her lip. Demetria sat at the machine next to her and glared at Minguita, who sat across the room at another machine, her project apparently forgotten, staring. Minguita lowered her eyes.

"Do they know yet who did this to poor Juan?" Delia asked Demetria quietly. Demetria shook her head, and glared again at the ladies across the room.

"It's such a shame," Emily said. "You and your husband were pretty friendly with Juan, weren't you?"

"He was Lorenzo's cousin," Delia replied, her voice rough. "We all grew up together. Juan was always so funny. He and Lorenzo were like brothers."

"It's sad," Demetria agreed. "Did you see Juan last weekend? Was he worried about anything?"

"He ate supper with us on Saturday. And he and Lorenzo went hunting on Sunday. For turkeys. But they didn't get any and Lorenzo and Juan were both back by three." She paused, and swallowed, the sewing project forgotten. "He was just like always, cracking jokes about that construction company he works for. Said the buses are so slow he thinks he'll never get home from work."

"Did Lorenzo speak to Sheriff Wilcox?" Emily asked.

Delia nodded and her dark eyes filled with tears. She stood abruptly. "I'm sorry, Miss Schwarz. I shouldn't have come to class. I need to go back to Auntie Juliana's."

Emily nodded assent and the young woman walked out of the room, leaving a sad silence behind her.

The two other ladies had started sewing and were talking together in low tones. Emily went over to see if they needed any help; their voices stopped as they saw her approach.

"Where'd Delia go?" Albertina asked.

"She went back to Atencio and Juliana's," Demetria answered. "Maybe she didn't feel comfortable here for some reason."

"Oh." Minguita gave Albertina a knowing look, but Albertina stared down at her sewing.

"I guess she and her husband were close to Juan," Emily said, trying to defuse the tension a little.

Minguita almost smiled. "Delia used to go with Juan in high school. Before he started trying to go with that girl from Cañada. Until their families put a stop to that. But by then Delia had married Lorenzo."

Emily made no reply to this and bent her head to look at Albertina's project. "You need to arrange these pieces so they are going with the grain of the fabric, not against it," she said, adjusting the pattern pieces on the calico.

Albertina nodded. "Thanks, Miss Schwarz." She started to re-pin the pieces. "Juan liked the ladies," Albertina added. "He was sure handsome, and the girls liked him right back. He probably had a girl in Albuquerque, too."

"And Cochiti. And Santo Domingo," Minguita said with a laugh.

"Do you think somebody would shoot him over that?" Emily asked.

"Maybe," Minguita replied, glancing over at the vacant sewing machine where Delia had been working. "If they got angry. People get jealous, you know."

"Let me show you how to gather those pockets," Emily said, not liking Minguita's tone. "There's a trick to it."

The class ended around eight o'clock. Emily and Demetria walked over together to Atencio's house. The funeral would be tomorrow morning but Emily couldn't cancel classes at a federal Pueblo Agency school for a Catholic funeral. Still, she wanted to pay her respects. She owed it to Juan and his family.

Light spilled out of the open doors and windows of the crowded house. Around the side Emily saw the cooking fires burning in the yard, and smelled the pungent scent of piñon and cedar smoke, mixed with cooking meat and chile. A few women moved nearby, shadowed by the firelight. They had already started cooking for the funeral and the people that would come to the house to eat the next day, after the burial. The aromas swirled around Emily and Demetria as they approached the door.

Inside the main room, through the crowd, Emily saw Juan's body, wrapped in a blanket, lying on the floor. Only his face was showing, and a pot of cornmeal sat at his feet. The brightly striped wool Pendleton was dusted with powdery white cornmeal, offerings from the mourners.

Emily and Demetria made their way through the room, closer to the body. People stood in the back, or sat on the packed dirt floor and on benches against the wall. Demetria approached the corpse, took a little cornmeal from the pot, and sprinkled it over the body, saying a prayer in her native language. Emily approached, feeling a little awkward. She crossed herself in front of the corpse and murmured a prayer that the boy would rest in peace. She saw Atencio and his wife, sitting on a bench near the body, along with Juan's little brother and sister.

"I'm so very sorry," she said, grasping each of them by the hand in turn. There wasn't anything else to say.

"Thank you for coming, Miss Schwarz," Atencio said. Juliana nodded, her eyes red. Atencio motioned towards a bench by the wall. "Sit down," he offered.

Some old grandmas almost filled the bench but they moved closer to each other to make room for Emily. She looked at the scene, and her throat tightened with unshed tears. The death seemed so raw. There was no coffin, no organ music, none of the trappings there would have been at a Catholic wake back home in Racine. Just a corpse, wrapped in a striped blanket, surrounded by grieving family and friends.

A bustle at the door heralded the arrival of several women from La Cañada, the members of the Marian society at the church there. They had come to say the Rosary. A few of the local women joined them, as the newcomers began to pray over the body in Spanish and Latin.

"Holy Mary, mother of God, pray for us sinners now and at the hour of our death." Emily joined in the familiar prayer, speaking English. Looking at the still face of Juan, wrapped in his woolen blanket, her eyes filled with tears.

The old woman sitting next to Emily smiled and reached out to pat Emily's hand as the Rosary ended. She said something to her in Keres, then took pity on Emily's blank look.

"Be strong," she told Emily in English, and Emily tried to smile back.

One of the women brought Emily a cup of coffee. Emily cradled the warm cup gratefully and sipped at the dark brew. An old man—Emily thought it was Atencio's father, Juan's grandfather—began talking to the assembly in Keres but Emily couldn't catch much of what he said. After a while he stopped talking. Emily rose and slipped out the door, intending to return to the schoolhouse and get a little sleep before the morning.

Gregorio stood in the shadows under the portal of the house, speaking quietly with some of the other men outside. He stopped talking when he saw Emily and approached her as she made her way across the porch.

"Miss Schwarz," he said, his tone grave.

"Hello, Gregorio," Emily said, not sure she really wanted to talk. "I'm just heading back. There's still school tomorrow."

"Do you have a flashlight?"

Emily nodded, feeling exhausted. She pulled it from her purse and pressed the button. It beamed weakly on the dirt before them. "The batteries are a little low, I guess."

"Here, I'll walk you. I just put new batteries in mine."

"The moon's out," Emily protested. "I'll be able to see."

"I'm the *fiscal*," Gregorio retorted. "Can't have the schoolteacher break her ankle on my watch."

Emily gave up. Gregorio said something to the other men and then walked with her across the plaza to the road that led the quarter mile or so to the schoolhouse.

"What did they find out in Bernalillo?" Emily asked him. "What did the autopsy show?"

"He wasn't shot with a rifle or shotgun. They pulled a slug out of his chest. They've sent it to ballistics for testing. Probably from a handgun, a .45 most likely. And they think it was point blank, at least that's what Sheriff Wilcox told me. There were powder burns. You get those at close range."

Emily shivered, from more than the evening chill. "Who around here has a handgun?"

Gregorio shrugged. "I guess the sheriff will be looking into that."

"So it doesn't sound like kids just fooling around." Not that Emily had heard of any kids with Juan that last Sunday. Just the turkey hunting with Lorenzo.

"No," Gregorio said flatly, but didn't add anything else.

Emily swallowed, her throat suddenly dry. There must be a murderer, then, here in San Antonito. She felt suddenly glad she wasn't making the walk down this quiet road alone.

They had reached the schoolhouse, the bulk of the brick building looming darkly in the night. Emily heard an owl cry, someplace down by the river.

"Goodnight, Miss Schwarz," Gregorio said. He waited outside until Emily entered the building and locked the door behind her. Emily heard his footsteps heading back towards the village. She listened in the dark silence for the owl, but didn't hear it again.

CHAPTER FIVE

Thursday. Most of Emily's students showed up for school, although the sound of the church bell tolling at nine interrupted their studies. It reminded Emily of the Mass and the burial taking place while she attempted to test the younger children on their spelling. Not that she had really been able to forget. The image of Juan's corpse in the river still haunted her.

Later, during recess, she glanced out the window of the brick school building and saw in the distance the procession of people walking to the camposanto, the cemetery, beyond the old mission church, the pallbearers carrying the wrapped corpse on a stretcher—a ladder, really—and the priest walking ahead, swinging the censer. She murmured a prayer under her breath: "May perpetual light shine upon him, Lord." Then she turned back to her class as recess ended and the children trooped in and took their seats.

That afternoon, her students dismissed, Emily got her notebook and reliable Parker Debutante pen, and sat at the kitchen table with her afternoon cup of coffee, laced with evaporated milk and sugar. No doubt she should leave the investigation of the murder to the sheriff but Juan's death nagged at her. Her dreams had been unsettled, filled with the image of the boy lying by the roots of the old cottonwood, and Juliana's tear-streaked face. Who had killed him, and why?

Emily wrote *Juan* at the top of the paper. Underneath she wrote: *Cañada*, *San Antonito*, and *Work*.

She put a big question mark under *Work*. Whatever Juan had been doing for McKee Construction, she didn't know. War work, folks said. What kind of war work would be happening in the mountains of rural New Mexico? Now if Juan had been working down in Albuquerque, at the Army Air Field, that would make more sense.

Under *San Antonito* she wrote: *Rough-housing. Handgun— who? Jealousy? Delia? Her husband?*

Under *Cañada* she wrote: *Romero girl? Her family?*

A knock at the door broke her concentration. Sighing, she laid down her Parker and took one more sip of coffee before rising. Probably it was just one of the pueblo families, maybe an invitation to a christening or something. There always seemed to be something happening in San Antonito. She supposed she should really stop by Atencio and Juliana's again. They would be feeding family and friends all afternoon, as folks came to pay their respects and offer sympathy. Birth, and death, she mused, as she walked down the hall to answer the summons.

It wasn't what she expected. Emily opened the door and saw a suited man, an Anglo, whose garb looked more suited to an Albuquerque courtroom than a New Mexico pueblo. A taller man stood behind him, wearing an army uniform. The suited man looked somewhat unassuming. Bland, Emily thought. A pleasant enough, slightly weathered face with neatly groomed brown hair, although Emily spied a hint of grey. He certainly didn't look old, though. Only the eyes, sharp and shrewd, belied the stranger's nondescript appearance. The taller man beside him, lanky with blond hair and a sunburned face, looked straight out of Racine.

"Miss Schwarz?" the uniformed man asked.

"Yes?"

"I'm Sergeant O'Toole, from Albuquerque. Kirtland Army Air Base, ma'am. And this is Mr. Shepherd. We're here about the boy that got himself shot."

"Yes?" Emily repeated, wishing she hadn't left her notebook open on the kitchen table. It wouldn't do for these strangers to see her musings.

"Sheriff Wilcox told us you found the body."

"That's correct," Emily replied. "What can I do for you?"

"We're just following up, ma'am," the other man interjected. "Juan Montoya worked for McKee Construction. They're based down in Albuquerque, you know. We just need to check on a few things."

"Shouldn't you be speaking with Sheriff Wilcox?" Emily asked. "Or Gregorio Cruz? He's the tribal sheriff, the *fiscal*."

"We know, ma'am," Mr. Shepherd said. "We've already spoken with Mr. Cruz. Now we'd like to speak with you."

"Well, I guess you'd better come in," Emily offered, her puzzlement growing.

"We won't keep you long, ma'am. Just a few questions, a few loose ends to tie up."

Emily nodded as she led the way into the kitchen across the hall from the classroom. She quickly gathered up her notebook, closed it, and gestured to the men to have a seat at the table.

"Would you care for some coffee?"

"Thank you, ma'am. That would hit the spot," Shepherd replied. Emily got down some of the blue willow teacups and poured them each a cupful.

"Sugar? Milk? It's just evaporated, not fresh."

Shepherd declined both, but the sergeant reached for the sugar bowl as everyone settled around the table. Emily waited while the men took a few sips of coffee, wondering what they wanted. Had they figured out who killed Juan? Why would they want to speak to her? Surely Sheriff Wilcox had told them everything.

Curious, she watched while they drank. Sergeant O'Toole had a pronounced Adam's apple that moved up and down as he swallowed. He drank his heavily sweetened coffee in big slurps. Maybe he was thirsty, or just had a kid's appetite. He didn't look that old. Mr. Shepherd took careful sips of his own black coffee. Although he looked innocuous, Emily had a feeling the man didn't miss much. She sipped her own coffee and waited for one of them to speak, suddenly a little nervous at the idea of being questioned again. Interrogated.

"So you found the body the other day," Shepherd said, setting the coffee cup back on its saucer.

"Yes, just this last Monday. It feels like a year ago."

"Where was he, exactly, ma'am?"

"Right near the creek bank, where the Chiquito passes a big cottonwood tree. One foot was over the bank, in the riverbed, the body just lying there in the roots of the tree. Juan and whoever killed him must have been arguing right by the water."

Shepherd nodded. "Who do you think that was?"

Emily felt her cheeks warm. Had Mr. Shepherd seen her notebook? "Who do I think killed him?" she asked.

Mr. Shepherd nodded and waited for her reply.

"I have no idea. It doesn't make sense that anyone here would do such a thing. Unless they had been drinking and then got into a fight over something. Although I did hear Juan had been dating a Spanish girl from La Cañada, that's the little town you pass through right before you head into the canyon here. None of the families involved were very happy about that."

Shepherd looked a little blank.

"The girl's family didn't want her dating an Indian, and I don't think Juan's family was thrilled about it either. They didn't like him dating a Spanish girl."

Shepherd nodded. "Anything else?"

"One of the girls in my home economics class, Delia Montoya, is married to Juan's cousin. Apparently, she used to go with Juan in high school before he started dating the Spanish girl. Delia was pretty upset at class last evening and left early." She paused, hating to pass on gossip. Still, it might be helpful. She wanted this mystery solved, she thought, before she continued. "Some of the women in my class mentioned Juan was pretty popular with the ladies."

"Oh? That might be worth checking into."

"So you don't know who killed him, either," Emily said.

"We're trying to find out, ma'am. Along with Sheriff

Wilcox. That's why we're talking to you," O'Toole interrupted. Shepherd looked on quietly, but didn't add anything.

"What did Juan do for that construction company?" Emily asked.

"We're checking into that, don't you worry, ma'am," O'Toole replied. Shepherd remained silent. "What about his friends here?" O'Toole continued.

She shrugged. "I don't know too many of the boys Juan's age. I've only been here three years, so I didn't teach him, or any of them. Juan was what—nineteen? He graduated last year. Most of the children go up to the Indian School in Santa Fe by the time they reach eighth grade. I guess that's where he dated Delia. But Juan and Delia's husband were close. They even went turkey hunting that Sunday, she told me. But she said they didn't catch anything, and then she saw them together before Juan took off."

The sergeant nodded. "Anyone else he was with over the weekend or on Monday, that you know of?"

Emily took a sip of her coffee before continuing. "Juliana thought Juan had planned to go to Albuquerque on Sunday, with some friends. And Paulina—a neighbor—said Monday that her son Charley had gotten some gas coupons and gone to Albuquerque. But I'm sure Sheriff Cruz already shared that information with you."

"Well, thank you, Miss Schwarz," O'Toole said, a little less abruptly. "You've been a great help."

She shook hands with the two men and they left. She decided not to walk into the village to the Montoyas' home; there was bound to be a crowd there after the funeral, and she was too tired to answer questions. She had been to the Rosary, she told herself. That would suffice.

Later, Emily wondered about the visit from Shepherd and O'Toole as she fried some Spam for dinner and ate it with two slices of tomato from the few plants she tended in the side yard. There was oven bread too; one of her students had brought her a round loaf of the yeast bread the women baked in the *hornos*, ovens built of adobe. Looking like little beehives, they dotted the pueblo. Each house had one, and sometimes two, outside, and often in the early mornings the air was scented with the smell of cedar and piñon smoke as the fires were kindled in them, burning down to ashes before the coals were swept out and the risen bread shoved inside with paddles to bake in the warmth of the hot rock-like structures.

Her dinner finished, Emily tried to settle down with her Daphne du Maurier novel but found she couldn't concentrate. It had been a long week. It seemed like a lifetime since she'd found Juan's corpse on Monday, and a lifetime since she had looked at the book. It no longer held the same interest, she felt like she'd left it far behind. She closed it with a sigh and looked out the window towards the camposanto. The light of a bonfire glowed, and she guessed the men were keeping watch over Juan's grave. She didn't know too much about the tradition; she'd only heard that the men watched over a grave for three nights until the spirit of the newly dead left for Heaven. Not quite Wisconsin Catholic, but it was New Mexico, after all. Still, wherever Juan's spirit was, Emily hoped it was at peace. But could it be, truly, with his killer still at large?

Saturday morning Emily walked over to the plaza, to Mr. Romero's shop. She told herself she needed to pick up another can of evaporated milk, but really she just wanted a little news.

"Good morning, Mr. Romero," she greeted the storekeeper. A girl was helping him today, a pretty teenager with permed dark auburn hair, wearing a pink dress and red lipstick. "Who's this?" Emily asked. She hadn't seen the girl before; she wasn't from San Antonito.

"Oh, Señorita, this is my niece, Consuela Romero. Her family has moved down to Bernalillo but sometimes she comes up to see her grandparents and help her old *tio*. Don't you, *mi hija*?"

Consuela nodded, and said hello to Emily, and then went back to stacking canned peaches, pears, and green peas on one of the shelves toward the back of the store.

"Do you have a newspaper, Mr. Romero?"

He sighed. "Just yesterday's *New Mexican*. Here, take it. On the house."

Emily tucked it into the crook of her arm and nodded her thanks. "What about yarn?" she asked. "I might do some knitting."

He gestured at the stock. "We only have this black wool. And a little green and red. The ladies like it for their embroidery."

Emily looked, unimpressed. "I was hoping for some blue. I thought I'd make a muffler for my brother Tim, I just wanted to do something for him." Señor Romero nodded sympathetically. "But since he's in the Pacific, he doesn't need it," Emily continued. "I'll knit more socks instead. For the Red Cross. It will keep my hands busy." She picked up a can of evaporated milk from the shelf. "I'll just take this for today."

He rang up the sale and took her money and ration

coupon. "You know, I think Señor Bateson said he might be going into Santa Fe today. Maybe you could ride up with him. I'm sure Beacham's, on San Francisco Street, would have a better selection of yarn, *que no?*"

"Have you seen the professor today? I heard he was up in the canyon, excavating something or other."

"He's back, Señorita. He just stopped in this morning."

"Thanks, Mr. Romero. I'll go ask him if he wants company." It was still early, and Mavis and Charles weren't to pick her up until five-thirty or so. She might well have time to go into Santa Fe. As she left the store, she spied Gregorio talking with some other men under the portal that shaded the front of the shop.

"Hey, Miss Schwarz," Gregorio greeted her. "How are you doing today?"

"Just fine, thank you. Have you seen Professor Bateson?"

"He's over at Atencio's house, I think. See. There's Anasazi, waiting for him there."

Emily looked. Bateson's dog was a strange combination, an unlikely mix of what could have been Springer spaniel, German shepherd, and Irish setter. Although how any of those breeds had wound up in San Antonito, Emily couldn't hazard a guess. Tourists, maybe? But the dog loitering by the Montoyas' was Anasazi, sure enough. The short reddish fur speckled with white patches looked out of place on a smallish German shepherd-type body, with shorter legs than usual, and a long-haired tail.

"I'll head over there, thank you," Emily said. "I haven't spoken to Atencio or Juliana since the Rosary."

Gregorio nodded. "Juliana will be there. The ladies are still cooking, over by the house."

Emil nodded and walked across the plaza toward the Montoya house. Outside, several women stood chattering while they stirred pots of stew simmering on grates set on rocks above the makeshift fire pits. They waved at Emily. She returned the greeting, but continued on into the house without stopping. Professor Bateson and Atencio were seated at the table, drinking coffee from blue tin enamel cups, apparently deep in conversation. Juliana stood at the counter washing dishes, helped by Demetria, who flashed a smile in Emily's direction.

Emily approached them and greeted Juliana, a little awkwardly. She crossed to the sink. "How are you doing?"

Juliana shrugged, her hands in the tin basin filled with dishwater. She lifted one hand out and wiped her forehead, leaving a smear of soap suds on her dark skin, then went back to her task.

"It's hard," she said, blinking back tears. "It's hard, but we have to be strong."

Emily nodded. Demetria gave Emily another smile and patted Juliana on the shoulder. "Miss Schwarz, would you like some coffee?" Demetria asked.

"That's all right, I had a cup before I came over," Emily said. "Actually, I needed to speak to Professor Bateson, but I wanted to check in."

"Well, the professor's right over there, asking questions." Demetria said something in Keres to Juliana and the other woman gave a short laugh, a laugh without any mirth.

Emily walked over to the table. The men were still intent on their conversation. Professor Bateson was doing most of the talking, asking questions in Keres, which Atencio answered.

The professor spoke Keres well. Not for the first time, Emily wondered if he might have time to give her some lessons. It would be nice to be able to say more than hello, thank you, and so on.

Professor Bateson finally stopped and Atencio looked up. "Good morning, Miss Schwarz," he said.

She returned the greeting. Atencio gestured to a chair and Emily sat, once again refusing an offer of coffee. "Actually, I was looking for you, Professor. Mr. Romero at the store said you might be going into Santa Fe and I wondered if I could tag along. I need to pick up a few things there. That is, if you're not coming back too late."

Bateson nodded slowly. "I imagine that could be arranged. I've got a long list of things to pick up for folks here, and just enough C-coupons to cover the trip. And I have to meet with someone at the museum. I'm planning to stick to business, and get back here by mid-afternoon. I'll pick you up at the school. Say in half an hour? Will that suit you?"

CHAPTER SIX

AN HOUR LATER Emily was seated beside Professor Bateson as his old 1927 Ford truck chugged up the La Bajada escarpment into Santa Fe. The road that climbed the bluff never failed to make Emily a bit nervous. The windows of the cab were open and the noise of the engine and dust blowing in the windows didn't do much to encourage conversation.

Professor Bateson's stooped academic shoulders seemed somewhat at odds with his tanned, weather-beaten visage. He wore a hat with a frayed brim, a flannel shirt, and old, worn jeans.

"It's a sad thing about Juan," Emily finally commented.

"What? Oh, yes. It's a sad thing to lose a child."

Emily nodded, and conversation lagged. The switchbacks on the way up the escarpment demanded some concentration, and she didn't want to distract the driver. After a time they made it to the top of La Bajada and the road flattened out. The rounded dome of Tetilla Peak rose on their left and further off to the right Emily saw the Cerrillos Hills, while up ahead, against a brilliant azure sky, the Sangre de Cristos rose before them, with the town of Santa Fe nestled against the peaks. Emily had been up to Santa Fe before, of course, but the mountains and expansive views never ceased to thrill her.

"What a gorgeous sight," she exclaimed. The road had improved, and conversation grew easier.

"It still amazes me," Bateson replied, "and I've been working out here for fifteen years."

"I'm just a newcomer, I guess."

"Yes, three years isn't very long at San Antonito. You'd still be an outsider."

Emily nodded. She often felt that way. Most villagers spoke Keres among themselves, although they politely switched to English when she was present. Folks were certainly friendly. Parents stopped by with food for the teacher and she was invited to share feasts celebrating christenings or First Communions. Still, she suspected she missed out on some things, although her work at the school kept her busy enough.

Her thoughts turned again to the murder. "I didn't know Juan, really, or who his friends were. Did you? Who could have wanted to kill him? He was just a boy."

"I knew Juan pretty well," Bateson answered. "He used to help me in the summers, when he was back at the pueblo from boarding school in Santa Fe. An intelligent boy, he could have gone on to college, but what with the war upending things, that didn't happen."

"And then he got that job with the construction company. Do you know what he was doing for them?"

The professor shook his head. "I really hadn't seen him much since he got that job. And I was in the back country last weekend; I didn't see him at all. There's a new site I'm excavating up in Bland Canyon. It might link the Pueblo people here with the natives who settled in Frijoles Canyon. The pottery looks right, the design motifs are similar."

Bateson droned on, talking about pottery shards and decorative styles as they followed a winding highway past a little village and, a few miles later, into the outskirts of Santa Fe. They passed some houses, a church—*St. Anne's*, Emily read on the sign in front—then a few blocks later another, older church, which Professor Bateson told her dated to the 1700s. Emily had seen it before, on other trips into town. The Sanctuario de Guadalupe. The old adobe structure had a simple beauty, although it didn't look anything like the brick Catholic churches Emily had grown up with in Racine. Finally, Bateson turned right and parked the car on Galisteo Street.

"There's a grocery nearby, if you need to pick up anything. I've got a long list of supplies to fetch, and a meeting at the museum with one of the conservators. I'll meet you back here," he checked his watch, "say around three o'clock? That should get you back down to San Antonito in time to meet your friends. I'll leave the truck unlocked for your groceries."

Emily nodded. She found a grocery store on Water Street and purchased what she needed, along with some other supplies she had promised to pick up for Demetria, and then stowed them in the back of the truck. Her ration book sadly depleted, she walked the two blocks up to the Santa Fe Plaza.

A cup of coffee sounded good, and maybe a sandwich at the little café near the dress shop on the plaza. But first, her yarn.

She found what she wanted at Taichert's on San Francisco Street, a nice wool that would make good socks. She bought an extra skein. Then she walked across the plaza, stopping to read a poster advertising the upcoming Fiestas de Santa Fe, when she heard someone call her name.

"Miss Schwarz?"

Emily turned, surprised to see Mr. Shepherd seated on one of the benches that stood around the plaza. He gave her a smile, and she noticed the crinkle around his eyes. It lightened his face in a nice way, she thought.

"Mr. Shepherd. Hello." Emily found herself smiling back at him. "What brings you up this way? I thought you and Sergeant O'Toole were based in Albuquerque."

"O'Toole is. But I'm usually up here. And you?"

"Oh, I needed to pick up a few things." Emily held her bag from Taichert's a little awkwardly. "I drove up with Professor Bateson; I need to meet him at three back at his car. He had to speak with someone at the museum, I guess. About pottery shards."

"Bateson?"

"The archaeologist. He's lived at San Antonito for ages, when he's not teaching in Chicago. I guess Juan used to work for him. Professor Bateson mentioned that today. Before Juan got the job with McKee."

"Is that so?" Shepherd folded up his newspaper and glanced at his watch. "It's twelve-thirty now. I was just going to grab a little lunch over at the hotel. Would you care to join me?"

"Oh, I wouldn't want to intrude," Emily protested, feeling oddly disconcerted. She really didn't know Mr. Shepherd all that well. Although lunch at La Fonda—well, that was a temptation.

"It's no intrusion, Miss Schwarz," Mr. Shepherd insisted. "I'd be delighted to have your company. It gets old, eating lunch by yourself."

Emily succumbed and agreed to go along, although she doubted Mr. Shepherd needed to eat lunch alone unless he preferred that. She herself rarely ate out, and of course there was no place to eat out in San Antonito. Occasionally she and Mavis came up to Santa Fe. They enjoyed eating at "the Inn at the End of the Trail," but it had been quite a while now since they had lunched there.

Emily walked with Mr. Shepherd over to La Fonda. It took her eyes a moment to adjust to the dark interior after the brightness outside. The lobby, with its distinctive Southwestern architecture, hummed with activity. They made their way to the La Plazuela dining room, and a waiter quickly showed them to a table. Mexican-style paintings of flowers and birds decorated the glass windows in the French doors surrounding the central dining area.

They ordered; a tomato and deviled egg sandwich for Emily, along with coffee. Mr. Shepherd ordered green chile meatloaf and mashed potatoes and string beans.

"What is it you do, exactly, Mr. Shepherd?" Emily asked as they waited for their food.

"Oh, this and that. Army procurement, mostly," Shepherd replied.

Emily laughed a little to cover her confusion. There weren't any factories in Santa Fe, so what was he procuring? "There's not too much of that in Santa Fe, I'd guess. Shouldn't you be in Chicago?"

"Probably." Shepherd laughed too but didn't say anything more about his work. "So how do you like San Antonito? It must be a big change from Michigan."

"Wisconsin," Emily corrected him. "Racine."

"Oh yes. Wisconsin. I'm sorry. What brought you out here?"

Emily hedged. Mr. Shepherd really didn't need to know her reasons for wanting to leave Racine. A father who drank too much and a hypochondriac mother weren't really proper lunchtime conversation with a stranger. "I guess I wanted to see a little bit more of the world than the Midwest," she replied.

Shepherd nodded. "You could always join the WACs," he commented with a smile. "You'd see a lot of the world that way."

"I guess I could. But I came out here before the war started, and was just settling in. They have to have a teacher here, anyway. Why not me?"

"Why not, indeed?"

The waiter brought their meals, and they ate in silence for a while. Emily worried a bit that Mr. Shepherd would think her a coward, or lacking patriotic sensibility. Of course, he wasn't in uniform either.

"I try to do my bit," she said, a little defensively. "The alcalde and I have worked together on some scrap drives, and you would be surprised what some people have hidden away in those rickety old barns. We got over five hundred pounds of scrap metal. And I've helped the elderly folks with their ration cards—it's hard for them to understand that system."

Shepherd smiled slightly and Emily felt embarrassed. Here Tim was off in the Pacific, perhaps even under fire this very day, while she rambled on about a few pounds of scrap metal. She glanced around the room. "Oh, look!" she said, grateful to change the subject. "There's Professor Bateson, heading towards the bar."

Shepherd glanced over. Bateson and a mild-mannered looking man with thick tortoiseshell glasses were crossing the lobby towards the lounge. Emily smiled in their direction but Bateson didn't see her.

"I guess that's the museum guy he's with," Emily said.

"Or some Santa Fe artist-type," Shepherd said, and returned his attention to his apricot pie. Some WACs and a few young men in army uniforms came in and took seats in the lobby, blocking Emily's view of Professor Bateson. Emily watched them order drinks, chatting and flirting. She wondered if perhaps she should have enlisted, but maybe she had grown too old for adventures at thirty-two.

She and Mr. Shepherd finished their lunch, and Emily glanced at her watch. "Oh, my goodness. I still have a long list of things to pick up before it's time to leave. I'd better get busy." She started to open her purse.

"I'll get this, Miss Schwarz. It would be a pleasure."

"Thank you," said Emily, feeling oddly flustered.

They parted ways outside the hotel on San Francisco Street and Emily headed down toward Beacham's to finish her shopping. Promptly at three o'clock she arrived at the car, her arms filled with packages, and found Bateson already there, waiting.

"I'm sorry to keep you," Emily said. "Did you find everything you needed?"

"Yes. More supplies. I'm headed back to the hills for a few days again, come Monday."

"Anasazi must like it out there."

Bateson nodded as he stowed Emily's packages in the back. "Did you enjoy La Fonda?" Emily asked. Bateson looked surprised, so she explained. "I ran into Mr. Shepherd and we had lunch together. I saw you in the lobby while we were eating. Were you with your museum consultant?"

"La Fonda does a good lunch," Bateson commented. "That was an old friend of mine, Mr. Greene. He moved out here about twenty years ago. A lunger. We often get together when I'm in town."

Emily knew what *lunger* meant—someone who'd come to the desert to "take the cure," usually for tuberculosis. Poor Mr. Greene. "How nice to have an acquaintance around," she said. Sometimes she felt a little isolated out in San Antonito. Of course, there was Demetria, and Mavis lived only a few miles away.

She and the professor didn't talk much on the way back to San Antonito, the rattle of the truck and the late afternoon heat precluding conversation, but Emily enjoyed the spectacular view as they descended La Bajada—the dark Jemez Mountains to the west, the Sandias to the south, and the vast lands that stretched between the two ranges. Once they were on the flatter road leading towards Cochiti, La Cañada, and San Antonito, conversation grew easier.

"What's this *fiestas* I saw posters for?" Emily asked. "I've never gone to it."

"It's a celebration of the re-conquest of New Mexico Territory from the Indians in 1692. After the Pueblo Revolt."

"What was that?" Emily asked. She didn't know much about the topic. She vaguely remembered a sentence from the sixth-grade history text she used, but she suspected Professor Bateson would know more. She wondered if her students would be interested in studying it in class.

"The native tribes united and drove the Spanish colonists out of New Mexico territory in 1680. They were led by a medicine man, Po'pay. He was originally from San Juan Pueblo, near Española, one of their holy men. The Spaniards had incarcerated him in the 1670s, and executed other religious leaders. At the Governor's complex, right there on the Plaza. You probably saw it today."

Emily nodded. The Palace of the Governors flanked one side of the Plaza. Native artists sold their wares under the shady *portal* of the building, but Emily hadn't had time to shop there today.

"Once released, Po'pay retreated to Taos and planned the revolt," Bateson continued. Emily felt a bit like she was back in college, listening to a history lecture. "All the pueblos were involved, including San Antonito. The tribes coordinated well, and runners traveled between the different villages, carrying knotted strings to count the days until the revolt. The natives took the Spaniards by surprise; they attacked Santa Fe, killing over five hundred people, and expelled the remaining colonists. The settlers retreated to El Paso, but the Spanish returned twelve years later, led by Don Diego De Vargas, and retook the territory. It's referred to as a bloodless re-conquest, but to my understanding that's not strictly true. There was some fighting at the end. At any rate, the annual Fiestas de Santa Fe celebrates the return of the Spaniards to New Mexico."

Emily had never heard any of this. "That's very interesting," she said, thinking she should include the story in her curriculum. Although she doubted there was much about it in the history textbook.

"The settlers saved a statue of the Virgin Mary, 'La Conquistadora' from the church in Santa Fe during the revolt," the professor went on. "They brought her back when they returned; you can see her in the Cathedral off the Plaza. Where was I? Oh, yes, they have a Mass, and a novena. They've added an historical pageant in the last few years. And they burn a big old puppet. Some local artist came up with that a few years ago, I believe. But anthropologically it is very interesting. The celebration isn't overly popular with the San Antonito people, although the little kids like the carnival.

"Of course they do." Emily could understand why the residents of San Antonito might not enjoy a celebration of the Spanish conquest of their land, but kids always loved a carnival. "When is it?"

"Labor Day Weekend."

"That's next weekend. It sounds fascinating. They burn a puppet?"

"Yes, a big old marionette. Old Man Gloom, they call him, or Zozobra. The idea is to burn all your sorrows so you can enjoy the festivities. Quite pagan, really. Interesting that it has taken root in such a Catholic community, from an academic viewpoint. But many of these old religious traditions have pagan roots as well."

Bateson continued talking about anthropology and Emily

stopped paying too much attention, just politely replying, "Is that so?" and "How interesting" whenever the professor stopped for breath, which wasn't that often. Still, the fiestas sounded intriguing. Maybe she would go, if she could catch a ride up the hill to Santa Fe.

CHAPTER
SEVEN

AFTER PROFESSOR BATESON dropped her off, Emily hurried to put her groceries and supplies away. She checked the clock; goodness, it was nearly five! The Millers would be along to pick her up in just a few minutes. She ran upstairs to throw a few items into her overnight bag. What did one wear to a dance in a little Spanish town, anyway? Although she and her parents had dined at the country club during her visit home, Emily suspected tonight's activities would require different attire. She finally settled on a flowered dress she had bought that summer in Racine and pulled her pair of pumps out of the back of the closet. She had barely finished packing when she heard a truck pulling up in front of the school. Hastily patting her hair into place, and wishing for a moment it wasn't such a boring brown, she glanced outside.

Mavis and Charles sat in the front of Charles's old pickup truck. Emily grabbed her bag and sped downstairs. Outside, she locked the door to the school and climbed into the pickup. Mavis squeezed over to make room and gave her a little hug. Emily caught a whiff of Mavis's perfume—Chantilly, Emily guessed.

Mavis patted her friend's arm as Emily settled into her seat. "How are you doing, dear? Have you recovered from the shock of everything? We heard about it in La Cañada, of course. Such a shame."

Of course word had gotten around. Emily resigned herself to answering a few questions. "Yes, Juan seemed like a nice boy. And it was a shock. I just wish—Why would someone want to shoot him? It just doesn't make sense."

"Maybe an argument over a girl?" Charles put in. "Didn't you know of a student a couple of years ago who got mixed up with an Indian boy, Mavis?"

"Oh, yes. Consuela. Her family moved to Bernalillo to get away from the boy."

Emily realized that must be the girl she had met that morning at Mr. Romero's store. "A boy from San Antonito?"

Mavis nodded. "I can't remember his name."

Emily wondered if the boy was Juan. She thought it likely, remembering the conversation between some of the ladies at her sewing class. She didn't mention that to Mavis, however. It wouldn't do to encourage pointless gossip, especially not when the facts about Juan's killing were still unknown.

The women chatted, comparing notes about their summers and the new school year, while Charles guided the truck up the road that led to Cochiti and points further south. They turned off the main road into the village of La Cañada, and in a short while pulled up in front of the Gallegos's home, a large old-fashioned Spanish style hacienda with a long front porch, or portal, hung with *ristras* of drying red chiles. Their sharp scent lingered in the air, the scarlet strands bright against the adobe walls of the house.

Mrs. Gallegos came out to meet them, wearing a calico apron over a housedress.

"Ah, Señorita Schwarz. And Señor Miller. Thank you for coming. The girls have been decorating the dance hall all day. Even with the *niños* gone we'll have a fiesta, *que no*?"

Emily nodded, and Señora Gallegos showed her to the spare bedroom in the back of the house. An iron bedstead and a simple washstand stood on the wide plank floor, against whitewashed adobe walls. A bright-colored quilt covered the bed.

"This is lovely, Señora Gallegos," Emily said. "Thank you."

"We'll have a little dinner shortly. Before the music starts over at the *salón de baile*. We old folks, and the children, will have some fun, *que no*, Señorita? Even though all the boys are off fighting." Señora Gallegos's eyes flashed with sadness, until she smiled resolutely at her guest. Emily remembered Mavis had mentioned the couple's sons had enlisted.

Emily nodded. Señora Gallegos left and Emily changed into her flowered dress. She put on a little lipstick and patted her hair a final time before leaving to find the kitchen. Mavis and Charles were already seated while their hostess set a bowl of steaming pinto beans down on the old pine kitchen table. "There's some fresh tortillas and red chile enchiladas for you," she told them, before turning back to the old woodstove to pull a casserole out of the oven. The savory, spicy, sharp scents of red chile and cheese filled the air.

The three guests sat at the table, enjoying the feast, while Señora Gallegos filled tin enamel mugs with steaming coffee. They were nearly finished eating when Señor Gallegos came in. "Have they burst yet from all the food?" he asked. "No one will be able to dance if you fill them so full!"

Señora Gallegos smiled at that and went off to change her dress. "Go along with Lorenzo," she told them. "It's just a little ways to the *salón*. I'll catch up."

Emily and the Millers thanked her. Señor Gallegos picked up his guitar case and they walked the short distance down the rutted dirt road, the main street of La Cañada. It had grown dark, but light poured out of the open doors of the dance hall and the windows of the homes they passed. They met other villagers, all walking in the same direction. Señor Gallegos, and to a lesser extent, Mavis, greeted other people as they met them in the street.

They entered the dance hall, which was getting crowded now with villagers. The floor, made of wide pine planks, looked to Emily as though it had seen some wear. A couple of bare electric light bulbs hung from the ceiling, the stark light glaring against the whitewashed adobe walls. A 1943 calendar from Purina Feeds hung from a nail on one wall. On a platform at the far end of the room the other musicians—a fiddle player and an accordionist—were busy tuning their instruments. They greeted Señor Gallegos, who hurried to join them. He took his guitar out of its battered case, and started to tune it up.

Two benches sat on opposite sides, perpendicular to the

stage. A few women and young girls sat on one bench; across the large room some men and teenaged boys, their dark hair carefully pomaded and combed, lounged against the wall. Emily didn't recognize anyone—she certainly didn't see anyone there from San Antonito. She guessed the boys were no older than sixteen, and the older men at least thirty-five or so. Most of the others, the boys in their late teens and twenties, she assumed, had enlisted. A table off to one side held a punch bowl and cups, along with cookies, but Emily noticed some of the men passing flasks around when they thought their wives weren't looking.

She followed Mavis over towards the bench where the women sat. Mavis introduced Emily to a couple of the ladies, Señora Romero and Señora Mondragon. Señora Romero's auburn hair was carefully curled, and she wore a pretty floral dress that could have come from the Sears catalogue. In fact, Emily thought she had seen it, and had nearly purchased it herself. Señora Mondragon, a bit older, perhaps in her fifties, wore a black dress and a shawl. Emily noticed that most of the older women wore black.

"That's my *hijo* over there," Señora Mondragon, told Emily. "Playing the accordion." The accordion player looked to be in his late thirties.

"He's very good," Emily commented as the band began to play a lively folk song. A few men and boys crossed the room and invited some of the girls and ladies onto the dance floor. The *baile* was underway.

There seemed to be plenty of young girls, but as Señora Gallegos had said, male partners were less plentiful. Emily thought about the war, and hoped before too much longer all the young men would be back home, dancing with their sweethearts. A few of the littlest girls danced with each other while some boys their age stood awkwardly on the other side of the dance hall, watching. Some of the older men valiantly dragged the teenaged girls out on the dance floor, despite their giggling and protests. Emily watched while a boy she judged to be about twelve, his hair carefully pomaded, danced gingerly with a girl about the same age wearing a pale pink dress. She thought of the ballroom dance classes she'd taken as a girl in Racine and how nervous she had been, dancing with boys.

Emily didn't feel the need to dance, although Charles insisted she dance one with him. The polka left her breathless and laughing as he brought her back to the ladies' bench, and then took Mavis for a turn on the floor.

"That was fun!" Emily exclaimed to Señora Gallegos. "I haven't danced in ages."

Before Señora Gallegos could answer, some more folks entered the salón. Emily recognized faces from San Antonito—mostly men. She saw Gregorio, and Charley, as well as Demetria's godson Lorenzo, and some others. There weren't too many women in the group, but Emily did see Delia, Lorenzo's wife, dressed in a pretty red shirtwaist. And, surprisingly, Paulina, Charley's mother, wearing a traditional cotton dress, with a brightly colored flowered challis shawl wrapped around her shoulders. Emily looked for Demetria, hoping to find her friend, but didn't see her in the group.

A little murmur arose from the Hispanic women as Paulina and Delia walked over to join the ladies. Emily saw several of the young men from San Antonito speaking with the Cañada men. The flask surreptitiously made the rounds again, and some of the men disappeared outside.

"They'll be gambling," Señora Gallegos said with a disapproving sniff. "Dice."

Emily wasn't sure what to say to that, so she relinquished her place on the bench to an elderly matron, who had just returned, smiling and pink-cheeked, from the dance floor. Emily made her way to where Delia and Paulina stood against the wall, not talking to the Cañada ladies, and greeted them.

"Lorenzo thought the dance would be fun," Delia said, patting her hair. "He wanted to come."

"And I'm here to keep an eye on Charley," Paulina added. But the boy had already disappeared outside. The women chatted and then Emily went and got some punch, served by an unsmiling grandma dressed entirely in black.

"How do you know those *Indios*?" the black-clad woman asked Emily abruptly as she handed her the cup.

"I'm the schoolteacher at San Antonito Pueblo Day School," Emily replied.

"There'll be trouble," the *vieja* continued, her tone dark and her face grim. "Wait and see."

Unsure what to say to that, Emily thanked the woman, took her cup of punch and a *biscochito*, and made her way back to the ladies' bench. The baile seemed trouble-free to her, just people enjoying themselves. Mavis was still on the dance floor with Charles, and Emily saw Lorenzo dancing with Delia. The girl's black hair was carefully curled and some pretty turquoise and silver earrings glinted in her ears. She laughed at something Lorenzo had said to her.

Emily's gaze drifted to Paulina's son, standing awkwardly against the wall. Abruptly, he lurched across the room and asked one of the Cañada girls to dance. She agreed, and they staggered onto the dance floor. Emily wondered if the boy had been drinking outside to get his nerve up. Very possibly. She heard a few quiet mutterings from son of the older women, but they spoke in Spanish, and Emily ignored them. Still watching Charley and the girl, she started, surprised, when Gregorio appeared in front of her.

"Would you like to dance, Miss Schwarz?"

Annoyed by the muttering of the old *viejas*, Emily agreed with alacrity. They had no right to be so narrow-minded. It was a harmless social dance, that was all. She let Gregorio lead her out onto the floor.

The dance was another polka-like number, and she and Gregorio laughed their way through the steps. Emily feared her parents had wasted their money on those ballroom dance classes long ago. She missed a few steps, and Gregorio wasn't much of a lead, but it didn't overly bother her, or apparently him either.

Gradually, Emily became aware of other noises besides the music—loud yelling and sounds of an altercation near the door. Gregorio heard it too, and steered her back to the ladies' bench as the musicians finished a verse of the folk tune.

"Sorry, Miss Schwarz," he said. "I think I'd better go see what's happening."

Emily nodded. Several other couples had also stopped dancing, although the musicians kept on playing. A crowd grew at the entrance to the dance hall as people thronged to see what was going on outside. Gregorio had disappeared into the throng. The music finally stopped, and Mavis and Charles appeared by the bench.

"What's going on?" Emily asked.

"I'm not quite sure," Mavis said in a low tone. "Let Charles go and check on things.

Emily nodded, and Charles headed off towards the entrance. The musicians did not start another song, and Emily saw Señor Gallegos set his guitar down and head towards the door. More shouting arose as folks inside, mostly men, shoved and crammed through the door, trying to get outside. A few of the ladies, both young and old, also headed towards the commotion.

"I wonder what the trouble is?" Emily repeated, anxiety growing in the pit of her stomach.

"Sounds like some kind of a fight," Mavis replied. "Too much hard liquor, and fists can start to fly. It's a shame, really. If they want to fight so badly, they should just enlist."

The crowd parted and Emily saw Señor Gallegos push his way into the dance hall, supporting a young man who stumbled weakly into the room. *He's just drunk,* Emily thought, but then she saw the splash of red staining the boy's white shirt.

Beside her, Mavis gasped. "Oh, goodness. He's been stabbed!"

Emily saw Gregorio come back inside, holding Paulina's son by the arms. The ballroom filled with noise as several men talked at once, a woman shrieked and cried, and other women murmured among themselves. One little old lady, the grandma in black who had been handing out punch, headed towards the knifed man and spoke urgently in Spanish to Señor Gallegos. He nodded. Some of the other men from La Cañada surrounded Gregorio, who still had a tight grip on Charley. Paulina herself headed over and looked to be arguing with Gregorio and the Cañada men.

Charles left the knot of men around Gregorio and Charley and walked back to where Mavis and Emily sat on the bench. They watched as a couple of men from town helped the injured boy out of the room, followed by the woman who had been serving punch and another older woman, who could have been the boy's mother.

"Just a fight," Charles said. "Seems like that boy from San Antonito got to arguing with the Cañada boys. About what, I don't know. The young fool pulled a knife."

"Is the injured boy badly hurt?" Mavis asked, her tone concerned. "It looked like a lot of blood on his shirt."

"It's just a flesh wound, honey." Charles put his arm around his wife's shoulders. "He'll be fine. That's the *curandera*, the local wise woman who went outside with him."

"Señora Cristobal," Mavis said.

He nodded. "She'll stitch him up and they won't even need to call the doctor."

Señora Gallegos broke away from the ladies talking by the doorway and came over to where Mavis, Charles, and Emily sat talking. "Oh, Señoras, I am so sorry. What a shame, this happening at our baile. Those young boys, they have straw for brains. But see, they're taking the hurt one home and *la curandera* will take care of him. I think there will be more music if you want to stay."

"What about the Indian boy?" Emily asked.

Señora Gallegos sniffed. "Well, it's not a good thing, *que no*? But the *fiscal* there says the tribal elders will punish the *niño*. And the boy here wasn't hurt too badly. His mama says he's a hothead, anyway." She paused. "Will you ladies stay for more dancing?"

Mavis and Emily looked at each other, and then Mavis nodded to Charles—one of those married couple nods, Emily thought, that conveyed so much.

"If you don't mind, Señora Gallegos, we might head back and turn in," Mavis said. "There's no need for you to leave, though. Stay and enjoy your husband's playing. He's such a fine musician. Charles will see us safely back."

Señora Gallegos protested at first, but finally agreed, telling them in detail where to find the matches for the kerosene lamps.

Emily looked for Gregorio and the others from San Antonito as she and Mavis and Charles left the dance hall and made their way back to the Gallegos's house, but she didn't see them. They had already headed back to the pueblo, she guessed, and that was undoubtedly a good thing.

CHAPTER EIGHT

THE NEXT MORNING, Sunday, Charles and Mavis dropped Emily off at the schoolhouse. They had left La Cañada early, despite Señora Gallegos's protests. Mavis pleaded papers to grade, and Emily concurred. Back at the schoolhouse by seven-thirty, she felt restless; the night before had been unsettling. The sight of the young boy with blood on his white shirt had brought back the memory of Juan's corpse all too strongly, although Charles had reassured Emily and Mavis that the boy would be fine. Still, Emily felt she had seen far too many bloody young men in the past week.

She said a silent prayer for her brother in the Pacific. She made a pot of coffee and glared at the stack of papers sitting on her desk in the classroom, and then decided to go to Mass at the old chapel on the pueblo. Perhaps the familiar ritual would settle her down. She put on her plaid jacket and walked over towards the old mission church.

The thick adobe walls of the building sloped irregularly upward, with the massive *vigas*, the beams, that crossed the ceiling supporting the flat roof above. She slipped inside and found a pew, and gave herself over to the service. The familiar Latin of the Mass soothed and comforted her. After the service was over, Emily left the church and walked over to the camposanto. She found Juan's grave easily enough. At San Antonito people were buried in the order in which they had died, not in family plots. Most of the graves did not have marble headstones; that didn't seem to be the way folks memorialized their dead here. Just simple wooden crosses, many with the names of the departed painted on them. Some families had placed artificial flowers on a few of the graves.

Near Juan's grave was some charred wood and ashes—the remains of the bonfires that the men who watched over the grave through the night had left behind. In the daylight, the graveyard was deserted. Emily saw a lizard dart behind one of the crosses, and the sun beat down on her as she stood by the brown mound of dirt that marked Juan's resting place under a deep blue sky. Juan's spirit didn't seem to be lingering here, but she said a quiet prayer anyway and then walked back to the school, where she settled down to her usual Sunday routine of grading some papers the older children had written and lesson planning for the week ahead.

She heard a car approaching, heading towards the main part of the pueblo. Glancing up, Emily glimpsed the Bernalillo sheriff's car through the classroom window as it sped past the school. She briefly wondered about it, but went back to her grading. Some of the fifth and sixth graders' essays, on the topic, "Why America Will Win the War and What I Can Do To Help" weren't too bad.

Emily had almost completed the essays when someone knocked on the door. She hadn't heard a car pull up; except for the sheriff's vehicle passing by earlier, the afternoon had been quiet. Emily laid down her red pencil and went to answer the door.

Her eyebrows rose when she opened up and saw who it was. "Demetria!"

Demetria's usually placid face looked distressed, her eyes red. Emily guessed she had been crying. "Miss Schwarz. Can I come in?"

"Of course. What's wrong? Here, sit down." Emily ushered Demetria into the kitchen and, without asking, poured her a cup of coffee. "What's happened?"

Demetria didn't answer immediately. Emily watched as her friend absentmindedly dumped a third spoonful of sugar into her coffee cup, and wondered what could have upset her so.

"They came—they took Lorenzo away," Demetria finally said.

"What? Who did?"

"The sheriff. He took Lorenzo in. He says Lorenzo shot Juan."

"No!"

"My godson would never do that. He's a good boy."

"I know, Demetria. He is."

"You've got to do something," Demetria pleaded. "Talk to the sheriff. Tell him you know my godson. Please."

Emily wasn't sure. Interfering in an investigation like that. But what harm could it do? Odds were the sheriff would just ignore her, anyway.

Demetria gripped her coffee cup. "I saw Juan with Lorenzo that day, after they came back from turkey hunting. They were laughing and joking. Lorenzo had no reason to shoot Juan."

"You don't think Lorenzo and Juan got in an argument," Emily said slowly, reluctant to hurt her friend. "Maybe over Delia?"

Demetria shook her head. "I know my godson. He loves Delia, but he loved Juan too. And Delia and Lorenzo are happy together. That Juan was a womanizer. He would have made Delia miserable, and she knows it."

Emily nodded. An argument between the two men didn't make any sense. Lorenzo was happily married to Delia, and she wasn't interested in Juan any longer.

"The sheriff said maybe they'd been drinking," Demetria continued, wiping her eyes with her hands. "But I saw them that afternoon, they hadn't been drinking. Lorenzo never drinks, never. Maybe Juan would have a beer sometimes, but not Lorenzo. Not after the way his dad died, drunk all the time." She looked straight at Emily. "So you've got to talk to the sheriff. You're educated. And the teacher. And—"

And white, Emily thought. Well, maybe the sheriff would listen to her. She'd have to try, for Demetria's sake.

But if Lorenzo hadn't shot Juan, who had?

Later that afternoon, Emily walked down the dusty road to La Cañada to use the pay phone at the mercantile there.

Nobody in San Antonito had phones. When she first moved there it had seemed odd, compared to life in Racine, but now Emily rather liked it. Life was generally quieter and didn't move as fast. As she walked, Emily savored the afternoon. The sky was deep blue above her, and a few leaves of the big cottonwoods down by the Rio Chiquito had just begun to turn gold. A jay squawked and scolded as Emily passed his tree, and the scents of chamisa sage and piñon mingled pleasantly in the air as she strolled along. She enjoyed the chance to stretch her legs, but she didn't much enjoy her errand.

The little town sat sleepy and peaceful in the afternoon sunlight. The excitement of the baile and the knife fight the night before might never have happened. She had Sheriff Wilcox's number on the card he had left with her after his visit.

She entered the general store, run by a brother of the Mr. Romero who ran the store in San Antonito. She recognized him from the dance, and they exchanged pleasantries. Emily asked after the boy who had been hurt, and the shopkeeper said he was doing well and would most likely go to work the next morning. As Emily made her way to the pay phone, she wondered what she could possibly say to Sheriff Wilcox. They must have had some kind of proof to arrest Lorenzo, after all. But what proof could they have? Demetria hadn't known of anything.

The phone sat tucked away in the back of the store, between a display of rope and clothesline, and another of kerosene cans. The cramped location did afford a little privacy, and Emily felt glad of that as she dialed the sheriff's number.

The call went through and a secretary answered. Emily gave her name and asked to be put through to Sheriff Wilcox.

The secretary asked Emily to hold and eventually she heard Wilcox's voice on the other end of the line.

"Miss Schwarz. How can I help you?"

"I wondered if I could speak with you again, sir. About Juan Atencio's murder."

"We have a suspect in custody, ma'am. Have you remembered something else?"

Emily was reminded of the times when, as a young girl, she'd had to coax her father into something. "Well, sir, I'm not absolutely sure—it's most likely not too important, but . . . I'd like a chance to tell you about it and let you be the judge of that."

Sounding somewhat mollified, Sheriff Wilcox agreed to come over and speak with Emily the next day. She thanked him and hung up. *Now, what am I going to tell him tomorrow,* she wondered, as she left the little store and started the two-mile walk from Cañada back to the schoolhouse.

She hadn't gone far when a dust cloud loomed on the road ahead. Emily stood off to the shoulder to let the old truck pass, but instead Gregorio stopped the vehicle and poked his lean head out of the open window. "Hi, Miss Schwarz."

"Hello, Gregorio. Hi, Florencita."

Gregorio's mother sat next to him on the front seat of the truck, her diminutive figure swathed in her sabana and an additional fringed blanket. Emily guessed some of the wrapping might have been an attempt to avoid the dust that, now the truck had stopped, began to settle again on every surface of the old vehicle.

"Where are you folks headed?" Emily asked. She hadn't

spoken with Gregorio since last night. She'd seen him at Mass—the *fiscal* had responsibility for the church, and therefore usually attended services—but they hadn't talked. She wondered what had happened to Paulina's son, but hadn't wanted to ask anyone.

"Just down to Cañada. Mom needed some lard and Señor Romero was closed since today's Sunday. She's going to bake tomorrow and the dough has to rise overnight. And you, Miss Schwarz?"

"I'm just on my way back. I had to make a phone call." She hesitated, then asked, "What happened to Charley?"

"The elders gave him a talking to. And some extra duties here at San Antonito. He has to plaster the church when he's not working for McKee. That might keep him out of trouble."

Emily nodded. "It's a shame that that happened. I don't know Charley well. Does he get into trouble often?"

Gregorio smiled. "He likes his beer. But he's a pretty good boy. If his mother would cut him a little slack he'd probably straighten out. He's got that job now, at least, working for McKee, the same as Juan did. I hear they pay pretty well."

"Well, that's good," Emily said, relieved to learn the boy wasn't a troublemaker. "I should get going."

"You want a ride back to the school?" Gregorio offered.

"It's not far. I'll be home before you've finished your shopping," Emily replied.

She continued walking back up the rutted road that led to San Antonito, while Gregorio and his mother continued down the road in the opposite direction. Emily wondered why Gregorio had never married, but he seemed perfectly at ease with his bachelor existence, so far as she could tell. His mother kept house for him, and Emily guessed the arrangement suited the both of them.

On Monday Sheriff Wilcox dropped by the school just as the children were released, as he had said he would. Emily had made some brownies the evening before, and had put on pot of fresh coffee in anticipation of the visit, but she was surprised to see both Sheriff Wilcox and Mr. Shepherd get out of the official car, marked with the Sandoval County shield, that the sheriff parked under the cottonwood outside the schoolhouse.

"Glad you've got some shade here," the sheriff commented as Emily opened the door.

"Sheriff Wilcox, thank you for coming," Emily said as she ushered them in. "And Mr. Shepherd too. I didn't realize you two gentlemen knew each other."

"Oh, I know a lot of folks," Shepherd said. Emily shot him a curious look, but Sheriff Wilcox interrupted.

"Mr. Shepherd here is helping with the case; he's a liaison between us and the military."

"I thought you worked in procurement, a war job," Emily murmured, feeling oddly betrayed. She wondered why the military would be interested in Juan's murder, but didn't ask.

"I do lots of things," Shepherd replied as he sipped his coffee. Emily remembered from their lunch at La Fonda that he took it black, with two sugars.

"So, Miss Schwarz, what is it you wanted to tell me yesterday?" Wilcox asked, after he'd worked his way through most of his brownie. "These are awfully good, ma'am," he added as he reached for a second one. "It was kind of you to go to all that trouble."

"It wasn't any trouble, Sheriff," Emily replied. "Thanks for making the trip out here."

"But back to your call. What did you want to tell me?"

"Well, Sheriff, it's just that I believe you've arrested the wrong man. Lorenzo is a very gentle boy, doesn't drink, and wouldn't hurt a fly. His godmother says he doesn't even hunt deer; he can't stand to see them suffer. I just can't imagine he'd commit murder. And Demetria—that's Lorenzo's godmother—said she saw the two of them back from the turkey hunt that Sunday, laughing and joking."

"Well, ma'am, we'd heard Lorenzo's wife used to go with Juan."

"Yes, that's true."

"And maybe still has a soft spot for him."

"She was upset by Juan's death, of course. But that doesn't mean she was still in love with him."

"Well, ma'am, jealousy can be a pretty powerful motive. A jealous husband, a young wife." The sheriff reached for a third brownie.

"No," Emily insisted. "I can't believe it."

"Well then, Miss Schwarz. Who did do it? Shoot a young man in the chest like that?"

The sheriff's words brought the image of Juan's dead body vividly back to Emily's mind. She blanched.

"I don't know. What about the girl in La Cañada and her family? They weren't happy about that romance."

"Well, neither was Juan's own family. And we've got Deputy

Duran investigating over there. He knows all the families and has connections in La Cañada."

"What has he discovered?"

"Nothing," Sheriff Wilcox said. "That's why we arrested Lorenzo."

"But you can't possibly have any evidence—"

"We'll find some."

Emily didn't like the sound of that. Wilcox continued, "Juan was shot with a handgun, probably a .45. We'll know for sure when the ballistics come back. A few of the old folks here enlisted and fought in that war; they probably kept their guns when they came back. Juan's dad, Atencio, and Lorenzo's dad, they were both in France."

"But you haven't found the gun," she guessed.

"No ma'am, not yet. But we will."

He was so definite, it got on her nerves. "Juan's mother thought her son had gone to Albuquerque with Paulina's boy Charley on Sunday. That's why they weren't worried when he didn't come home Sunday night. And Charley didn't come back from Albuquerque until Monday evening. I guess he missed a day of work. He works for the same construction company that Juan worked for. He likes to drink some, although he's a good boy." Her voice trailed off. "At least that's what people say."

She had the feeling Sheriff Wilcox wasn't paying her much attention. His bored reply—"Is that so?"—reinforced her suspicions.

Mr. Shepherd, who had been listening quietly, spoke up. "Miss Schwarz, exactly why do you believe Lorenzo didn't do it?"

"Because it doesn't make sense. Demetria—that's Lorenzo's godmother—saw them at about four o'clock on Sunday afternoon. The two of them had come back from turkey hunting up in the hills. She said they were laughing and joking, in good spirits. And then Lorenzo went on home, but Juan said he had to go talk to someone, so he left Lorenzo and Demetria and headed the other direction."

"Who did he want to talk to?"

"I don't know. He didn't say."

Sheriff Wilcox sighed and put down his brownie. "Well, I'll speak with this woman, Demetria. See what she says. Maybe she'll remember some detail that will be helpful."

"Thank you, Sheriff," Emily said, in her most placating tone. "If you could manage it."

"I sure hope it's worth my time," Wilcox added. "But I'm keeping that boy in custody for now."

Emily nodded. Her neck felt tight and strained. At least the sheriff had agreed to something, although it wasn't much. It seemed as though he felt he had his suspect. And Emily was sure the boy was innocent.

Wilcox pushed his chair back from the table and stood. "Well, let's get going. Are you coming, Shepherd?"

Mr. Shepherd put his coffee cup down. "Just a second, Sheriff. You go on ahead, I'll be right there."

Sheriff Wilcox left the schoolhouse and headed out to the car, leaving Emily alone in the kitchen with Mr. Shepherd.

"I just had one more question," he said.

"Yes, Mr. Shepherd?"

"This weekend is the fiestas up in Santa Fe. There are parades. They even burn a big puppet."

"Yes, I've heard about that. Professor Bateson mentioned it. I guess a few of the people from San Antonito go up—the kids enjoy the carnival." Emily wondered what this had to do with Juan's death, and what Mr. Shepherd was getting at. It made her uneasy. She picked up the dirty coffee cups and put them on the counter while she waited for Mr. Shepherd to continue.

"Well, would you like to go up with me on Friday? That's when they burn Old Man Gloom. That's the puppet. And in the meantime you could keep your eyes open here, let me know if you can find out who else Juan might have visited that evening. Maybe this woman Demetria will tell you more than she'll tell Wilcox."

"I don't know," Emily hedged. She wondered what Mr. Shepherd wanted. Was he asking her to spy on her friend? And why ask her to come to Santa Fe with him? What was his angle? "I think Demetria would do anything to help her godson," she finally replied. "I'm sure she'll tell Sheriff Wilcox everything she can."

Mr. Shepherd looked at her, but didn't directly reply. "So what about it?" he asked after a moment. "Zozobra. Will you come?"

Emily bit her lip, then surprised herself by saying yes.

Mr. Shepherd flashed a smile. "I'll pick you up on Friday, then. About four-thirty, that will give us time to get up to Santa Fe and look around a bit before they burn that puppet. I hear he's going to look like Hirohito this year."

"Well, I'd be happy to see that man burn up," Emily said.

Mr. Shepherd smiled again, making the small wrinkles around his eyes crinkle pleasantly. "I'll see you on Friday," he replied, and left to join Sheriff Wilcox.

Emily followed him outside as far as the porch. The shadows were lengthening in the canyon and soon it would be getting dark. Emily stood on the front stoop, smelling the scent of ponderosa pines and watching the dust cloud as the sheriff's car drove off down the dirt road towards La Cañada.

CHAPTER
NINE

O<small>N</small> W<small>EDNESDAY</small> <small>NIGHT</small> Emily saw Demetria at her home economics class. Afterward, Demetria stayed behind to help Emily tidy up, so they had a chance to chat a bit.

"I spoke with Sheriff Wilcox on Monday after school," Emily volunteered. "Did he speak with you?"

Demetria nodded. "He wanted to know if I knew who Juan went to see that evening. I'd told you everything, and I told him again. After I saw Juan and Lorenzo that Sunday, Juan headed north up towards the canyon, away from the plaza. Lorenzo went the other way, home." She scoffed a little. "That sheriff, I don't think he was too interested in what I had to say, though. He's certain who did it."

Briefly, Emily laid a hand on her friend's shoulder. "I wish we could convince him. What would it take?" She wound up a few final bits of yarn into a ball. The project that evening had been knitting, making socks for the troops. "I wonder where Juan was going that afternoon? After all, he'd just been up in the woods. Why would he head back there?"

"Maybe he lost something? And didn't want to say so?" Demetria replied.

"You don't think he met up with Charley and went to Albuquerque with him?"

Demetria shook her head. "I think Charley had already left by then. Nobody saw Juan after he headed back north."

"Do you think he mentioned anything to Lorenzo or Delia?" Emily asked.

"Lorenzo's in jail. We can't ask him. But Delia's here."

Lorenzo's young wife hadn't come to class tonight. Emily had overheard a fair bit of gossip among the ladies who had attended about Lorenzo's arrest. She had noticed a coolness tonight between Demetria and those women, and she imagined that was why. Emily guessed Delia just hadn't wanted to deal with the innuendos and sly looks, and truthfully, Emily didn't blame her one bit.

"It's not that late," Emily observed. "Do you think Delia's still up? Let's stop by." She cast her gaze around the room and saw some extra yarn and needles. "I'll bring her this and tell her about tonight's project."

Demetria snorted. "I don't know if I'd be happy to have someone show up on my doorstep late at night with those darned socks. I'm not much good at knitting, and I don't think Delia likes it either. But let's go. I'll bet she's still awake."

The two women left the schoolhouse and walked towards the plaza. A quarter moon rose over the canyon walls, lightening the darkness just a tad.

The little two-room adobe house Delia shared with Lorenzo was at the far end of San Antonito, a little off the main plaza. The families of the couple had collaborated to build it for them. It had been a nice gift and meant the newlyweds wouldn't have to share a place with either set of in-laws. Emily saw lamplight through the front window as she and Demetria approached. The house had real glass windows, not selenite like many of the older homes in the pueblo.

"It looks like she's still up," Demetria said, and knocked on the door. "*Guw'aadzi!*" she called.

After a minute, the door opened. Delia stood there, her hair up in curlers with an old flowered scarf tied around her head. "Auntie Demetria. And Miss Schwarz." Emily guessed Delia hadn't been expecting company, and she didn't look thrilled to see them. Delia hesitated a moment, biting her lip. "Come on in," she finally said. "I'll get you some coffee."

Emily looked around the house as they entered it. An old table stood against one wall along with a treadle sewing machine nearby. It looked like Delia was making a man's shirt. She'd used some old white flour sacks for the fabric; Emily could see a scrap with the blue bird logo on the floor by the machine. A bench lined the other wall, and some colorful wool blankets hung against the plastered adobe. The kerosene lamp sitting on the table cast a warm glow over the scene.

"We're sorry to disturb you so late," Emily said, as Delia brought them some coffee and gestured for them to sit.

"I can't sleep anyway," Delia replied. "I was sewing. A shirt. For Lorenzo. He'll need it, when he gets out of that place." She looked at her visitors. "What do you ladies want? What is it, Auntie?"

Emily looked at Demetria, who nodded slightly. "We missed you at class," Emily said.

Delia sniffed. "Those women. I didn't want to be around them, with all their talk."

"They were pretty quiet tonight," Demetria told her. "I made sure of that. They just want to gossip."

Delia didn't reply, but Emily thought she glimpsed tears in the girl's eyes.

"We've started knitting socks for the troops," Emily interjected briskly, "so I brought you some yarn and needles. Your auntie can show you how to get started."

"Thanks, Miss Schwarz." Delia didn't look too happy to receive the yarn.

Emily plunged ahead. "Demetria said that after Juan and your husband came back from turkey hunting on Sunday, Juan went back north, out of the pueblo. Did he say why, or where he was going?"

Delia looked confused. "Lorenzo told me Juan said he dropped a knife out there someplace. I think he was going to look for it. That's why he didn't come back."

Demetria frowned. "That's not what Juan said when I saw him and Lorenzo a little earlier. He said he had to go talk to someone."

Delia shrugged. "I don't know. I'm just telling you what Lorenzo told me."

Emily didn't think Juan had a knife on him when she'd found the body that awful day. Of course, she hadn't seen everything. Maybe they'd found the knife when they examined the corpse in Bernalillo.

"It was a good knife," Delia was saying. "One Atencio had gotten for him, with a nice elk horn handle."

"And you and Lorenzo didn't see him after that?" Emily asked, using the stern voice she usually reserved for sixth graders.

Delia shook her head no. "Miss Schwarz, the sheriff has the wrong man."

As Emily walked back to the schoolhouse a bit later, her mind buzzed with theories about what could have caused Juan to head back into the woods late that Sunday afternoon. She had passed the plaza, and was so intent on her thoughts that she almost bumped into a tall figure heading towards her. She stepped back, surprised and a little alarmed, but after a moment realized the man approaching her in the dark was Gregorio, leading his old horse behind him.

"Hello, Gregorio," Emily greeted him. "You startled me." She looked at Flossie. "Did she run away again?"

"Busted right through the corral," Gregorio replied. "Of course, that gate was pretty rickety. Never got around to mending it. I should sell this horse. Maybe to somebody down in Cochiti. Or Santo Domingo." He laughed. "No, I won't. Everybody knows about Flossie. Nobody would buy her. Besides, I kind of like the old girl." He laughed again and Emily chuckled with him. She knew Gregorio doted on the horse. "But what are you doing out, Miss Schwarz?" Gregorio continued. "It's late. Anything wrong?"

"No." Emily explained that she and Demetria had gone to check up on Delia. "She told us Juan headed back up the canyon that Sunday, after he and Lorenzo came back from turkey hunting, because he left a knife in the woods. Did he have a knife on him when the body was examined?"

"Nope," Gregorio said. "I sure didn't see one."

"Delia said it was a good knife, with an elk horn handle. Atencio had given it to him."

Gregorio shrugged. "Maybe he didn't find it."

"So what did he find—or who? Surely he wouldn't get shot over a knife."

Gregorio nodded. "I don't think anyone here would do that. Unless they'd been drinking. You never know what folks will do when they're drunk."

Emily shuddered, then collected herself. "Sheriff Wilcox told me Juan was shot with a handgun. Who around here has one of those?"

"Most folks have rifles, and shotguns for hunting. Not so many folks have handguns. Atencio and his brother both fought in the last war, so either of them might have an old army-issue gun around someplace. They didn't have citizenship, couldn't vote, but our men enlisted and fought for their country. A couple of other boys from San Antonito served, too. Guillermo, and Florentino. Either of them might have brought a handgun back from the front with them."

Emily nodded. "But Lorenzo didn't have a gun."

"Not of his own, I don't think so, but Guillermo was Lorenzo's dad."

"Has anybody asked Guillermo about it yet?"

Gregorio shook his head. "Guillermo's gone now. He died about four years back. I don't know what happened to his gun. But Sheriff Wilcox will think of it sooner or later, and investigate."

"Why don't you call him and tell him about the other men who served, so he can find out where their old guns are? There's what, three of them besides Guillermo? Or at least mention it to Atencio. He's the governor. Let him tell the sheriff. And the sheriff should know about Juan's missing knife, too."

Gregorio nodded, but Emily had a feeling he wasn't going to do as she asked. She imagined Gregorio saw her as bossy, but honestly, what was the harm in letting the sheriff know about other possibilities? The sooner the better.

"I'll keep my eyes open for that knife," Gregorio finally said. "Do you want me to walk you back to the school, ma'am?"

"I'm almost there. I'll be perfectly fine." Emily's exasperation showed in her voice.

"I'll apologize in advance, then."

"For what?"

"When I found my horse back there, she was eating your dahlias."

The next morning Emily surveyed the sad remains of her dahlias over her morning coffee. Lord knew it was hard enough to grow things out here, when it was so dry. She had loved the flowers, their bright lushness against the dry dirt. Then her first students arrived, and she had no more time to mourn the blossoms. School began. Some of the talk at recess, she noted, was of the carnival that weekend up in Santa Fe.

She wondered, not for the first time, what had possessed her to agree to go up to Santa Fe with the mysterious Mr.

Shepherd. She told herself Professor Bateson's comments on Old Man Gloom had piqued her interest. A giant puppet, burned to banish cares, would surely be something she'd never have seen if she'd stayed in Racine, Wisconsin.

CHAPTER
TEN

O<small>N FRIDAY, ONCE</small> her pupils were dismissed, Emily fidgeted a bit with her appearance. She told herself it wasn't for Mr. Shepherd's benefit. It was just, whatever did one wear to a pagan puppet burning, anyway? She settled on a dark print dress and jacket—the September evenings sometimes had a chill in them—and then put on some lipstick and fussed with her hair a little more before she heard the sound of a car outside. She grabbed her hat, ran downstairs and opened the front door. Mr. Shepherd was parked behind the wheel of an older Dodge. Emily realized that most times she'd seen him, he ridden to San Antonito with someone else—Sheriff Wilcox, or that army officer O'Toole.

Shepherd got out and opened the car door for Emily. She settled in the passenger seat and they started on the hour-long drive up towards Santa Fe.

"So are you based in Santa Fe?" Emily asked. "Or in Albuquerque?"

"Mostly Santa Fe, these days," Shepherd replied. "But they'll send me all over the state. Procurement, you know. I chase after all kinds of things. You'd be surprised."

"I'm sure I would be," Emily answered, a little primly. To her disappointment, Mr. Shepherd didn't volunteer any other information about his job. Instead they talked about the news from the Pacific, the buildup of troops in England, and the Allies' invasion of Sicily. Mr. Shepherd, well informed and intelligent, proved a good conversationalist—and when speech lagged, the views of the Sangres looming ahead over Santa Fe, and the golden aspens and cottonwood trees they passed, blazing against the deep blue sky of the New Mexican autumn, made up for it.

The ride passed quickly and it seemed very soon that they arrived in Santa Fe. Mr. Shepherd parked the car on Don Gaspar Avenue, near some car dealerships and, surprisingly, pulled a picnic basket out of the back seat.

"I brought a blanket," he explained. "But we need something to eat. Maybe we can pick up something on the plaza. They have vendors there, selling food."

People were crowding the streets already, strolling toward the city plaza. There were lots of family groups, some with their own picnic baskets. Emily saw women in bright, ruffled, Spanish-style dresses trimmed with rickrack, wearing silver and turquoise Indian jewelry, and she felt very Midwestern and prosaic in her print dress and jacket. Mr. Shepherd wore his standard suit, like some of the men in the throng, but plenty of others had on jeans and plaid cotton shirts, cowboy hats and boots. As they walked through the plaza, Emily noticed many booths set up, selling food—hamburgers, tortilla burgers and burritos, hot dogs. The scent of roasted green chiles and grilling meat filled the air.

"Are you hungry?" Mr. Shepherd asked. "I could do with a burger."

They got in line and ordered two hamburgers, with cheese and green chile, and Coca-colas. Their food arrived and Mr. Shepherd asked for a paper bag. He deposited the food and sodas in his picnic basket.

"Let's head on up to the ball field. It's still pretty early, and we can get a good spot."

They walked the few blocks up to Fort Marcy and filed into the ballpark. Lots of families had spread out tablecloths on the field and sat on the ground, picnicking. Up at the front of the ballpark, she saw the giant puppet and gasped.

"There it is," Mr. Shepherd said. "Old Man Gloom himself. We'll have a good view from here."

The thirty-foot tall figure, made of paper, did look like Hirohito, with glasses and a Hitler-esque mustache, and was dressed in a long white robe with black buttons and belt. Emily glared at the giant a moment, thinking of her brother and all the other families, people who had sons and brothers fighting and sometimes dying in the war. There certainly seemed enough gloom and doom this year, that was for sure. It would be good to get rid of some of it.

Little boys raced around the ball field, ignoring the cries of their parents. The space was quickly filling up with families. Most looked to be from Santa Fe, although Emily saw a few WACs and army folks, along with some people wearing more conservative attire who kind of kept to themselves. They looked a bit out of place among the Santa Fe natives. A few people in the crowd were dressed more extravagantly, the women in cocktail gowns with silk embroidered piano shawls around their shoulders, and the men in fancy dress. That group drank something poured out of cocktail shakers and seemed to be having quite a fine time. Artists, maybe.

"They're calling him Hirohitlimus this year," Mr. Shepherd said, referring to the puppet. Emily didn't answer right away, thinking about her brother, in the thick of the fighting. She hadn't heard from him in a long while, and wondered if her parents had received any letters.

"I don't see anyone from San Antonito here," Emily said after a minute, rousing herself. "Look at those folks over there," she added, indicating one group. "They don't look native to Santa Fe. I wonder who they are."

"Tourists, most likely," replied Shepherd, glancing over in that direction. "From back East."

The sun sank lower in the sky, and some musicians started to play up on the rise where the giant effigy stood. The musicians wore suits decorated with silver buttons and big sombreros, and they played traditional Spanish songs. Emily and Mr. Shepherd sat and ate their burgers while the sky grew darker and the ballpark grew more crowded. Their parents, Emily noted, had now corralled most of the children.

She finished the last bite of her burger and wiped her mouth on the paper napkin. "Mr. Shepherd," she asked, "why did you ask me up here tonight?"

Shepherd laughed. "Do I need a reason? I wanted to. You

mentioned you'd never seen fiestas, and I had some extra gas coupons."

She wasn't quite sure how to respond to that. "Well, thank you," she said after a minute. "This is something pretty unusual."

"You wouldn't see this in Wisconsin," Shepherd teased, and Emily agreed, laughingly, that he was correct.

The mariachis stopped playing, and the lights around the stage dimmed. Some little kids, dressed up in white sheets like ghosts, came out dancing and capered around at the foot of Hirohitlimus. Emily felt the crowd's anticipation increase; people stopped chatting and watched, alert and excited.

"Those are the glooms," Shepherd explained. "And here comes the Fire Dancer." A man wearing a red and orange leotard, his costume resembling flames, emerged from behind the figure and danced too, appearing to taunt the effigy, whose arms moved and whose groans, amplified by loudspeakers, filled the air.

She and Mr. Shepherd stood, along with most of the rest of the audience, and pressed forward, edging into the mass of people to try and find a better view. From the crowd Emily could hear shouts of, "Burn him! Burn him!"

"Professor Bateson was right," she said to Shepherd, raising her voice so he could hear her above the increasing noise. "It really is quite pagan." The thrill and excitement felt contagious, intoxicating, uncontrolled. She'd never experienced anything quite like it.

Shepherd nodded. "Have you seen Bateson? I don't imagine he'd want to miss this." Emily just shook her head no. It was noisy, hard to converse.

Some fireworks erupted at the base of the figure. The Fire

Dancer took a lighted torch and pranced around with it, the swinging torch leaving streaks of fire against the dark sky.

The crowd's roar had increased to a mad frenzy. "Burn him!" Emily found herself screaming with the others, caught up in the excitement. Burn up gloom, burn up war, burn up all death and destruction and sadness. There had been far, far too much of it this year.

Another cascade of fireworks went off. Emily smelled the sulfur and smoke amid the crush of humanity. The Fire Dancer continued his capering until the crowd had reached a fevered pitch, then finally touched his torch to the white front of Hirohitlimus. The paper caught immediately, and Emily heard more fireworks as the huge puppet burst into flames. His arms waved and writhed in agony and a groaning voice played over the loudspeakers.

"Burn him!" Emily cried again, along with the rest of the chanting crowd. Her nose filled with the scent of ash as the fireworks continued. "Burn him!"

Then it was over. The last glowing remnants of the gigantic marionette fell in ashes to the ground. People clapped and cheered, then began retrieving their paraphernalia before slowly exiting the park.

"Well." Mr. Shepherd looked curiously at Emily. "That was something, all right."

Emily felt herself flush. She had really lost control. She didn't even know if Mr. Shepherd had joined in the shouting.

She hadn't paid any attention to him, caught up in the moment, and now she felt a bit embarrassed.

"It sure was," she answered him. "I've never seen anything like it. Certainly not in Racine. I guess I got a little carried away."

"You and a few thousand other people," Shepherd observed dryly. "Do you ever go to any of the Pueblo dances?" he asked, as they found their abandoned picnic spot. He began to fold up the blanket.

"San Antonito has corn dances in the summer. And they dance at Christmas—the Matachines, I think they're called. I've seen the deer dance, too. But this was different."

Shepherd smiled, a crooked grin, as he tucked the folded blanket in the picnic basket. "Leave it to the Bohemians," he said. "Fiesta used to be mostly a Mass, and some historical and religious processions. Then about twenty years ago, the artists got into the act. Will Shuster designed the first Old Man Gloom, along with Gustave Baumann. You may have seen Baumann's prints in the museum here. Anyway, Shuster still creates Old Man Gloom for the community, every year."

"You seem to know Santa Fe pretty well," Emily observed.

"My lungs brought me out here about sixteen years ago. They got better but I liked it and stayed around. Now the army has me in this procurement job, so I'm here for the duration."

They filed out of the ballpark and made their way down to the plaza along with the rest of the noisy crowd. A band played Mexican music and some couples danced near the bandstand on the plaza while other folks lined up at the burger stands.

"I guess I should think about getting you back down La

Bajada," Shepherd said, and Emily agreed, although it didn't look like the party was going to break up anytime soon.

They left the plaza and started back towards the car. A few other people were making their way home, walking to the residential area just the other side of the Paseo de Peralta. Emily and Mr. Shepherd turned down Old Santa Fe Trail at La Fonda, following the crowds, and walked down to Alameda Street, which followed the course of the tiny Santa Fe River back towards Don Gaspar. The crowds had thinned out a bit when Emily spied a familiar figure.

"Professor Bateson!" she called out, but Bateson didn't hear her. He continued walking in the opposite direction, up towards the Old Santa Fe Trail, and then turned towards the plaza.

"He didn't hear me. I wonder where he's headed?" Emily said to Shepherd.

"Probably just back to his car," Shepherd replied, "or to La Fonda for a nightcap."

"I thought he was out in the back country."

"I guess he couldn't stay away from the pagan spectacle. It was just too tempting," Shepherd said lightly. Emily giggled.

They turned onto Don Gaspar Avenue and soon reached the car. "It's too bad he didn't hear me," Emily said as she settled herself into the passenger seat." "You wouldn't have to drive me all the way back down to San Antonito. It's a long trip."

Shepherd looked at her oddly. "I don't think I'd beg off, Emily. I'd like to make sure you get home safely."

Flustered, Emily didn't reply. She didn't quite know what to say and hoped Mr. Shepherd didn't think she had been rude. It had been a while since she was on a date with anyone. She supposed that's what this was, although it certainly wasn't anything like the picture shows she had gone to with boys in college.

They set off on the two-lane road out of town, passing through the little villages of Agua Fria and later La Cienega, before they finally reached La Bajada. A sliver of bright moon, just past new, shone in the west, almost setting in front of them, as they drove down the switchbacks.

Emily didn't say too much. She felt somewhat awkward. And tired. The excitement of the fiesta, and the burning of Old Man Gloom, seemed to have caught up with her, leaving her drained. She closed her eyes a moment, then opened them as she caught Mr. Shepherd's glance at her. They finally came down the escarpment and passed through the little village named after the rugged cliffs above. A dog barked from someplace, and the light of a kerosene lamp burned in one of the homes; someone sat up late inside. They sped past, down the road to cross the Rio Grande, and then turned away from the road that led south to Cochiti, instead going up north towards La Cañada and San Antonito.

"Thank you," Emily said as Shepherd stopped the car in front of the San Antonito schoolhouse. "I can truthfully say I've never spent an evening quite like this!"

"My pleasure, Miss Schwarz," Shepherd said. He got out and opened the passenger door for her. He made no move to kiss her once she was out of the car, and Emily wasn't sure if she was relieved, or sorry.

"I'll wait until you're safely inside," he added as Emily unlocked the door to the schoolhouse. "Good night, Miss Schwarz."

"Good night," Emily replied. She turned on her flashlight, went inside, and lit the kerosene lamp on the kitchen table. By the time she finished, she heard the noise of Mr. Shepherd's car fading away in the distance as he headed back down the road to Cañada.

CHAPTER
ELEVEN

Emily slept late that next morning. She had glanced at her wristwatch before she went to sleep; it must have been a little past midnight when she'd gotten home. She figured Mr. Shepherd wouldn't have gotten back up to Santa Fe until at least one-thirty or two. She imagined he would be sleeping in this morning too, then quickly banished that thought as she focused on her chores. Laundry today, grading papers, lesson planning. She supposed she should really write a letter home, to her parents in Racine. She realized she hadn't written them since before she found Juan's body, and wondered what she should tell them about that. *Dearest Mother, I found a corpse on my afternoon walk a few days ago.*

But first, coffee. She went into the kitchen and started a fire in the wood stove. It could heat while she dressed for the day. While the fire caught, she filled the percolator, then realized she was out of evaporated milk. She really didn't like black coffee. Well, the store on the plaza would have some milk, she hoped.

She dressed in denim trousers, a gingham blouse, and her oxfords, and, after banking the fire, set out towards the main plaza. A truck passed going the opposite direction, filled with children in the open back of the pickup. Emily recognized some of her students.

"Miss Schwarz!" they called to her. "We're going to Santa Fe! To the carnival!"

Emily waved back. "Have fun," she cried, but the truck was already out of earshot.

People were busy this Saturday. She smelled the warm, yeasty odor of fresh baked bread as she walked. Looking over, she saw some women pulling round loaves out of the hornos, the outdoor ovens. Emily greeted the ladies and continued up to Mr. Romero's shop. As her eyes adjusted to the dim interior after the bright morning light outside, she saw the shopkeeper's niece behind the counter.

"Hello, Señora," Consuela said. "What can I get for you today?"

"Just a can of evaporated milk, please. Here's my ration card." Emily found the card in her purse and handed it to Consuela. "You're still here," she commented, hoping it didn't sound like an accusation. "You must be a big help to your uncle."

"Yes, sì. Especially since he caught a summer cold, and now it's gone down into his chest. He's back in La Cañada, in bed today. And since I'm done with high school, it's good to be able to help out here. My parents don't mind, now."

106

Emily guessed what that "now" meant. "Did you grow up in La Cañada?" she asked.

"Sì, ma'am. We just moved down to Bernalillo last year. My senior year of school. I don't really like it too much. It's big, not so big as Albuquerque, but it still seems big to me. And the kids at school weren't too friendly. The shops are nice, though. And there's even better shops in Albuquerque. Here's your milk, ma'am."

"Why did your family move?"

"Oh…" Consuela glanced away. "My dad and mom just wanted a change."

Emily knew hedging when she heard it. Time to change the subject? "That's a pretty lipstick. What shade is it?"

Consuela licked her lips. "Do you like it? It's a Helena Rubenstein. Victory Red. I got it in Albuquerque."

Emily wondered what else she could shop for. She wanted to keep talking with Consuela. "You know, I just remembered I need some flour. And sugar. Do you have any cocoa? I was thinking of baking one of those Wacky Cakes, that don't need eggs."

"Just let me look, Señora. I think we have cocoa." Consuela rummaged through some supplies behind the counter.

"I might take some cake over to Atencio and Juliana," Emily continued. "Did you know their son, Juan?"

Emily heard a sharp clang as Consuela dropped several cans on the wooden floor. "I'm sorry, Señora, this will just take me a minute."

The girl busied herself collecting the dropped items and restocking them on the shelf behind the counter, her back turned to Emily. But Emily noticed the girl's hands were trembling as she restacked the cans.

"Here it is. Here's your cocoa." Consuela put the box on the counter, finally turning towards Emily, who couldn't tell if the girl had tears in her eyes or not. Emily waited.

"Yes, I did know Juan," Consuela finally said. "He was a couple of years older than me, but so handsome. He used to help my dad some with our cattle when he was in high school."

"His death must have been a shock," Emily said quietly. *When you're young, you don't ever believe your friends can die.*

Consuela nodded, biting her poppy red lips. "I had just seen him. He was fine."

"When did you see him? That weekend?"

Consuela's eyes shifted away from Emily. Emily turned to look at the empty shop. "We're alone," she said, facing Consuela again. "You can tell me if you want to."

The girl bit her lips again. "Well, that's why we moved down to Bernalillo," she finally confided. "Juan and I got to know each other when he was working for my dad, and we fell in love. But my folks didn't approve. They're old fashioned. Neither did Juan's parents. They are really traditional, they like the old ways. They just didn't understand, any of them. They didn't want to understand, either. So my dad moved us down to Bernalillo. And Juan and I broke up."

"But you still saw him sometimes?"

Consuela shook her head. "I hadn't seen him in months. But just last month my tio needed extra help in the shop, and I couldn't find a job in Bernalillo, so finally my father let me come back up. At first just during the week. They knew from Tio that Juan was working for McKee and wouldn't be around during the weekdays. But that weekend Tio had to butcher a pig and he convinced my folks to let me mind the store."

"And you saw Juan?" Emily persisted. Maybe Consuela could shed some light on Juan's murder.

Consuela nodded. "He and Lorenzo came in that Sunday before they went hunting. And I promised Juan I'd meet him after I closed up the store at four o'clock."

Emily nodded. That probably explained where Juan had gone after he got back from hunting. "Did you meet him?"

Consuela nodded. "There's a little canyon off the road that leads north out of the village. It's not too far away. I grabbed an old sabana my tio had in the back room and put it over my head, so I'd look like some woman from here if anyone saw me. But nobody really noticed me; there weren't many people around. I waited a little while, and then Juan showed up."

"How long did you stay there?"

"Not too long. We talked a little; he said he hadn't forgotten me. And I surely hadn't forgotten him. But we just kissed some—I'm a good girl, Señora, you've got to believe me. Finally it got late and I knew my tio would be wondering about me, so I said I had to go. And then I left."

"Did Juan have his knife with him? The one with the elk horn handle?"

The girl tilted her head. "Why?"

"He told Lorenzo and Delia he had to go back to look for it."

"That was just an excuse. But I didn't see the knife; I didn't pay any attention to that. We were busy." Consuela smiled, remembering.

"Why didn't you tell the sheriff all this?" Emily said gently.

"He didn't talk to me. He didn't ask."

"But you know they've arrested Lorenzo for the killing. You might be able to clear him."

Consuela swallowed. "My parents would kill me. Or send me to a nunnery. The Carmelites up in Santa Fe."

"Surely not."

"Oh, but they would! I don't even know why I went to meet him—it's just—" Consuela's green eyes filled with tears. She rubbed at them. "Juan was so handsome. And special— what we felt was special. My folks said I'd get over it—get over him. But it's been a year now—"

"And now he's gone. He's been killed," Emily said severely. "And his good friend is in jail for the murder."

Consuela started crying in earnest now, tears rolling down her cheeks.

"What about Deputy Duran? Would you talk to him?"

Consuela blanched. "He's my *primo*, my cousin. I can't tell him. He'd just call me a *puta*, a tart."

Emily waited while the girl composed herself somewhat. After a while she said, "Maybe you could talk to Sheriff Wilcox at the schoolhouse and your parents wouldn't need to know. But your information could clear Lorenzo."

Consuela wiped her eyes and sniffled. Her tears subsided, and she took a couple of gulping breaths. "Lorenzo's a good guy," she finally said. "If you can get the sheriff to agree, I'll talk to him with you. But I don't want my primo to be there."

A bit later, Emily left and headed back towards the schoolhouse, her evaporated milk and un-needed baking supplies in a brown paper sack and a sadly depleted ration book in her purse. She felt bad about having been so stern with Consuela, but if the girl's testimony could clear Lorenzo it would be worth it. She thought of her students, especially the older ones. Sometimes you had to be strict with people, for their own good. Consuela had eventually agreed to meet with Sheriff Wilcox, and Emily had agreed to contact him for her. Mr. Romero, in bed with bronchitis, wouldn't even need to know, and neither would the girl's parents.

The only phone was down at the mercantile in La Cañada. Emily dropped off her groceries at the schoolhouse and then continued walking down the road that led to the little Hispanic town. The sun shone high in the sky, the cottonwood leaves were beginning to turn gold, and the sky that deep, deep blue that you saw mainly in autumn. The scent of chamisa sage filled her nostrils. About half a mile down the road she saw a car pulled off to the side, and she recognized Shepherd's old Dodge. What was it doing here? Hadn't he gone back to Santa Fe the night before? They hadn't discussed it, but Emily had assumed he would. Telling herself not to fret, she hurried over to the car. It was Shepherd's, the picnic basket still sitting in the back seat.

The car sat empty, unlocked. Puzzled, she checked the wheels. No flat tires. She looked around and saw a few footprints in the dust of the road, leading away from the vehicle and off towards the Rio Chiquito, heading upstream.

Emily tried to follow the prints but lost them in the cottonwood leaves that littered the ground. "Mr. Shepherd!" she called. "Mr. Shepherd!" No one answered.

Whatever could have happened? Concerned, Emily

decided to head on down to Cañada and call Sheriff Wilcox. At least Consuela's testimony might help clear Lorenzo, assuming the sheriff agreed to come speak with the girl. And then Emily would find someone—maybe Gregorio—to help look for Mr. Shepherd.

At the Cañada mercantile Emily made her call, and was lucky enough to reach Sheriff Wilcox despite it being a Saturday. She told him about Consuela's new information. Somewhat grudgingly, Wilcox agreed to drive up later that afternoon, once Emily stressed that Consuela would only talk with him, not Deputy Duran. As Emily hung up the phone, she thought she heard a car pass by, heading down towards Cochiti, but by the time she reached the door of the shop it had disappeared.

Relieved that her call had been successful, Emily left, blinking in the sunlight as she came out of the dim shop. The dog sleeping in front of the mercantile hadn't budged. As she headed back up the road to San Antonito, Emily wondered again what had happened to Mr. Shepherd. She hoped he hadn't come to any harm. It was late when he'd headed back to Santa Fe, of course, but he hadn't seemed all that tired. Although maybe it had caught up with him, and he'd stopped for a catnap by the side of the road. But where was he now?

Emily rounded the slight bend in the road, right by the place where she had seen the old Dodge. The car was gone.

CHAPTER TWELVE

I MUST BE GOING *crazy*, Emily thought. She knew she had seen the car, but now the road looked utterly deserted. Then she glimpsed tire tracks in the dust, and felt relief. The tracks headed towards La Cañada, and back to the main road towards Santa Fe. At least she hadn't been seeing things. But why hadn't Shepherd answered her when she called out to him? And why had his car still been in San Antonito so many hours after he dropped her off?

Emily continued up the road, kicking at some inoffensive dark basalt pebbles in her way. Her irritation carried her along, and in what seemed like just a few moments she was back at the schoolhouse. She still had a few hours until Sheriff Wilcox was due to arrive. And there were assignments to grade. Always, she thought, papers loomed over her "free" time. She grabbed a pile of third- and fourth-grade arithmetic homework, settled herself at the kitchen table with her red pencil, and started in.

A bit later she heard a knock. Thinking it was Consuela, she headed down the hall, but she saw Gregorio's lean face when she opened the door.

"Hi, Gregorio. Can I help you?"

"I'm looking for Sheriff Wilcox. I heard he might be stopping by."

"Now, how did you hear that?" Emily asked, exasperated.

"My Auntie Tonita was just passing by Romero's shop when she heard you speaking with Consuela this morning."

"And she didn't come in?"

Gregorio shrugged. "She said you were talking, and Consuela sounded upset. She didn't want to interrupt you. At least that's what she told me."

"How considerate." Emily's frustration made her tone stiffer than normal. But she knew there were few secrets in San Antonito. "Yes, Sheriff Wilcox did say he'd stop by today. Why?"

"Well," Gregorio said, "I was talking to some of the other guys that work for McKee and took the bus with Juan. Thought he'd like to know what they said, especially if Lorenzo's in the clear."

Emily thawed a little bit. She sighed. "Yes, if what Consuela says is true, Lorenzo couldn't have killed Juan. But can you ask your aunt to stay quiet about it all? Consuela—well, she doesn't want her folks to find out and I promised her she could speak with Sheriff Wilcox privately."

"I don't think my aunt would tell anybody in Cañada what she heard," Gregorio replied.

"What about her friends here in San Antonito?"

Gregorio shrugged. "You know how ladies like to gossip."

"Well, if you can ask her not to say anything . . . It might be important," Emily said, with little hope that it would do any good. She checked her watch. It was still early, just after two-thirty. "Would you like a cup of coffee?"

"Sure, thanks, Miss Schwarz." Gregorio followed Emily into the kitchen and seated his lanky frame at one of the chairs by the table. Emily poured him some coffee and he added three spoonfuls of sugar. "No milk, thanks," Gregorio said. "It upsets my stomach."

Emily nodded and got herself a cup of coffee, with evaporated milk. Then she sat down across from Gregorio.

"So what did the guys from McKee say?" she asked.

"There's three other guys from San Antonito that work for McKee: Goyo, Ben, and Charley. And three guys from Cañada, but I didn't talk to them."

"Maybe Deputy Duran can speak to them."

"Yeah, he'd probably get more information. They might not talk too much to the San Antonito *fiscal*. A deputy sheriff will have more clout."

Emily nodded and took a sip of coffee. Deputy Duran would probably be more successful talking to the La Cañada folks. He was one of them.

Gregorio's eyes lit on the pile of papers Emily had been grading. "Arithmetic, huh? Those poor kids." He grinned. "I never liked school much, Miss Schwarz. But I graduated high school."

"Good for you," Emily said. Education was vital, she thought.

"My mother said she'd belt me if I didn't," he added with another grin.

The vision of Gregorio's elderly mother chasing him around with a belt made Emily chuckle.

"She went to boarding school up in Santa Fe," Gregorio continued. "She didn't want to go, and tried to run away and come back home. She actually walked all the way back here. But they made her go back, and she had to stay up there."

"But she must have valued her education, in the end," Emily said. "If she made sure you graduated." That's why she had gone into teaching, Emily thought, to make a difference in the lives of the children she taught. That was part of what had lured her out to New Mexico, to teach for the UPA.

"I guess. Or else," Gregorio said with another smile, "she just didn't want me hanging around all the time, eating all her chile."

Emily laughed again. "Where did you go to high school?"

"Up at the Indian School in Santa Fe. Just like my mother, I guess."

"Did you run away?'

Gregorio shook his head. "Just to downtown Santa Fe for cigarettes. Played hooky some, but I stuck it out."

Emily nodded. "That's good."

"But boy, did I hate math class. Those poor kids of yours. Multiplication tables, long division. I feel for them."

"Don't waste your sympathy." Emily reached for the coffee pot. "Do you want another cup? What did the men say, the ones that worked with Juan?"

Gregorio stirred sugar into his fresh coffee. "So like I said,

116

there's three fellows from here that work with McKee, besides Juan, I mean: Goyo, Ben and Charley."

"Paulina's son. He's the one who got in trouble at the dance," Emily said. "And?"

"Well, we had to go for wood this morning, up in the hills. Ben and Goyo went along; all the men did, really. We went up in the mountains, up that back road that leads out of San Antonito Canyon—there's some nice piñon and juniper up there. The ladies like juniper for cooking, it burns real hot."

Emily nodded and took another sip of coffee.

"But this is wood for the practice house, where we practice the songs and dances," Gregorio continued, "not for the ladies. So we wanted piñon. Maybe even pine. Big pine logs burn a long time. There's some downed ponderosas up there, they make good firewood."

Emily nodded again. She wished Gregorio would get to the point, but she had begun to learn, in her time at San Antonito, that some things were best not hurried.

"Anyway, so Goyo and Ben rode in the truck with me."

"And?"

"It was just the three of us. We'd loaded up the truck and were headed back, and we got to talking about Juanito and how he was found. Poor kid."

"Did they know anything?"

Gregorio shrugged. "They just said they were at work one day, week before last. It's some kind of government job—war work. They can't say what, can't even say where they're working. Sounds like it's up in the mountains someplace."

"What kind of war work would be going on in the Sangres de Cristos?" Emily wondered.

117

"Who knows? Radar? Maybe it's some kind of POW camp, maybe they're going to move those Japanese guys out of Santa Fe. Anyway, they can't talk about it."

"So what did they say?"

"Well, they were off in the mountains like I said. Sounds like they were working on a fence or something. Way out in the middle of nowhere. Juan needed to—" He blushed a little. "Well, nature called. Excuse me, ma'am. There's no outhouse out there."

Emily nodded.

"So he went off. Goyo said Juan came back a few minutes later, looking real nervous."

"Did Juan say why . . . what happened?"

"Ben asked him if he'd seen a bear or something. But Juan said no, said he'd tell them what happened later."

"Could he have seen a snake?" Emily always felt anxious about that when hiking. She didn't like snakes much, and there were occasional rattlesnakes around the pueblo, as well as the more common red racers and bull snakes. Of course, the last two weren't poisonous, but red racers moved fast. One of those had surprised her behind the schoolhouse in August, and she'd actually screamed.

"I don't know," Gregorio answered. "Ben said they never got the chance to finish the conversation. Charley was working with them that day, too, but they didn't talk about it at work, or on the bus home. Juan didn't say a word. I think if he'd seen a rattler, or a bear, or a mountain lion, he would have told people."

"I wonder what he did see?"

"I don't know," Gregorio said again. He drained the last of

his coffee and set the cup down on the table. "But if you could send Sheriff Wilcox up my way, once he's finished talking to Consuela, I'd appreciate it."

"Gregorio—"

"What, Miss Schwarz?"

She told him about seeing Mr. Shepherd's car on her walk down to Cañada. The *fiscal* didn't seem too concerned. "He probably just got tired and took a catnap. Or maybe he was off taking care of nature's business—excuse me, Miss Schwarz—and didn't want to answer when you called. I wouldn't worry about it too much."

That made sense, Emily agreed. After Gregorio left, she busied herself grading more papers while the sun crawled across the canyon sky towards the west. Close to four o'clock, Emily heard a car drive up from Cañada and come to a stop outside the schoolhouse. Sheriff Wilcox, she thought, and carried the stack of graded papers into the classroom, leaving them on her desk. Consuela hadn't arrived yet, and Emily hoped the girl hadn't changed her mind.

About a half hour later Sheriff Wilcox, seated at the kitchen table in the day school, drained his coffee and set his cup down with a thunk. "Well, Miss Schwarz, where is she?"

"I'm so sorry, Sheriff. Consuela said she would stop by after the shop closed, on the condition she could speak with you privately. What she told me would clear Lorenzo."

"Then where is she?" Sheriff Wilcox usually seemed fairly easygoing, but there was a tightness in his face as he spoke that made Emily anxious.

"She might have gotten cold feet." Emily tried the placating smile that had often worked with her father back in Racine. "Maybe I should walk up to the shop and see if she's still there. By the way, Gregorio was asking for you. He has something to share too—some information from a couple of Juan's buddies who also worked for McKee."

"Well, I guess since I'm out here on a wild goose chase . . ."

Emily cringed at that. "Would you like another brownie, Sheriff?"

He looked somewhat mollified. "Don't mind if I do."

"And just a little more coffee?" Sheriff Wilcox nodded and Emily continued speaking as she poured him another cupful. "If we both head up there, I'll look around for Consuela—you know what teenage girls can be like—while you speak with Gregorio, if you think it's important enough. If I find Consuela, I can let you know."

"Fair enough." Wilcox swallowed the last chunk of the brownie and washed it down with a gulp of coffee. He stood and walked out of the kitchen, followed by Emily. They left the schoolhouse and walked the short distance up to the plaza. But Romero's store was dark and locked up tight, and Emily saw no trace of Consuela.

CHAPTER THIRTEEN

EMILY LEFT SHERIFF Wilcox at Gregorio's and returned to the schoolhouse. It had been a long, tedious day, filled with unexplained disappearances. She imagined Consuela had just walked on back to La Cañada. At least Emily hoped so. The silly girl had probably chickened out about speaking with the sheriff. Surely nothing bad could have happened, not here. San Antonito was such a sleepy, peaceful place. Then Emily remembered Juan's corpse, and shuddered.

Trying to relax, she heated up some stew—one of her students' mothers had brought it over, along with a round loaf of oven bread—cut herself a slice of the fresh bread, and settled down to dinner, intending to read her neglected du Maurier novel as she ate. It would do her good to get her mind on something else. But she couldn't concentrate on the plot, and after a few minutes she closed the book with a dissatisfied thump and tried instead to focus on the pungent flavors of the green chile, tomato, potato, and corn in the stew. It got dark and she lit the kerosene lamp. It cast a pool of light in the darkening kitchen.

Emily supposed she should do something constructive, since she didn't feel like reading. Ironing, maybe, for next week. Or, of course, there were still more papers to grade. But instead she sat at the kitchen table, the dishes undone, puzzling over the day's events. What had Mr. Shepherd been doing at San Antonito this morning? And why had Consuela changed her mind? Or could something have happened to her? Who had shot Juan? She supposed Consuela might have, if the girl were jealous enough. But Juan's body had been found below the village, while Consuela had said they met further up in the canyon. Had the girl been lying?

Emily guessed she'd have to talk to Sheriff Wilcox again soon. That thought made her tired. Nettled and frustrated, she washed up and prepared for an early bedtime, but found she couldn't sleep. When she finally did doze off, her dreams were a confused mess of red lipstick, gun barrels, and flat tires. She did not have a restful night.

The next morning, Emily dragged herself out of bed, put on her Sunday dress, and walked up to Mass at the little chapel located just off the San Antonito plaza. As the pueblo shared a priest with the town of Cañada, the Mass was early, at eight o'clock, and usually sparsely attended. The schedule gave the priest time to walk the two miles back down to La Cañada in time for their Mass at nine-thirty. Gas rationing made weekly driving impossible.

Emily found a seat towards the back of the church. It was chilly inside the old adobe building. The whitewashed walls gently rose above the dark wood benches that served as pews, to meet the massive vigas that supported the roof. On the walls hung some Victorian era prints of the Stations of the Cross, in handmade frames decorated with native designs. Wooden *bultos*, traditionally carved statues of Christ on the Cross, the Virgin Mary, and Saint Anthony, the patron saint of the pueblo, stood in niches set in the plaster walls at the front of the church. Mary wore an Indian sabana atop her European-style gown. A simple table covered with a striped blanket served as the altar, elevated on a platform that stood two feet above the packed earth floor of the chapel.

The attendees this morning were pretty much the usual. Some older folks—Emily saw Gregorio's mother but not the *fiscal* himself. Juan's parents sat towards the front of the church, but Delia was not in attendance, nor was Lorenzo's mother. Emily was happy to see Demetria there. She caught her friend's eyes and smiled. They would talk after Mass ended, Emily thought with pleasure. Demetria would be glad to hear of Consuela's information. It would clear her godson.

Emily's musings returned to Consuela as the Mass began. What if the girl had shot Juan? If so, why should she help clear Lorenzo with the story she'd told Emily? That didn't make any sense, though it might explain why Consuela hadn't shown up to talk to the sheriff yesterday.

Emily remembered one student she'd had, back in Racine. The child, a tow-headed boy from a bad family, often told lies, but the lies had been cleverly woven into truth. It was harder to catch a lie out that way. Maybe Consuela had shot Juan in a fit of anger. Emily wondered if Consuela's uncle, or father, had fought in the last war and still had their army-issue guns. She'd have to ask Gregorio about that.

Mass finally ended, with a prayer for the men fighting overseas. The tribal official spoke a few words in Keres, dismissing the people, and the little congregation filed out into the churchyard. Emily caught up with Demetria outside the church and the two women stood chatting a moment. "Why don't you come over to the schoolhouse and have a cup of coffee," Emily said. "I've got some news."

Demetria accepted the invitation, wrapping her sabana around her against the morning chill, and the two women set off towards the schoolhouse. Father Simon passed them, walking quickly down towards Cañada, and they waved. He waved back but didn't slow his pace.

"I spoke with Consuela yesterday." Emily told Demetria what the girl had said. "But then she didn't show up to talk with Sheriff Wilcox like we'd agreed."

"If she can clear my godson, that would be great. Maybe she's just scared."

"Or maybe she shot Juan."

Demetria's eyes widened and she stayed silent at first. "I don't know that girl very well," she finally said. "I guess that's possible—if it's true, no wonder she wouldn't want to talk to the sheriff."

"Do you know if Señor Romero or his brother fought in the last war?" Emily asked. "Gregorio told me Juan could have been shot with an old handgun."

"I'm not sure," Demetria said, "but Gregorio will most likely know. He doesn't always come to Mass, for all he's in charge of the church and is supposed to be there. He has his assistant dismiss the congregation. I guess that man just doesn't like to get up early. But we could probably find him at his mother's." Demetria grinned. "I'll bet Florencita already has some coffee made."

Emily smiled back. "Well, we might as well stop by. It would save me starting a fire in that big cook stove back at the schoolhouse. And Florencita should be used to folks dropping by. She's the *fiscal's* mother, after all. People are always needing him for something or other, aren't they?"

Demetria nodded. Actually, Emily thought, most people in San Antonito didn't mind neighbors dropping in. The coffeepot was usually on the stove, and nothing was so pressing that people didn't have time to sit and chat, even if they'd just stopped by to borrow a tool or a ladder or something.

"And if Gregorio doesn't know who fought in the first war, I'd bet his mother would," Demetria continued. "She was a young girl back then."

The two women changed direction and headed towards the little house Gregorio shared with his mother. As they approached, they saw Gregorio's horse in the corral nearby.

"There's Flossie," Demetria observed. "So it looks like Gregorio is home."

They knocked on the door and Demetria called out "*Guw'aadzi.*"

"*Guw'aadzi.*" Florencita's voice echoed from inside, a second before she opened the door. "Come on in. Oh, Miss

Schwarz. Come in and have a seat. And Demetria. I just made some *atole*, have a cup."

The two women soon were seated on a bench at Florencita's table. The old mica windows in the thick adobe walls didn't let in too much light. Emily smelled a pot of beans cooking, the scent mingled with those of coffee, blue cornmeal, and the piñon fire from the wood-burning stove.

"Thank you, Florencita," Emily said, as Gregorio's mother handed her an enamel mug filled with the blue cornmeal drink. "This looks delicious."

"It's good on a cool morning," Florencita replied. "Warms you up."

"And yours is so creamy," Demetria added. "Mine always has little lumps in it."

"You have to add the meal to the water when it's still cold," Florencita told her. "If you wait until it's boiling, you get lumps." The two women lapsed into Keres for a bit. Emily guessed they were going over the finer points of making atole, but then Demetria spoke in English again.

"Is Gregorio around?"

Florencita nodded and answered in the same language. "He's just outside getting some more wood. You ladies drink up."

Demetria and Florencita caught up on some of the local news, switching back and forth between their native language and English. Emily looked around. The wood stove and kitchen table where they sat were at one end of the big room. Brightly colored Pendleton blankets hung against the plastered surface of the thick walls. At the other end sat some more benches. Nails in the whitewashed adobe supported some old baskets hanging on the other side of the room, along with a few necklaces of turquoise and red coral. It looked pretty, and colorful, Emily thought. So different from the dark wallpaper and gilt-framed family portraits in her parents' house in Racine.

Emily sipped at her atole, enjoying the nutty taste of it. She'd never tried to make it herself but she knew the housewives of San Antonito roasted the blue cornmeal a little bit before they added it to the water.

Just then they heard a noise at the door.

"Here you are, Ma. Here's some more wood," Gregorio said as he entered the house, his arms full of freshly split piñon. He dumped the wood in the bin that stood near the stove in the kitchen area. Then he looked around the room and saw the two visitors. "Hello, Demetria, Miss Schwarz. Mass is over already?"

"Yes," Demetria said. "Your assistant dismissed us. He said you had a stomachache."

"It's better," Gregorio replied.

"Maybe you just can't stomach the priest," Demetria said with a laugh. Gregorio muttered something in Keres that Emily didn't catch. She raised her eyebrows and looked at Demetria, who leaned toward her.

"He just said he thinks Father Simon drinks a little bit too much of the Communion wine," Demetria whispered. "Come to think of it, he does have a tremor." Emily bit her lip to keep from laughing and tried to look serious.

Gregorio took the cup his mother handed him and sat down at the table, across from the two women. His nostrils widened as he breathed in the scent of the drink. He took a sip. "Nothing like atole on a cool morning. Do you like it, Miss Schwarz?"

"Yes. Yes, I do," Emily replied, surprising herself just a little. Florencita beamed, and brought some fresh flour tortillas, butter, and hot roasted green chile over to the table.

"Have some tortillas, Miss Schwarz," she said. "Sorry we don't have eggs today to offer you. Those chickens haven't been laying much lately."

"This looks delicious," Emily replied, buttering a tortilla and putting some of the peeled roasted chile inside.

"Make sure you get most of the seeds off," Demetria cautioned. "They make it real hot."

"Unless you like it hot," Gregorio added with laugh. "Then leave the seeds in. And add a little salt. It brings out the flavor."

Emily, a little flustered, made sure most of the chile seeds were removed and added some salt before she took a bite. The fresh tortilla, the melting butter, and the hot green chile blended tantalizingly on her tongue. The three ate in silence a moment, while Florencita stood at the stove, making more tortillas.

"Did you speak with Sheriff Wilcox yesterday?" Emily asked Gregorio. "Consuela didn't show up. I don't know what happened."

Gregorio nodded. "He found me. He said Consuela hadn't come by, but she wasn't at the store either. It was all locked up at the usual time."

"She must have just walked on back to La Cañada," Emily said.

"Probably." Gregorio buttered another tortilla.

"Well, she needs to talk to that sheriff," Demetria put in.

128

"If she can clear my godson, she needs to do it." She set down her cup emphatically. "I feel like walking down to Cañada and giving her a piece of my mind."

Emily looked at Demetria in surprise. She was usually pretty soft-spoken. This wasn't like her. Demetria bit her lip, said "Thank you," to Florencita, and got up from her chair, taking the cup over to the counter where the wash bin sat.

"Are you really going to walk down to Cañada?" Emily asked.

"Oh, I don't know." Demetria bit her lip again. "I guess Señor Romero usually opens up the store at noon. And he's in bed with that bad cough. Maybe I'll just wait and talk with that girl when she's here."

"That might be best. If you confront her in Cañada she might just deny everything, especially if her folks are around."

"She might still deny it even if you talk to her here," Gregorio added. "But she did talk to you, Miss Schwarz. So maybe both of you should go this afternoon."

Emily nodded her agreement. "Oh, by the way," she asked, "do you know if Mr. Romero fought in the Great War? Or other men from Cañada who went?"

"Huh. I'm not sure. Mom, do you remember?"

"What?"

"What Spanish boys from Cañada fought in the last war? The one Atencio fought in."

Florencita stopped patting out dough for more tortillas, and thought. "Well, Atencio and Guillermo went from here. And there were two or three boys from Cañada too. Huberto, Roberto, and Carlos. Carlos Duran. That's that deputy's father. And Pedro, Pedro Romero—he was Carlos's cousin. But he didn't come back. Carlos did, though. And Huberto. They made it back, but then Huberto got sick and died when he got home. That flu, that's what killed him."

"And Roberto?" asked Gregorio.

"That's Señor Romero's brother. Roberto. He's Consuela's father. The one who just moved his family down to Bernalillo."

It sounded like there might be some old army-issue guns in Cañada as well as in San Antonito. "So Consuela might have gotten her hands on one of those old guns. Maybe her father's?"

"Consuela?" Gregorio laughed. "You think she killed Juan?"

"I don't know. If she saw him again, and was angry enough, she could have. The body was found down from the plaza, not north of it. They could have walked down the Rio Chiquito towards Cañada, argued, and she shot him. And then she just kept going downriver to La Cañada."

"What about Hilario? He was working his field. Maybe he saw something," Demetria suggested.

"Juan had been dead awhile before you found him, Miss Schwarz," Gregorio said, and Demetria's face fell. "It would have to have been Sunday night. The body had been lying there all day. I doubt Hilario saw anything. He would have said something."

"It wouldn't hurt to ask," Emily insisted.

"You're right, ma'am. It wouldn't hurt to ask. I'll get right on it."

Emily scowled at Gregorio. He just smiled, maddeningly. From his tone of voice, she felt sure he wasn't going to rush to speak with Hilario. But she and Demetria would be sure to talk to Consuela this afternoon. Thanking Florencita again, the two women left.

A little later Emily waited impatiently with Demetria on the San Antonito plaza for Consuela to open up her uncle's shop.

"I'm going to give that girl a piece of my mind when I see her," Demetria said again.

"She's probably just scared," Emily replied. "I had to pressure her pretty hard before she agreed to talk with the sheriff. I felt like I was lecturing a schoolgirl. I hope I didn't say too much."

The plaza sat quietly this early Sunday afternoon. A couple of dogs lounged under the big cottonwood tree that shaded the south side of the square. Another dog, spotted dusty brown and white, kept them company; from the look of the dog's swollen nipples Emily guessed she had pups someplace nearby, but apart from the three dogs the plaza was nearly deserted. The sun had come out and the day had warmed up. The golden leaves of the cottonwood blazed against the deep blue sky, and the smell of the piñon, juniper, and sage from the mesa blended with the scent of manure and horses from the corrals.

"Let's sit down," Demetria finally said, settling herself on the rickety bench outside the store.

"I guess you're right," Emily agreed. "Pacing won't make her arrive any earlier." The two women sat and waited, but no one came to disturb the Sunday quiet.

Paulina came into view on the other side of the plaza, saw

the two of them, and hurried over, her sabana wrapped tight around her. Her bangs framed the forehead of her round face, with the rest of her hair tied up in a bun, a *chongo,* in the back. Emily and Demetria greeted her.

"Are you waiting for Señor Romero?" Paulina was missing two front teeth, but it never stopped her talking.

"Yes," Emily replied.

"He's not coming."

"I know he's been ill, hasn't he?"

Paulina nodded. "He's real sick. Too sick to open up."

"That's too bad. We thought maybe his niece would do it," Emily explained.

"Nope." Paulina looked eager as she dropped her bombshell. "The girl has disappeared."

CHAPTER FOURTEEN

"**B**UT I JUST saw her yesterday," Emily protested. "Where has she gone?"

Paulina shrugged. "I don't know. But she didn't come back to La Cañada last night."

"How do you know? Where did you hear this?"

"My son went down to La Cañada this morning, went with Juanita. That's my mother, Miss Schwarz," Paulina explained. "She missed Mass here this morning, but wanted to go, and so he walked down with her. I didn't go. I was baking bread."

"And?" Demetria asked.

Her clear impatience didn't faze Paulina. "Well, after Mass, people were talking but they didn't say anything to my mother about it. But my son, that's Charley, he needed to pick up some cigarettes and thought he'd see if the mercantile was open.

That's kids, wasting money on smokes. But he won't listen to me. At least he's got that job with McKee, so it's his own money he's wasting."

"Kids are like that," Demetria said. "But what happened?"

"Well, so the mercantile was closed, but Deputy Duran's car was pulled up next to the Romeros' house there, right by the store. And there were a bunch of people standing around there."

Demetria nodded, gnawing her lip.

"Well, it turns out that Consuela hadn't come home from the shop last night. So they're looking for her. They'll probably be up here soon." Paulina smiled her gap-toothed smile again.

"Oh no!" Emily exclaimed. "I just saw her yesterday afternoon."

"And Señor Romero's still sick with his chest. So I don't think the store will open today. You might as well go home."

Paulina left them and headed back over to her house on the other side of the plaza. Emily and Demetria stared at each other. "What could have happened?" Emily wondered. Now she felt worried, and responsible for the girl's disappearance.

"Well, maybe she got scared and ran off."

"To where? Santa Fe?"

"I don't know."

"But she'd have to go by Cañada, the highway goes right past the town. Surely somebody would have seen her."

Demetria shrugged. "The road turns off into town. Or maybe she didn't keep to it, and took a trail. A shortcut. Maybe she didn't want anyone to see her."

They heard a car engine, and Deputy Duran's car drove up

and parked near Atencio's house. The dust settled as the car door opened.

"Hello, ladies," the deputy said, tipping his hat in their direction as he knocked on the governor's door.

"Does he know you spoke with Consuela yesterday?" Demetria whispered after the deputy had gone inside.

"I'm sure he must. Surely Sheriff Wilcox told him."

Demetria's brow furrowed and Emily added, "I hope she's OK," mirroring the other woman's unvoiced thoughts.

The sat on the bench by the shop until the door to Atencio's house opened again. Gregorio came outside and approached the two women.

"I guess I might have been a little hasty," he said to them. "It looks like that girl has disappeared. Miss Schwarz, you were one of the last people to talk with her yesterday. Would you mind coming inside with me? Deputy Duran wants to talk to you."

"Of course," Emily assented. "I'll see you later, Demetria." She walked with Gregorio back towards the governor's house, her heart thudding and her stomach fluttering. What could have happened to the silly girl?

Inside, Emily saw Atencio, Deputy Duran, and several other men she recognized as tribal elders seated around the table near the kitchen area. They looked solemn; Emily didn't see a single smile.

"Miss Schwarz."

"Hello, Deputy. Gentlemen. How can I be of help?"

"Well, Consuela's disappeared. And the sheriff told me you spoke with her yesterday."

"Yes, at the shop. We had quite a long conversation and,

in the end, Consuela said she wanted to speak with Sheriff Wilcox."

"About what?" Duran's voice sounded crisp.

Emily bit her lip. She hated to betray Consuela's confidences, but the girl might be in danger. Finally, she said, "Consuela had information that could clear Lorenzo in Juan's murder. She said she spoke with Juan that Sunday afternoon, after he left Lorenzo and Delia."

"Hmm. Why didn't she come forward earlier?"

"She said nobody asked her, Deputy. And her family had forbidden her to see Juan. She didn't want to get in trouble. At least that's what she told me."

"Hmm," Duran repeated.

"It's a bad thing for a young girl to disappear here in San Antonito," Atencio said gravely. The other men seated around the table nodded. Most wore their hair in the traditional manner, with bright cotton headbands and bangs cut straight across their foreheads, with a chongo in back. "Let us send some men out to look for her," Atencio added. "This is our land. We know these canyons. We will find her if she is here to be found."

Duran nodded, and Atencio said something in Keres to Gregorio and the other men. Gregorio got up. "With your permission, sir," he said to Duran, "I'm going to get some search parties organized."

Duran nodded again. "The Cañada men are already searching down by the Rio Grande, so you folks can concentrate in the canyon up here." Gregorio nodded, then left.

After a bit more discussion, Deputy Duran got up to leave and Emily did also. She walked with him towards his car, repeating the details of what Consuela had said the day before. "She was very reluctant to come forward," Emily concluded. "She told me she was concerned about getting in trouble with her family—she didn't want you to know about it either, but finally agreed to speak with Sheriff Wilcox. But then she didn't show up."

"Well, I'm her cousin." Duran's face looked set and grim. "And I know her mother and father were dead set against the match. They did their best to break it up. We thought they'd succeeded. Silly *chica*, full of romantic notions."

Emily sighed. That reaction was exactly what Consuela had been afraid of. And now Emily felt responsible for the situation. "What do you think happened to her?"

Duran stood, his hand on the car door handle, indecisive. "I don't know. She knows this area. She grew up around here. She could be hiding out someplace, or maybe she hiked down towards Cochiti and then hitched a ride back home to Bernalillo." He shrugged. "I sure hope so."

"Well, surely you would have heard if she's shown up at home."

"You would think so, *que no*? We have an all points bulletin out for her on the radio. So hopefully if she got a ride, or someone saw her, they'll call the office, or come in."

"You don't think she had anything to do with Juan's death, do you?"

Emily watched a muscle in Deputy Duran's cheek twitch. "Well, if my cousin's guilty, why would she have told you about her meeting with Juan?"

Emily shrugged. She didn't know.

"And this disappearance—*Dios*," the deputy continued. "I hope the stupid girl is OK."

"I heard Juan was shot with a handgun," Emily said. "Maybe an old army-issue gun."

Duran's cheek twitched again. "Where'd you hear that?"

Emily didn't answer. "So?" he finally said, and spat on the ground.

"So, did any of the men from La Cañada fight in the last war?" Emily persisted.

"My dad for one, Carlos Duran. I was just a baby. And Pedro, but he got killed in France. And Huberto, he made it back home. Then the influenza killed him. Uncle Roberto served too. So there could be some old army-issue guns around there. But that doesn't mean my cousin shot Juan, or that anyone from La Cañada did. We won't know anything about the gun until we get the ballistics report. And that lab is busy, and understaffed. Everybody that could enlisted."

He spat again, the spittle leaving a darker mark in the dry dust. "Just wait till I find that girl."

Emily watched Duran. He sounded irritated, but perhaps his tone hid worry for his cousin. She didn't, however, think he'd view more conversation favorably.

"Well, thank you, Deputy. I've taken too much of your time. I won't keep you." Emily turned and walked back down towards the schoolhouse as the deputy got in his car and started the engine.

This weekend seemed to be one for unanswered questions. Where was Consuela, and what had Mr. Shepherd been doing yesterday at San Antonito? Maybe Consuela had run off with Mr. Shepherd. For some reason that thought irritated Emily and she kicked a rock from the dirt road into the ditch. Then, feeling like one of her own students caught out in some act of mischief, she hurried down the road to the day school.

CHAPTER FIFTEEN

THEY DIDN'T FIND a trace of her. The men of San Antonito scoured the canyons. The Cañada men searched the lower lying areas, where the fields of La Cañada sloped down towards the Rio Grande, and the sandstone cliffs that rimmed the river. Not a trace.

The men kept at it until dark and then resumed the search early the next morning. Deputy Duran had set up an unofficial headquarters at the mercantile in Cañada. Emily learned that news when one of the San Antonito mothers walked her young son, a first grader, over to the school that next morning, bringing the teacher a gift of tamales and oven bread.

As the school day progressed, Emily attempted to keep her mind on her instruction but didn't entirely succeed. The girl's vanishing gnawed at her while she assigned spelling words for the week and listened to her younger students read out loud. After Emily dismissed her class, she headed up towards the plaza. If Mr. Romero was minding the store, perhaps he'd have news. And if the store hadn't opened today, Emily thought she could count on Paulina for the latest.

Some ladies stood outside the mercantile, Minguita among them. Minguita nodded at Emily as she passed, then said something in a low tone of voice to the other women. Emily guessed they were gossiping about Consuela. She pulled on the old screen door and entered the shop. Inside, Mr. Romero was reaching for a sack of flour for Paulina. He heaved the sack up on the counter and gave a hacking cough, then took a sip of water from a tin cup sitting by the cashbox. He looked pale, Emily thought, and anxious too.

"You should be home in bed, Mr. Romero, with that bad cough," she observed.

"Thanks, *hija*, but someone's got to open the shop. Miss Paulina needs her flour, after all. You ladies have to make bread and tortillas, don't you?"

Paulina grinned and handed Mr. Romero her ration book and a crumpled dollar bill. "Yes, Señor. Our families would go hungry and nobody wants that."

"Can you carry that by yourself?" the shopkeeper asked, giving Paulina her ration book and some change.

"My son is outside. He will help me." Paulina stepped out onto the porch to call to her son. "Charley, get in here."

Charley entered, came over, and reached for the sack. Emily guessed he was about nineteen, the same age as Juan; she had never taught him at the day school.

"Hi, Charley," Mr. Romero greeted him. "Miss Paulina,

you should get that boy a Coke for all the work he's doing."

Paulina snorted. "He don't need a Coke. There's water at the house, he can drink that if he's thirsty."

"Hi, Señor Romero. Hi, Miss Schwarz." Charley looked at Mr. Romero. "Hey, did you get any smokes in? I don't know about the Coke, but I sure could use some cigarettes."

"Sure did. Lucky Strikes and Camels. Do you want a pack?"

Charley smiled. He had the same teeth as his mother, Emily noticed, but more of them. His were just a little crooked on the right side. "McKee doesn't pay until Friday. I'll hold out until then, I guess. Thanks, though. Save me a pack, OK? Lucky Strikes?"

Mr. Romero nodded. Emily remembered Gregorio had said Charley worked for McKee. "So you were off today?" she asked.

"He was sick," Paulina interrupted, speaking for her son. "He was throwing up something awful. Anyway, I needed help with some things, so he stayed home and helped me."

Charley smiled, a little self-consciously, Emily thought. She didn't think he looked very ill, certainly not like Mr. Romero, who had started another coughing spell.

"You should get some cough syrup for that," Emily suggested.

"I've got *osha*. That's all you need," Mr. Romero replied.

Paulina nodded. "That's right," she said. "That osha is good for the cough. Better than those medicines from the Health Services. They don't know what they're doing, those ones."

Paulina and Charley left, and the screen door shut behind them with a bang.

"Have you heard anything about your niece?" Emily inquired, after the dust settled.

"Oh, you've heard about that?"

Emily nodded in sympathy.

Mr. Romero shook his head. "Deputy Duran—he's my nephew—is leading the search. He'll find her but the crazy chica has just vanished. I can't think what could have happened to her. It's got me worried sick." He coughed again. Emily didn't like his pale color.

"Mr. Romero, you should be home in bed."

"I can't. Who would watch the shop? You have to do what you must, *que no*?"

Emily took her copy of the paper. "Well, let me know if there's anything I can do to help." Then she had an inspiration. "Do you think those men out searching would like some brownies when they get back?"

"*Porque no*?" Señor Romero replied, shrugging. "Everybody likes brownies."

"In that case, I might need a small package of sugar too. I'll bring brownies down to Cañada later, and leave some here for the San Antonito men." That would give her an excuse to find out the latest news.

Señor Romero smiled, but the smile didn't erase the concerned look from his eyes. Feeling guilty, as though Consuela's disappearance was her fault, Emily paid, took her paper bag of groceries, and headed back towards the schoolhouse.

Two hours later Emily made her way down the road to

the Cañada mercantile. She carried a large platter of warm brownies, hopefully enough for all the searchers. The sharp scents of piñon and ponderosa pine lingered in the cooling evening, mixing with the chocolate smell of the brownies, and the sun skimmed the canyon walls to the west. The walk to Cañada went quickly in the pleasant evening. As Emily approached the mercantile, she saw a number of men sitting on the wooden bench under the portal, several holding beer bottles.

"Miss Schwarz!" Antonio Romero, Mr. Romero's brother, greeted her. The family had been in the mercantile business for a long time, and owned the shops in La Cañada as well as the pueblo. "Welcome. What brings you down this way?"

"I thought the men who'd been out searching for that poor girl might enjoy some brownies." Emily held the dish out to Antonio. "Have they found any trace of her?"

One of the guys set his beer down next to him on the bench. "Not a trace of her. *Pobrecita.*"

"Oh, Pedro, she knows every trail from here to La Bajada," another man said, taking swig of his own beer. "You're acting like an old *vieja*. The silly girl probably just hitched a ride into Albuquerque."

"I don't think so, Carlos," the other man replied. "And don't be calling me an old woman."

"Where's Deputy Duran?" Emily broke in. She'd broken up enough playground fights to recognize the signs of impending conflict.

"Gone back to Bernalillo for the night. Maybe somebody called in some information from Albuquerque to the station there," Pedro said. "Or maybe she showed up at home and her *padre* is taking the bullwhip to her. Silly girl."

Emily shrugged and motioned to the platter of brownies, which Antonio had set out on the bench before heading inside his shop. "Well, enjoy these, after all your hard work."

"Thank you, Señora," Pedro said. Carlos didn't say anything, but Emily noticed he'd almost finished another beer, and she thought she should take her leave. She picked up the untouched platter of brownies. "I'll just take these inside," she said, and went into the shop to say goodbye to Antonio.

"I can't understand what's going on around here," she heard him say as she entered the store. "First that shooting up in San Antonito. Now this. The world's gone mad these days. Do you want another beer, Marcos? And *gracias* for those brownies, Miss Schwarz. They'll taste real good. Those two outside, well, they'd rather drink than eat, but we'll enjoy them, *que no*, Marcos?" He reached for one and took a bite. "If you get tired of teaching school you can bake for the shop, Miss Schwarz."

Emily laughed and then quickly left, taking the road back up towards the day school and the pueblo beyond it. The sun had set now and the canyon rapidly grew darker. She walked quickly, feeling uneasy in the deepening twilight. From someplace further up the Rio Grande she could hear the faint yips of coyotes. The sharp wildness of their calls made her more anxious, and she started moving faster.

A car engine growled behind her. Without breaking stride, Emily fumbled in her basket for her flashlight and turned it on. The engine hummed louder now, closer, and she stepped off to the side of the road to let the auto pass. Her heart pounded loudly, but she told herself sternly not to be so fanciful. It was just somebody returning home late to San Antonito.

But who? There weren't that many cars in San Antonito, and gas rationing made trips even more of an event. She saw the headlights of the car sweep past her, the shape looming in the dark. A Dodge. Then it slowed, pulling over to the shoulder in front of her, and stopped. The driver's door opened and Mr. Shepherd stepped out, neatly attired in his usual suit, tie, and hat.

"Miss Schwarz! Can I give you a lift?" Shepherd said, as if it were the most normal thing in the world to be passing by on the rutted, lonely dirt road to a tiny godforsaken native village.

"Mr. Shepherd. What are you doing here?"

"Working late, actually. I had some business with the governor and couldn't get down here before now."

"I thought you said you were in procurement."

"War work, Miss Schwarz. Most of it is procurement."

"Did you sleep in your car the other night?" she asked. "I came down to San Antonito on Saturday morning and saw it parked by the road. Right about here, in fact. And then it was gone. If you were that tired after they burned the puppet—" Emily paused awkwardly, realizing she might sound too forward. "Well, I'm sure someone around here could have put you up."

Shepherd didn't answer her question and Emily had the sudden, surprising urge to smack him. "You gave me a start just now," she continued. "I didn't really expect to see anyone on this road so late."

"Well, let me at least give you a lift as far as the schoolhouse. To make up for my many sins," Shepherd said with a slight smile.

Emily gave up and got in the car. Shepherd followed suit.

"What were you doing down here Saturday morning?" she demanded as he pulled back onto the road.

"Oh, I needed to talk to somebody about something," Shepherd replied. "Don't worry about it."

"That's a lot of gas," Emily said, thinking of rationing.

Shepherd smiled again. "Well, I'll have to stay home next week to make up for it, I guess."

Emily fumed, doubting that he meant what he said. Silence reigned until they pulled up in front of the schoolhouse. "Thank you," Emily said.

"You're welcome. Say, would you feel like taking in a movie sometime? Some weekend, a Saturday or Sunday matinee?"

"I don't know." Emily wasn't sure how she felt about the man. Could she trust him? He certainly didn't give straight answers. "I . . . I have lots of schoolwork on the weekends. Grading papers, preparing lessons, you know."

"I'm sure. And I've just about used up that gas ration, too, as you pointed out. Well, I might ask again in a week or two; see if your schedule opens up."

Emily nodded, a little curtly, and got out of the car. She went into the schoolhouse and busied herself lighting the kerosene lamp until she heard Shepherd drive away. Exasperating man. And what could be bringing him down to San Antonito at this time of night?

The second plate of brownies for the San Antonito men was still sitting on the kitchen table. The clock's hands stood at just past eight. Emily decided to go ahead and take them up to the alcalde's house. Maybe the searchers had found some trace of Consuela. She might have dropped her lace handkerchief on the trail for them to find, Emily thought sourly, surprised by her own cynicism. Or that Helena Rubenstein lipstick. She was in a foul mood, and the thought of running into Mr. Shepherd again didn't improve it one little bit.

Still, the brownies would get stale if she waited until tomorrow. She covered the plate with a kitchen towel, got her flashlight, and started up the road to the governor's house.

CHAPTER
SIXTEEN

A T THE MONTOYAS', Emily was surprised to see that Shepherd's car wasn't outside. The elusive Mr. Shepherd. Emily wondered what he did, really. She would bet her best jewelry it wasn't strictly procurement. But light streamed through the house's old-fashioned mica windows, and the door was propped open just a bit to let in some air. Emily heard men's voices inside, speaking Keres. She knocked on the door and went in.

"Miss Schwarz. You're out late," said Atencio, greeting her. "Come in." The voices of the other men died down to silence.

"Thank you," Emily replied. "I really can't stay; I just made these for the men who've been out searching for that poor girl." She set the platter of brownies down on the oilcloth-covered table.

"Thank you," said Juliana, handing Emily a cup of fresh coffee from the enameled tin pot on the stove. "They'll eat them up in no time, won't you?" she added, addressing the five or six men who sat at the table. Most were just finishing some bowls of beans and *chicos*. Emily saw Gregorio sitting at the far end, wiping out his bowl with a piece of tortilla. He smiled at her and she nodded back. "You work up an appetite in those canyons," Juliana continued. "Here, Miss Schwarz, have a seat. Did you eat?"

Emily told Juliana she had, but sat down on the bench next to Hilario, squeezing into the empty spot next to his broad bulk. "Did you find anything?" she asked the searchers.

"Not a thing," Gregorio said. He had swallowed the last bite of his tortilla, and now reached for a brownie. "Not a footprint, not a hair ribbon. She's not up in the canyon."

Emily looked at Atencio. "I saw Mr. Shepherd. He said he wanted to speak with you. Did he stop by?"

"Yes. We told him the same thing. He just left."

He hadn't passed Emily on her way up to the village. Which way had he gone, then?

"That's a long way to drive, just to check up on a missing girl," Hilario said. "He must have a lot of gas coupons."

"He does some kind of war work," Emily volunteered. "Procurement. At least that's what he says."

Nobody said anything for a minute, then one man muttered something in Keres that Emily didn't catch.

"He mentioned he needed to talk to Professor Bateson about something," Gregorio offered. "He said he was heading over that way when he left."

Emily frowned, puzzled. "I thought Professor Bateson was

still in the back country. We saw him up in Santa Fe on Friday night, though."

"Oh yeah," Gregorio said. "The puppet-burning. I'd forgotten all about it, what with that girl going missing."

Emily finished her coffee and said her goodbyes. She picked her way carefully down the dirt road that led from the plaza to the schoolhouse, the way dimly illuminated by the beam of her flashlight. Overhead, the sky was filled with bright stars, visible between the canyon walls and the black shapes of the cottonwoods and ponderosa pines, but Emily could only see a few feet ahead of her. She felt the same way about this whole business—Juan's murder, the missing girl, all of it. She didn't know what to make of any of it, and had no idea how to find her way forward.

The next day, Tuesday, left Emily with little time to worry about either Consuela or the annoying Mr. Shepherd. Her students were fractious, her lessons boring. One of the third graders, Atencio and Juliana's younger son Gilbert, fell and scraped his knee at recess, and two fifth-grade boys got into a scuffle. She set the malefactors to work writing lines—"I will not fight in school" a hundred times each—and assigned the other upper graders an essay on "The Importance of Honesty." The younger students wrote sentences using their spelling words. The classroom grew quiet except for the sound of pens scratching on paper, punctuated by an occasional quiet groan.

Emily sat at her desk in the front and surveyed the class. Good kids, really, all of them. All they needed was to learn to apply themselves. The hands of the clock crawled towards dismissal time. Emily collected the completed papers, assigned homework, and finally rang the bell, ending the school day. She stood on the schoolhouse porch watching her students, now freed, head up the dusty street towards the plaza, the older boys still rough-housing, the girls chatting with each other and admonishing the little ones to keep up.

Emily sighed and went back inside. She realized her ladies' home economics group would meet the next evening and she hadn't yet planned an activity. She sighed again, and headed into the school kitchen for her ritual after-class cup of coffee . . . a needed pick-me-up, and one well deserved, she thought. Especially after days like this.

A short while later, as she sipped her coffee, a knock on the front door disturbed her reverie. Irritated at the disruption, despite her efforts not to feel so, Emily dragged herself out of her chair and went to open the door.

Demetria stood on the porch in the late afternoon sunshine, holding a basket on her arm. Emily's annoyance vanished at the sight of her friend, and the spicy aroma coming from the basket. At least it wasn't more bad news. "Come on in and have some coffee," Emily said. "This morning's, but it's warm. I heated it up."

Demetria smiled and came inside. In the kitchen, she took a seat across from Emily at the pine-board table. "Tired?" she asked. "Did those kids wear you out today?"

Emily nodded.

"I heard something about Minguita's grandson."

"He was fighting at the lunch recess with another boy, one of the Mondragons. They said they started out playing Japs and US Army, but it degenerated into a free-for-all, and Federico wound up with a nosebleed."

"He'll survive," Demetria said, unconcerned.

"I suppose so," Emily agreed. "They both might be suffering from writer's cramp; I had them write lines. But what brings you over here?"

Demetria nodded at the basket. "I brought you some red chile stew, with beans and potato. And some tortillas."

"That sounds wonderful. I'm too tired to cook anything this evening," Emily said, realizing how true that was as she spoke. "Thank you, Demetria."

The two women sat in quiet, drinking their coffee. "Have you heard anything about Consuela?" Demetria asked after a moment. "They still have my godson locked up."

Emily heard the unsaid accusation and felt her face flush with guilt. Not that it was her fault, she thought. "Until Consuela shows up, I guess they have to hold him. But I told Sheriff Wilcox and Deputy Duran what the girl told me. They must not feel it's enough to release Lorenzo."

Demetria took another sip of coffee. "I hope that girl shows up soon. I want my godson out of jail."

Demetria sounded determined, and stubborn. Emily felt a headache coming on, a tight band around her temples. "I know," she said. "But I can't do anything about it. I tried, Demetria, I did." She drank more coffee, hoping it would help. "By the way, have you seen Professor Bateson?"

"He's around. I saw that dog of his on the plaza today. Why?"

"Oh, I don't know. He's in the back country a lot. I guess I wondered if he'd seen any trace of Consuela."

Demetria stood and pushed the wooden chair in to the kitchen table. "That's a good idea. Maybe I'll stop by and ask him if he's noticed anything. The men have called off their search."

"Oh, dear. And she's still missing." The tight band of tension around Emily's head throbbed more insistently. It *was* her fault, all of it. "It couldn't hurt, I guess, speaking with Professor Bateson. Do you want me to come along?"

"No, you're tired. I'll see you tomorrow night at class."

Emily felt secretly relieved. What she wanted most right now was an aspirin. She said goodbye to her friend and went in search of one.

The next afternoon Emily readied the home economics room for the upcoming class. She had been busy all day with her students, and hadn't heard from Demetria. She hadn't really expected to, and imagined she would catch up with her after the evening session.

Instead of a sewing project, they were going to be canning, so a lot of the activity would take place in the kitchen. Emily put away her dinner dishes and made sure the counters and the table were clear. Some early apples had ripened, so they were going to can applesauce. Emily started the water heating in the big enamel canner. She put the glass jars, lids, and rings, along with the apples, cinnamon, and the sugar she had managed to round up, on the big wooden worktable and waited for her students to arrive.

The ladies trickled in, starting a few minutes before the clock marked seven. Demetria had not yet arrived but Emily began the lesson, not waiting for any latecomers. Her students cut up the apples and stewed them. Then Emily showed the ladies how to use the food mill—simple enough, really—add sugar and cinnamon to the mix, and how to get the jars, lids, and sealing rings ready for the applesauce. The kitchen filled with the aromas of spice and fruit.

Demetria still hadn't shown up, which made Emily uneasy. "Demetria's not here," she said to Minguita. "Have you seen her? It's not like her to miss class."

Minguita shrugged as she stirred the applesauce. "I haven't seen her all day."

"Delia's not here either."

"Well, that husband of hers is still in jail. She must not want to show her face around here. Imagine, shooting his own cousin like that. And over *her*, too. That's what people say."

The women chattered as they poured the hot applesauce into the jars, set the sealing rings and lids in place, and lowered the jars into the hot water in the canner with special tongs.

"Now the jars have to process for twenty-five minutes," Emily told her students. "We start timing after the water comes back to a simmer. I'll set a kitchen timer—you just turn the dial to twenty-five, and the bell will let us know when the time is up."

The women talked among themselves while they did the dishes and the water in the canner bubbled against the glass jars. Emily tried to ignore the worry that nagged at her as she helped put the dishes away. Demetria never missed the Wednesday evening sessions. "It's not like Demetria to skip our get-togethers. I hope she's not ill."

Minguita shrugged. Just then the timer went off, and everyone grew busy removing the hot jars from the canner and setting them on the table to cool. The women listened with satisfaction as the lids began to ping, indicating the jars had sealed properly.

"These will keep for at least a year," Emily told the ladies. "It's a good way to deal with a bumper crop of apples."

A short time later the ladies left, each carrying a quart jar of applesauce to take home. Emily made sure everything was put away and damped down the fire in the kitchen range. Then she went into the classroom, checking that all was ready for the next day's lesson.

She thought about Demetria, and eyed her watch. It was a little before nine. It wouldn't take too long to walk up to the plaza and check on her friend. Demetria's husband Joe served in the army, someplace in the Pacific. Demetria hadn't said much about Joe lately, and Emily hadn't wanted to pry. She chided herself for her nervousness, but got her flashlight and left the school anyway, starting up the road to the plaza. She could easily check on Demetria and be back in half an hour.

The moon hadn't yet risen and Emily had to mind her footing on the rutted road. Light shone from the windows of some of the houses she passed, but others were dark, the occupants already asleep.

She approached her friend's house, just past Mr. Romero's store. No light shone from the window. A dog barked nearby, startling Emily so that she almost dropped her flashlight. As if in answer, she heard the yipping of coyotes from further up the canyon. She knocked on the wooden door. "Demetria?" Emily heard the slight quaver in her own voice with surprise. "Can you hear me? Demetria?"

No answer. Emily pushed on the door. It creaked open. She shone her flashlight around the small house Demetria shared with Joe. The woodstove. The table, clean and covered with a tablecloth. Nothing looked out of place. The bed in one corner, made up, the blankets smoothed. A few western-style dresses hung on pegs on the wall, while a hanging pole suspended at both ends from the ceiling held some mantas—the traditional dress of the San Antonito women—a Pendleton blanket, and some fringed shawls.

"Demetria?" The dark and empty house did not reply, the faint yip of the coyotes the only response to Emily's call.

She left the house, uncertain what to do next. Demetria wasn't a child. But Consuela's disappearance, combined with this, increased Emily's anxiety. She decided to speak with the alcalde, or at least find Gregorio and tell him. She walked across the plaza to the old house Gregorio shared with Florencita. Light shone through the mica window. Relieved they were still awake, Emily knocked on the door. From the corral nearby she caught a whiff of horse dung, and heard Flossie whinny, before the door opened.

Gregorio seemed surprised to see her, but he greeted her with a smile. "Miss Schwarz. It's late."

"Yes, I know. Gregorio, I can't find Demetria."

"What?" His smile vanished. "Come in. What happened?"

Emily went in. Florencita sat at a bench, sewing. Emily waved aside the old woman's offer to sit down. She paced the length of the table, then back again. "It's Demetria," she repeated. "She's gone. She didn't come to class tonight, so I went to check on her. She's not home. She's disappeared."

"Check at her mother's house," Florencita advised quietly. "Agapita might have called her over for something."

Gregorio nodded. "That's right. Mothers are always wanting something or other."

Florencita smiled. "Don't you forget that, either."

Emily sighed with relief. She hadn't thought of Agapita. "That must be it. But she never misses home economics class. And with Consuela vanishing—"

Florencita snorted. "That one probably ran out of nail polish and went into Bernalillo to get some."

"I don't think so," Emily said.

"Well, let's just go see what's what." Gregorio said something to his mother in Keres. She replied with a long speech. Emily wondered what she had said, but Gregorio didn't say. He took an old-style kerosene lantern and lit it, and then he and Emily left. "Let's check her house again," Gregorio suggested.

"I'm sure she's not here," Emily protested, but she followed the sheriff across the plaza.

At Demetria's house, Gregorio pushed the door open. "*Guw'aadzi.* Demetria?" he called. "Are you in there?"

The house stood silent in the night.

"She's not here," Gregorio said.

Emily nodded. She had told him that already.

He closed the door. "Come on."

Emily followed him across the street and down another alley, to where Agapita lived. At least that's where she assumed Gregorio was taking her. She had never visited Demetria's mother, although she had met her a time or two.

"Here's her place." Gregorio stopped in front of an old adobe house, small, sandwiched between two other buildings. The homes down this street seemed to slump against each other, as if for support. The walls gently sloped, although the last house in the row looked to have been newly plastered. It had plate glass windows and its door looked freshly painted, in sharp contrast to the middle house. Agapita's home had old style windows, small ones, set with mica, and the blue paint on the door had faded and largely flaked off the wooden frame. Light shone through the mica, a dim orange glow.

Gregorio knocked on the door. "*Guw'aadzi*. Agapita?"

"*Guw'aadzi*. Come in." The door opened, revealing a tiny woman, seemingly ancient. She wore a traditional cotton dress, its calico print of pink flowers on a light blue background faded with time. Three flowered challis shawls enveloped her shoulders, and she had two flowered silk scarves tied over her head and knotted under her chin. "Gregorio. Miss Schwarz. Come in and shut the door. The cold out there makes my ears ache. I have to bundle up. What do you want here, so late at night?"

A kerosene lantern sat on the table, casting a faint glow around the simple one-room house. An old iron bedstead sat in one corner, and on the whitewashed, mud plastered walls hung some *tablitas*, traditional headdresses worn by San Antonito dancers, along with an old religious engraving of Jesus of the Sacred Heart. Some embroidery in traditional native designs—the red, green and black yarn a bright contrast to the white background of the fabric—lay on the table.

"Hello, Auntie," Gregorio said respectfully. "We're looking for Demetria. We thought maybe we would find her here."

Agapita replied to Gregorio in Keres. Emily looked at Gregorio, confused.

"She says she hasn't seen her all day, not since yesterday noon time. She said we should look at her house."

"She's probably already asleep," Agapita said in English. "What do you want with her this time of night, anyway?"

158

"Oh, we just had to check with her about something," Emily improvised. "About the ladies' classes." She didn't want to worry Agapita, although she herself was getting more concerned by the minute.

"Sorry we disturbed you, Auntie," Gregorio said.

The old woman nodded toward the embroidered lengths of fabric. "I was still working on these. Albertina wants them for her son, for his dance costume. Gregorio, you tell your mother to tell Albertina I should have them ready by next Friday."

"OK, Auntie, I'll let her know."

They left, and Agapita shut the door behind them.

CHAPTER SEVENTEEN

"**W**HERE COULD SHE have gone?" The nervous flutter in Emily's stomach churned upwards, setting her heart racing. She took a deep breath. "Demetria said she was going to ask Professor Bateson if he had seen Consuela. But that was yesterday."

"Well, let's head over there and check with him. I think he got back yesterday from his last expedition. At least I saw Anasazi hanging around the plaza today. He's usually with the professor when Bateson's out in the back country."

"It's late."

"Don't worry about that. I see his light on at all hours. That man is a night owl."

Gregorio led the way towards the edge of the pueblo, away from the plaza on the north side, to Professor Bateson's little adobe house. Emily smelled the nearby corrals, faintly visible in the starlight. Piñon and juniper trees loomed dark on the hills beyond. This far up the little canyon there wasn't much agricultural land. Cliffs narrowed down over San Antonito like black sentinels in the night, guarding the pueblo.

As Gregorio had predicted, light shone through the glass windows in the house. Anasazi barked once, then came up, sniffed at Gregorio, and wagged his tail, whining a bit in greeting. The door opened, letting brightness pool on the shadowy ground in front of the house, and Emily saw Professor Bateson stick his head outside.

"Anasazi, cut that out!" Bateson must have seen their lantern because he squinted in their direction. "Who's there?"

"Professor Bateson, it's Gregorio. And Miss Schwarz."

"You'd better come in. Why are you folks wandering around at all hours?" Bateson opened the door wider and gestured to them to come inside. Anasazi led the way.

In the main room, unruly piles of paper fought for space with old pot shards on the wooden table. A bookcase crammed with scholarly volumes stood along one wall. Emily noticed a copy of Bandelier's *The Delight Makers* as well as more abstruse archaeological tomes, many in foreign languages. She saw some journals, mostly the *American Journal of Archeology*, but also a few from something titled *Society for the Study of Primeval Ideas*. A book on Native American pottery motifs lay open on the table.

"You're back," Gregorio observed.

"I got back yesterday. In the evening. I've found a very interesting site just up Bland Canyon a bit. A small settlement, but the pot shards are similar to those Bandelier found at Frijoles Canyon."

"How long were you up there?"

"Just a few days this time. Why?"

"Oh . . . I thought I saw you up in Santa Fe over the weekend. When they burned that puppet," Emily said.

Professor Bateson's face relaxed. "Yes, I was there; I couldn't resist going. I went upcountry the next day. I didn't see you in Santa Fe, though. Not surprising, there was such a crowd. And such a pagan experience. Amazing, really. I'm tempted to write a paper on it, but it would take too much time from my studies here. I'll have to leave it for one of my colleagues. You don't have an interest in the social sciences, do you, Miss Schwarz?"

Emily demurred, saying education was more her area.

He nodded. "Yes, well, someone will fill the void, I'm sure. But surely you two didn't seek me out this evening to discuss Zozobra?"

"Actually, we're looking for Demetria Gonzales," Gregorio said. "She mentioned yesterday she was coming over to ask you about something and we wondered if you had seen her."

"Demetria?" Bateson said blankly.

"Yes. Old Agapita's daughter. Married to Joe, who's off fighting now." Gregorio sounded impatient. "Didn't he help you with your research a couple of years ago?"

"Oh, yes. Joe. I was sorry when he enlisted. Not to sound unpatriotic, we all have to do what we can for the war effort, but he was an excellent research assistant. He's careful, meticulous."

Emily hoped Joe was meticulous, flying bombers in the Pacific.

"Yes. Well, we're looking for his wife. Have you seen her?"

"No. I haven't seen anyone since yesterday evening, really.

I spent today cataloguing some of the shards I brought back. Would you like to have a look?"

"It's pretty late, Professor Bateson, and I've got to teach in the morning," Emily replied. "Maybe another time? I'd love to, someday."

"Well, all right then. Good evening."

"And to you."

"Come on, Miss Schwarz, let's leave the man in peace. Goodnight, Professor Bateson, Anasazi." Gregorio briefly petted the dog on its mottled brown head before they left the house. The outside seemed even blacker as Bateson shut the door and Emily heard the deadbolt click shut behind them.

"He's got a lot of locks on that door," Gregorio observed. "A padlock. And a deadbolt."

"I'm sure he just wants to make sure his research is safe when he's out in the field."

"Yup. Wouldn't want kids to get in there and trash the place."

"No," Emily agreed. "But what could have happened to Demetria?"

"Agapita's sister is married down in Cochiti. Maybe Demetria went down there to check up on her old auntie."

"Maybe." Emily felt dubious.

"Tell you what. I'll ride Flossie down there tomorrow. I'll let you know right after school, OK?"

Emily nodded, uncertain. But tomorrow would arrive soon enough. Gregorio insisted on accompanying her back to the school, and she didn't protest. Two women had vanished in just a few days. First Consuela, and now Demetria.

They approached the wire fence that surrounded the schoolyard and Emily opened the gate.

"I'll bring you some aster plants, Miss Schwarz."

"Why?"

"You can plant them where those dahlias were. Or whatever you call them. Those purple and orange and red flowers you were growing. They gave Flossie horrible colic. Asters won't bother her tummy one bit."

Emily laughed, despite her concern, and shut the gate behind her.

The next day dawned far too early. Emily's alarm jarred her out of slumber while the morning sun shone in through her second-story window. She had slept poorly, worried about Demetria, and finally drifted off around four or so. Of course, she was worried about Consuela too, but Demetria was the closest thing she had to a real friend here in San Antonito. Still, her students would show up at eight-thirty whether she had slept well or not. She dragged herself out of bed, skipped breakfast, drank three cups of coffee instead of her usual two, and left the coffeepot on the stove. It could be a very long day.

The classroom filled, and the day's lessons commenced. Most of her students were good kids, she mused after recess. She'd only had to break up one argument during that period and admonish little Gilbert, for perhaps the twentieth time, not to draw dinosaurs on his math paper. She picked up the paper with a little smile. Gilbert, the Montoyas' younger son, was an introverted, quiet nine-year-old and definitely better at drawing than arithmetic. A lifelike Stegosaurus filled the bottom margin of the paper, while a Tyrannosaurus rex adorned the left-hand margin.

Emily put the paper in a stack as the students came back from recess, and moved on to spelling, trying to ignore the sound of a horse and rider—Gregorio most likely—as they passed the school and headed down the road to Cañada and Cochiti.

School ended, and Emily hadn't heard from Gregorio, or Demetria. She decided to walk up to the plaza and see if Gregorio had returned and what he had discovered. She drank another cup of coffee with plenty of milk and sugar, neatened her hair, and started out. Her shoes scuffed up little clouds of dust as she walked up the dry, dirt road. It was unusually warm for September, and she felt a faint sheen of sweat on her forehead as she walked.

The usual men lounged around the porch at Romero's store. Emily noted happily that the store was open for business. Hopefully Mr. Romero was feeling better, and over his cough.

Emily greeted the men. She recognized the short, somewhat stout figure of Hilario among the group. "I was looking for the *fiscal*," she said to Hilario as she approached. "Have you seen him?"

Hilario took a swig of his Coke. "He went to Cochiti."

"He's not back yet?"

Hilario shook his head.

Emily tried again. "You haven't seen Demetria Gonzales, have you? Joe's wife."

Hilario shook his head again.

"Well, thank you," Emily said, flushing awkwardly. She made her way past the men and entered the shop. "Mr. Romero,

I'm glad to see you up and about. You're feeling better?"

Mr. Romero's cheeks still looked pale, but he nodded. "Still a bit of a cough, *que no*? But much better. The osha root is helping. Osha will cure anything, Señora. That, and *yerba buena.*

Emily wasn't convinced but she promised Mr. Romero she would try some the next time she was feeling poorly. She ordered a root beer, and took a nickel out of her pocket to pay for it.

"Has Demetria been in today?" she asked, hopeful her friend had turned up.

"I haven't seen her," Mr. Romero answered, "but she's always busy, that one, baking bread or this and that. Sewing. She likes to sew, she's always coming in here for thread."

Emily took her root beer and started to leave, but paused on her way out the door. "Still no word about your niece?"

Mr. Romero's face flushed, and he coughed a bit into a handkerchief. Emily felt bad she had asked, as the man shook his head.

"No. I think she's run away to Albuquerque. They haven't found a trace of her here, and the silly chica was always carrying on about friends she'd made in Bernalillo last year who moved to Albuquerque. But she didn't tell me their names. She needs a whipping, that girl, for all that she's my own niece. She's *loca*, crazy."

Emily nodded, thanked him, and left. She detoured slightly to pass by Demetria's house, but it looked abandoned. Worried, Emily took a swig of her soda and continued back to the school. She was about halfway there when she heard hooves plodding up the road towards her. Looking down the road, she saw Gregorio, on Flossie, ambling back towards the pueblo. Gregorio saw her, waved, and encouraged Flossie to move at a slightly quicker pace. It wasn't too long before they reached Emily. Gregorio looked solemn, his usual smile absent.

"Miss Schwarz."

"Hello, Gregorio," Emily replied. "What happened in Cochiti?" Suddenly no longer thirsty, she toyed with the bottle in her hands, passing it from one hand to another.

He hesitated before answering. "Demetria's not there. Not at her auntie's anyway. Nobody's seen her."

"Oh, no."

"I'm going to call out some search parties. She's got to be somewhere. Maybe she tripped looking for clay, and couldn't get home. Sprained her ankle or something."

"I hope so." Demetria hadn't said anything about looking for clay when she left Emily in the afternoon two days previously. In fact, Emily had never heard her friend mention it at all. "Clay?" she asked Gregorio. "Demetria's not a potter, is she?"

"No, but her mother is."

Emily hadn't known that. Gregorio hadn't shaved, and Emily noticed faint stubble on his chin. His dark eyes looked tired. "This is bad, these ladies disappearing," he said.

Emily nodded. She could feel sweat in her armpits, and it wasn't from her walk. Somebody was targeting women, women involved with Juan's murder. And she herself had found the body.

"Go on back to the school," Gregorio ordered. "But bolt the door, Miss Schwarz. Don't open it up until you know who's there."

"But what about Demetria?"

"The men will know where to look. You stay safe; at least that way I won't have to worry about some poor Meleca disappearing too."

Emily wasn't sure how she felt about Gregorio referring to her as "some poor Meleca." She knew Gregorio often referred to white people as Melecas; she guessed it came from the word Americans. Gregorio had told her it was a Zuni word. He had an aunt in Zuni and he'd said he had picked up the word there. She shrugged. It didn't seem like a day to quibble over nicknames. She really should be out looking for Demetria, too, but she didn't know the country as well as the men of San Antonito did. Finally, apprehension prevailed. "Come and let me know when you find her."

Gregorio nodded and Emily left him, walking rapidly back to the schoolhouse. When she arrived, she locked and bolted the main door and then checked the back one. After that, she tried to settle down; there were papers to grade, of course, but Emily found it hard to concentrate and didn't get much done.

CHAPTER
EIGHTEEN

EVENTUALLY EMILY MADE a pot of coffee, hoping Gregorio would show up with news of Demetria, or possibly with Demetria herself, and they could sit around the table joking and talking, as they used to do. In the midst of this daydream, her papers still ungraded, the sound of knocking on the front door startled her. She glanced at her watch; it read close to seven. The light in the narrow canyon outside was fading quickly.

The knocking continued, insistent. Hoping it was Gregorio with Demetria, Emily went to the door. "Who is it?"

"It's Mr. Shepherd, Miss Schwarz. May I come in?"

Mystified, Emily opened the door. Despite the cool evening, Mr. Shepherd had his suit jacket off, slung over one arm, and his white shirt unbuttoned at the neck.

"Mr. Shepherd. What brings you this way?"

"I had to speak with the governor about some business and thought I'd check up on you."

"I am fine." Emily knew she sounded prim, but the nerve of the man. Her irritation goaded her. "Tell me the truth this time. What was your car doing on the road between here and Cañada?" she demanded abruptly.

"Saturday morning?" Shepherd smiled, which made Emily even more annoyed.

"Yes. I walked down to the mercantile. Your car was there; I saw the picnic basket in the back seat. Then you took off. I must have heard you driving away while I was in the shop."

Shepherd didn't look at all contrite.

"So. What were you doing there?" Emily felt like she was interrogating one of her fifth graders.

"Well, it was late after I dropped you off. I just got sleepy and decided to pull over for a catnap. Next thing I knew it was seven AM."

"But you weren't in your car when I spotted it."

"Just went for a little walk to clear my head. I'm sorry I missed you, though. Did that puppet give you bad dreams?"

"Not in the slightest," Emily replied, prim again.

"Do I smell coffee?"

"I've just made a pot." After a moment she added, a bit grudgingly, "You're welcome to a cup."

"Thanks, I'll take you up on that." Shepherd flashed a smile. Truthfully, Emily didn't feel like she'd had much say in the matter. Between Shepherd and Gregorio she didn't feel like she'd had much choice in anything lately.

"Did you see the *fiscal* when you were at Governor

Atencio's?" she asked, after they were seated at the kitchen table and Mr. Shepherd had taken a sip of his coffee.

"No. This hits the spot, by the way," Shepherd said. Emily nodded. "Atencio said something about somebody going missing?"

"Two people. First Consuela Romero, from Cañada. She disappeared on Saturday afternoon and hasn't shown up yet. They had search parties all over the place but nobody found a thing. Now Demetria has disappeared, too. She left here Tuesday afternoon; she was going to talk to Professor Bateson. But she never arrived."

Shepherd's eyes narrowed and he raised one eyebrow.

"We asked the professor about it last night, but he hadn't seen a thing. Then Gregorio thought maybe she'd gone down to her aunt's house at Cochiti, so he checked today. But she wasn't there, so now they've got men out looking for her too." Emily heard the tremble in her own voice and for a moment she was afraid she would burst in to tears. It had been a relief to talk to someone about all of it, although Mr. Shepherd seemed an unlikely confidante. Still, he listened intently to her.

"No wonder you're a nervous wreck," he observed when she finished.

"I am not—" Emily began, and then her lips curved upwards despite herself. "Well, maybe a bit," she conceded. "And you, Mr. Shepherd," she added after a pause. "What brings you down to San Antonito this evening?"

"I had to talk to Governor Atencio about something."

Emily wondered what that was.

"Have you talked to Professor Bateson lately?" she asked. "He said he hadn't seen Demetria, but I can't imagine where she could have gone."

"I haven't spoken with him since last Sunday."

A knock sounded, and Emily answered the door. Gregorio stood outside. Beyond him, Flossie was tied to the schoolyard fence.

"You didn't find her," Emily said.

"No."

Emily bit her lip. "Well, come on in. Mr. Shepherd stopped by too. You look like you could use a cup of coffee and there's a fresh pot on the stove."

Gregorio nodded and walked with Emily down the hall, his normally erect posture sagging. Like a tired old man, Emily thought, as if seeing him for the first time.

In the kitchen, Gregorio sat at the table, and Emily got him a cup of coffee. Shepherd looked at him. "Rough day?"

Gregorio nodded. "Two missing women. And no sign of either one."

"What about Sheriff Wilcox?" Shepherd asked. "Can he help?"

"He's been looking for Consuela, that girl from Cañada. We haven't called him in yet about Mrs. Gonzales. We hoped we'd find her before that was necessary. Besides, he wouldn't do much about that. It's our jurisdiction, not his. A tribal matter."

"You don't think the two disappearances are connected?" Shepherd asked, his voice alert.

Gregorio shrugged. "Consuela Romero's a girl raised in these parts. And Demetria knows this area well. There's no reason for either to go missing."

"Except Consuela had information that would have cleared Demetria's godson," Emily interjected tartly.

"So the sheriff still has Lorenzo in custody," Shepherd said.

"Yes, and you think he's going to let him go?" Gregorio laughed bitterly. "He's got his suspect. As far as he's concerned the case is closed."

Emily wondered whether Wilcox would have been so eager to close the case if the victim had been a white man, but she didn't remark on it. Gregorio sounded upset enough already.

Both men left shortly afterward. Gregorio had offered to take Mr. Shepherd up to Atencio's before it got too late. Emily felt perversely glad to see them both to the door, which she then carefully locked and bolted as Gregorio had suggested.

Thoughts and questions buzzed in her brain like the large black flies that settled around the garbage pail outside. Where was Demetria? Shepherd's explanation for his car on the side of the road didn't make much sense. What was he hiding? What was his job, really? A procurement officer had little business in San Antonito. What did he want with the governor? Where was Consuela? Who had killed Juan, if it wasn't Lorenzo? Would the killer strike again? Emily had found the body. What if she was next?

She feared her ruminations would prevent her from sleeping, but she dropped off the moment her head touched the pillow. Thankfully, she did not remember her dreams.

The next morning, Emily's students seemed strangely subdued. The older ones no doubt had heard of the disappearance of "that girl from the store" and Auntie Demetria. Emily heard whispers about it during recess, but she endeavored to ignore them. The day crawled by, Emily's anxiety about Demetria a nagging undercurrent to her lessons in arithmetic, spelling, and geography.

At recess she noticed Gilbert Montoya sitting alone under the big cottonwood, the only shade in the dusty playground area. Curious, she walked over to him.

"Drawing more dinosaurs, Gilbert?"

Gilbert looked up, his round face serious. "No, Miss Schwarz."

"Don't you want to go play with the other boys? They're playing dodge ball."

"I don't like dodge ball."

"Why not?"

"I always get hit. Then I'm in the middle of the circle forever."

"Oh." Emily looked over at Gilbert. With a stick, he drew something in the dirt by his side.

"What are you drawing, then?"

"Anasazi. That's Professor Bateson's dog. I like dogs." Gilbert smiled shyly.

Emily smiled back. "I do, too. What's Anasazi doing in the picture?"

"He's with that lady that went up the canyon."

Emily felt the hairs on her arm prickle. "Who was that, Gilbert?"

"Just some lady. I don't know. She was kind of far away. But the lady and Anasazi went up the canyon the other day, up to that pool where there are salamanders. Maybe she likes salamanders. I like salamanders. And dinosaurs."

"Oh, really?" Emily replied, her heart pounding. Could the woman have been Demetria? "Look, Gilbert, recess is just about over. I'm going to ring the bell. Why don't you be the first to line up."

Gilbert stood up and dusted off his overalls. He flashed another furtive smile, gone almost as soon as it appeared, and then raced over to the playground gate while Emily rang the large hand bell that signaled the end of recess.

The school day finally came to a close. Emily watched as the students walked up the road to the main village, some jostling each other, nearly running in their attempt to begin their weekend, others—girls, mainly—walking more slowly, chatting or gossiping.

Emily neatened up the classroom and then repaired to the kitchen for her post-class cup of coffee. She had a plan. Since none of the men in the pueblo had found Demetria, she would look for her. Gilbert's picture had convinced her. Perhaps Professor Bateson had seen Demetria and Anasazi head up the canyon, and it had slipped his mind; if she saw him, she could ask him about it.

Emily changed into denim dungarees and filled her aluminum canteen with fresh water. She gathered together her father's old compass, a flashlight, and her Girl Scout pocketknife, and put them in her rucksack. She tied her hair back with a scarf, then left the school and walked up past the plaza, waving hello to people she saw outside their homes. Most waved back. She didn't see Gregorio, or the other men who usually lounged outside the store. Maybe they were out searching for Demetria.

She passed through the plaza and down the little road that led to the north side, up the canyon. Professor Bateson's house looked quiet, and his truck wasn't parked there. From that house, on the edge of the pueblo, a little track led up the narrowing canyon. Really more of a trail than a road, only the ruts in the pale dusty dirt showed that cars or trucks infrequently passed this way.

Emily had heard that the trails led out of the canyon, to an abandoned silver mine, and then to rough back country. She guessed that must be where Professor Bateson did his excavating, up in the mountains. The area abounded with ruins. She knew that, a bit further up the Rio Grande, a Swiss archaeologist named Bandelier had excavated some extensive ancient settlements in the late 1800s. Emily kept meaning to go up and see them. She'd heard there was a lodge too, that took in visitors. It might be a fun little side trip, but she hadn't yet found the time. She stayed pretty busy in San Antonito, and didn't have much leisure for sightseeing.

The afternoon sun shone pleasantly on her back, and the mingled scents of ponderosa pine, piñon trees, cedars, and junipers filled the air as Emily left the pueblo behind her. The village noises of horses, cows, donkeys, and people faded away and she walked in quiet, broken only by the sound of her shoes crunching twigs on the path, the occasional caw of a raven circling overhead, and sometimes, the squawk of a piñon jay.

As she walked, she scanned the trail, looking for tracks. Or anything to show that Demetria had passed this way. She saw nothing. No footprints, no helpful scraps of fabric from Demetria's dress snagged on nearby brush. Emily stopped and took a drink of water from her canteen. Had Professor Bateson lied about seeing Demetria? If he had, why? Or maybe Gilbert had seen someone else, not Demetria at all.

After a while the trail branched, and through the trees

Emily heard running water. A little creek ran through this part of the canyon, and Emily took the left fork, heading towards the distant sound. If there was a pool with salamanders, as Gilbert had suggested, this must be the way to it. But would Demetria have gone that way? She hadn't been looking for salamanders. She'd been looking for Consuela. Emily felt sure of that.

She shrugged and continued down the left fork, eventually reaching a little place where some animal, a beaver most likely, had dammed up the creek. Some of the water had spread out, forming a little marshy area with a small pool. She didn't see any salamanders, but to tell the truth she didn't feel much like turning over all the muddy rocks and sticks in the little pool to find them. She didn't see any trace of Demetria, either. Or of Anasazi. Again, no footprints. No trails of white pebbles or breadcrumbs either, Emily thought ruefully, remembering the fairy stories she sometimes read to her younger students.

The shadows lengthened, and the air started to chill down as the sun sank behind the canyon walls. Disheartened, Emily turned around and began to make her way back to the village. She suddenly felt nervous about being alone in the woods as darkness came on. She berated herself for thinking she would have found Demetria when all the men of San Antonito, who knew this land so well, hadn't. All because of some silly picture a child had drawn in the dirt.

The trail looked different heading back towards San Antonito. Funny how that worked, Emily thought. Rooks took on different shapes when viewed from the opposite direction; it could almost be an entirely different path. As the darkness strengthened, Emily pulled out her flashlight from the rucksack she carried and switched it on. How much further was it to the village? Maybe half a mile?

Emily heard a twig crack and a rustle in the brush along the right side of the trail. Alarmed, she swung the flashlight towards the brush. The light caught the white spikey fur of a young skunk scurrying back into the undergrowth. Going to meet its mother, she guessed. It hadn't looked too large. Feeling thankful she hadn't been the one to meet the adult skunk, she moved the flashlight beam back to the dirt of the trail ahead.

Something metallic glinted at her. Something that shouldn't have been there. Emily bent down and picked up a silver earring. It had lain in some leaves, almost covered. If it hadn't been for the beam of her flashlight, Emily never would have noticed it.

She rubbed the dirt off of it. A silver earring, a simple hoop design. Traditional enough. Emily tried to remember if she'd seen Demetria wear earrings like that, but she didn't think so. Or Consuela? She wasn't sure. Still, she had found something.

She pocketed the earring and piled up a few rocks to make a small cairn, marking the spot where she had found it. Then, unsure what else to do, she continued back towards San Antonito. She couldn't find Demetria on her own, not in the dark. She guessed she'd have to search out Gregorio.

CHAPTER NINETEEN

Emily found the *fiscal* at his house. Florencita stood at the sink, a tin tub set on the pine table, washing up the dinner dishes by the light of a kerosene lamp. Gregorio sat on a bench at the table, finishing a cup of something Emily assumed was coffee.

"Miss Schwarz," Gregorio said, looking up to where she stood in the open doorway, "you're out late again."

"I found something. I don't know whose it is." Emily pulled the earring out of her pocket and showed it to Gregorio and his mother.

"I remember that." Florencita spoke slowly. "That girl had it on. The one at the shop."

"Consuela?" Gregorio asked. "Señor Romero's niece?"

"The one who used to run around with Juan." Florencita

nodded, as if to confirm her identification. "She used to wear them at the shop. Silver hoops, like this. Fancy. She likes jewelry, that one does."

"They haven't found her yet, have they?" Emily asked, although she was pretty sure she would have heard if there had been any good news. Or bad news, for that matter.

Gregorio shook his head. "It's on the radio out of Albuquerque. On KOB, and I think Wilcox put it in the paper too. But, so far as I've heard, nobody has come forward with anything." He looked at the earring more closely. "Where did you find this?"

Emily told Gregorio what Gilbert had said, about Anasazi and "a lady" heading up the canyon together. "So I went up that back trail, to see if I could find anything. I saw this when I was walking back. It was on the trail, mostly covered with leaves. The flashlight beam picked it out."

Gregorio's eyes narrowed. "Which trail?"

"The one that goes up to the back of the canyon. I've never been up there. But Consuela said she met Juan around there, late in the afternoon on the day he died. She could have lost it then, not later. Not after she disappeared."

"Maybe," Gregorio said. Emily couldn't be sure what he was thinking. "I'll take another look up there tomorrow."

"I'll come along," Emily volunteered, then glanced at her watch. "It's late. I should get back."

"I'll walk you. We don't need anybody else going missing."

Emily protested, but Gregorio insisted, quietly stubborn, and eventually she acquiesced. He got up, she said goodbye to Florencita, and they left.

"I'm sorry to put you to the trouble," Emily said again,

as they walked down the little alley that led from Gregorio's house to the plaza.

"It's OK, Miss Schwarz. Like I said, we just don't need anybody else disappearing."

The moon hadn't risen yet and Emily was glad of the kerosene lantern Florencita had insisted Gregorio bring along. A few lights shone out from the windows of some homes, but the town, without moonlight, sat dark and still. Quiet. Most folks had already gone to bed, Emily guessed. She and Gregorio walked across the plaza without speaking and headed down the road that led to the school. Emily heard coyotes yipping from someplace further up the canyon, and an owl hooted closer to the Rio Chiquito.

"That's the night grandfather," Gregorio commented, breaking the silence between them. "The owl. That's what my Zuni auntie told me. He'll guard your house for you at night."

"That's interesting," Emily replied. The comment sounded vapid even to her. "And the coyotes?" she asked, trying to sound less prim.

"They're tricksters. We've got lots of stories about Coyote. Ask the kids sometime. They'll tell you."

Emily nodded, although she typically read other stories to the children in school. Classics. The older students were reading *Treasure Island* now. But maybe she'd ask them about the coyote legends.

"Some lady anthropologist even came down to Cochiti about twenty years ago, collecting stories," Gregorio continued. "She put them in a book. There might be a copy someplace in the school."

"I'll look," Emily said. There were some old books stored on the second floor at the schoolhouse. That might be something the older students would enjoy. Something of their culture, that was meaningful to them. Maybe she didn't need to only focus on English classics.

They reached the schoolhouse and Gregorio waited while she unlocked the door.

"Goodnight, Miss Schwarz."

"Goodnight, Gregorio. Thank you."

For a moment, Emily watched the lantern bobbing in the dark as Gregorio headed back towards the village. Then she went inside and locked the door behind her. She was glad the next day was Saturday. Maybe she would sleep in. Then she remembered she had insisted on helping Gregorio with the search the next morning. He had said to meet on the plaza at sunrise.

By eight the next morning Emily and Gregorio, along with several other San Antonito men, had returned to the trail that led from the backside of the village up the canyon to the mountains above. After a quick survey of the left-hand fork, Gregorio confirmed there were no tracks to be found there. The party took the right-hand fork instead, which led, the *fiscal* told her, to an abandoned mine. This trail climbed steeply, switchbacking a bit as the canyon narrowed and gained some elevation. The sun, higher in the sky now, blazed down and Emily felt sweat trickling down her back and between her breasts. She wished for a moment that she had stayed back at the schoolhouse, but she pushed that thought quickly to the back of her mind. Surely this wasn't bad, this was nothing compared to what the troops in the Pacific went through every day.

"How far is it to the mine?" she asked when they stopped for water at a little spring. The rivulet trickled down from further up the canyon, a few scrub trees and chamisa bushes shading the water from the sun as it ran over the rocks.

"About four miles," Gregorio said. "But it's all uphill. It's OK, Miss Schwarz," he added as he saw her face. "We've already covered two of them."

"That's not so bad," Emily replied stoutly, and filled her canteen at the spring. The water had a somewhat alkaline, mineral taste, but it cooled her off. They started walking again, and the trail climbed higher. After another hour or so of climbing Emily glimpsed a few weathered wood buildings through the pines and junipers.

"That's it up ahead," Gregorio said in English. One of the other searchers said something in Keres that Emily didn't catch, and Gregorio answered him in the same language, laughing. Emily looked at him.

"When were these mines abandoned?" she asked.

"Oh, maybe thirty, forty years ago. There were lots of mines in these mountains. Here, and up in Bland Canyon, too. A lot of the men from San Antonito used to work up in them. My grandpa did. And yours too, eh Hilario?"

Hilario nodded. "He said it was hard. He didn't like the tunnels. But the money was good."

"Why did they close the mines?" Emily asked. They had entered the area now, a small abandoned settlement of several weathered and collapsing board buildings. A screen door hung forlornly askew from one door and it seemed that no one had disturbed the place for years.

"The silver ran out, and then the company went bust," Gregorio explained. "Check the buildings," he ordered, and the San Antonito men separated, inspecting the abandoned structures. Emily stood in the center and wiped her forehead with her blue bandana.

"What about Professor Bateson?" she asked Gregorio. "Isn't he excavating some ruins nearby? I'm surprised he doesn't use this as a base camp."

Gregorio just shrugged.

Emily went inside one old cabin. It took her eyes a moment to adjust to the darkness. A couple of rickety chairs stood in one corner, and the building smelled strongly of some wild, musky scent. Emily didn't know for sure what it was, maybe a fox's den. Spiderwebs and cobwebs festooned the walls and dust blanketed everything. Nothing seemed to have been disturbed for many years. Emily hoped snakes wouldn't come in to get out of the heat. Nervous, she exited the building, and stood outside blinking in the bright early afternoon sun while the men completed their searches.

They didn't turn up anything. Everything looked as if no one had been back since the miners had left it so many years ago. Although they did find remnants of an old fire just outside the settlement, some blackened rocks circling old ashes and nearby, some empty broken beer bottles and a few rusty tin cans marked with shotgun holes.

"Just kids," Gregorio decided. "Sometimes kids from Cañada come up here, hunting." It didn't look like anything to do with either of the missing women, and Emily had to agree with the *fiscal's* assessment.

"Well, this is as good a time for a lunch break as any," Gregorio said.

The men began pulling the lunches their wives had packed out of old knapsacks; burritos made from thick, homemade tortillas and mashed pinto beans. One man had tamales. Emily ate her peanut butter and jelly sandwich and an apple left over from the applesauce lesson earlier in the week. Everyone rested for a while, sitting in the meager shade cast by the wooden buildings as the sun crossed the zenith and began its afternoon descent to the west. A few clouds built up, fluffy white against the deep blue sky, and Emily found herself hoping the trip home wouldn't be quite as hot as the hike up had been.

By five o'clock Emily was back at the schoolhouse, soaking her feet in a tin basin of hot water and Epsom salts while she sat at the kitchen table. She had a pile of arithmetic papers in front of her to grade, but so far had only completed one of them. Gilbert's. His dinosaurs were really quite good, Emily thought. Maybe she should have him paint a large one for a bulletin board. A big Brontosaurus, maybe. Weren't they the largest?

The arithmetic papers and the prospect of a new bulletin board did little to assuage her disappointment and worry. They had found no trace of Consuela or Demetria. Hilario and Antonio had taken some other trails back, little hunting trails and tracks made by the mule deer and elk that wandered the canyons, but no one had found anything to report when everyone gathered back at Gregorio's house. Florencita had offered food—*posole* stew with red chile and pork, along with more tortillas—but Emily had declined, bone-tired after the long hike. She had limped her way home. Most of the other searchers had headed home as well, leaving Gregorio to fill Atencio in on the day's search.

So Consuela must have lost that earring the day she met Juan—nearly three weeks ago now. But where had the girl gone? And, even more worrisome to Emily, what had happened to Demetria Gonzales?

Emily picked up her red pencil and began doodling on a piece of scrap paper that had gotten mixed up with the children's assignments. Juan's murder. What if whoever killed Juan had shot Demetria also? There were lots of places in the mountains to hide a body. But if that was case, why hadn't the killer hidden Juan's body three weeks ago? Why leave the corpse lying by the Rio Chiquito for anyone to find?

So if Lorenzo hadn't murdered Juan, who had? Who had a reason to kill him? Consuela, if she was jealous enough, and if she could have gotten her hands on a gun. Emily realized she hadn't heard anything about the investigation into the guns— who in Cañada and San Antonito owned old weapons from the Great War, and if any had gone missing. She would have to ask Gregorio the next time she saw him.

She doodled a picture of a gun, like her father's old revolver. Who else might have killed Juan? If Consuela had gone up north in the canyon to see Juan, surely she wouldn't have shot him and left the body down on the river, south of San Antonito and so much closer to Cañada. Unless she and Juan had agreed to meet later that evening, closer to her home. If that was it, Consuela could have shot him and then run away, panicked, after she and Emily had spoken last Saturday.

Who else? Maybe Sheriff Wilcox was right. Maybe Lorenzo had shot Juan, jealous over Delia. Emily wasn't sure, but the

186

sheriff and Deputy Duran seemed convinced. Of course, neither man was from San Antonito. It would probably suit them to have it be a tribal killing, something in the pueblo, nothing outsiders needed to worry about.

But neither of those theories shed any light on Demetria's disappearance. What had happened to her friend? Gilbert said he had seen her . . . or at least, someone that might have been her. But that couldn't be true, now she thought about it. Professor Bateson and Anasazi hadn't returned until Wednesday evening, and Demetria had already gone missing by then. So Gilbert must just be confused. He was a good boy but a scatterbrain at times. Emily looked at Gilbert's paper again. He certainly didn't have the multiplication tables correctly memorized, despite his love of dinosaurs. Six times six was not sixty-three.

The water in the basin had grown cold. Emily put her pencil down and pushed the chair away from the table. Her feet felt better after the soak, but she certainly didn't intend on hiking anyplace the next day.

She dried her feet on an old towel and put on her comfortable old slippers, then dumped the water outside by the back porch. She gathered the children's papers and wearily headed towards the classroom. Maybe she would get more work done at her desk.

That night Emily dreamed she was back in Santa Fe, at the burning of Zozobra. But they weren't burning that puppet, they were burning Demetria—like a scene from an old movie she'd seen once, of Joan of Arc burning at the stake. Demetria screamed, "Help me!" and although in the dream Emily couldn't hear the words, she knew what her friend was saying. "Wait," she said, "I'll get Mr. Shepherd," but when she turned around Mr. Shepherd had vanished. Emily grew desperate, surrounded by the yelling crowd. Then she saw Mr. Shepherd up on the dais. *Surely he'll rescue her*, she thought, but instead Mr. Shepherd took the torch from the fire dancer and set fire to the pyre himself, while the crowd pressed against Emily, screaming "Burn her! Burn her!"

Emily sat up in bed, her heart pounding frantically. A dream, just a bad dream. About Demetria. And Mr. Shepherd.

She checked her watch. Four-thirty, too early to get up. But she didn't think she could go back to sleep after that nightmare. She fumbled with her flashlight, then some matches, and finally lit the old kerosene lamp on the bureau. She looked at the neglected novel lying on the nightstand—the Daphne Du Maurier book she'd been reading weeks ago, before all this had started. She opened the book and read a page or two, but put it down again and lay in bed, watching the glimmer of the lamp. She didn't want to dim the light.

CHAPTER
TWENTY

Sunday morning Emily attended Mass in the little mission church dedicated to Saint Anthony. The patron saint of lost things, she thought wryly. Maybe he'd help them find the missing women. Or maybe the saints had bigger things on their minds, what with the battles in the Pacific and the Nazis overrunning Europe like an infestation of rats. She said a prayer anyway, and found the familiar Latin somewhat soothing. Emily left the church in a slightly better mood, despite her previous cynicism. Surely the saints could hear every prayer, even those for a silly teenager and a missing Indian woman.

After Mass she asked Gregorio what he'd discovered about the handguns in San Antonito. Lorenzo's father had an old service gun, as did a couple of other men. Hilario had one he'd gotten from his father, who had died a couple of years previously. "But they're all accounted for," Gregorio concluded, "and none of them look like they've been used in years. Although Hilario had to use his awhile back when a rattler got in the house."

Emily shuddered.

"What about La Cañada?" she asked. "Did Deputy Duran give you any information?"

Gregorio shook his head. "Nope. Do you want to go ask him about them? You could bake some more brownies." He laughed when he saw Emily's face. "Those were good, Miss Schwarz. We ate them all up."

Emily didn't reply. Two women were missing. Was baking brownies all she was good for? The nerve.

Her annoyance must have showed in her face, because when he spoke again, his voice sounded tentative, not his usual tone. "I mean it."

He paused, and she took her chance. "Surely Deputy Duran will let you and the governor know what's happening with the investigation," she replied, her voice stiffer than she wanted it to sound. She took a deep breath and asked another question. "Gregorio, what do you know about Mr. Shepherd?"

"Not much. He says he does procurement work, war work."

"That's what he told me, too," Emily said, "but he's always showing up at odd times. He says he needs to speak with Atencio. You don't think he could have anything to do with this, do you? He surely seems interested in it . . ."

"For a guy who works in procurement," Gregorio finished her sentence. "Well, I don't know. I can ask Atencio about it. I know the guy's stopped by his place sometimes, since all this happened. I don't remember seeing him around before he showed up with that army sergeant."

"Yes, Sergeant O'Toole." Her brows furrowed as she thought. "But Juan was killed southeast of the schoolyard. If the killing happened at night, Shepherd could have met him down there without being seen at the village."

"Maybe, Miss Schwarz." Gregorio sounded doubtful. "He doesn't seem the type to go shooting Indians in the middle of the night for no reason, though. Just my opinion, of course. And there are all kinds of war work. But next time I see Deputy Duran, I'll ask him about those guns in Cañada."

"Good. Then I won't have to bake any more brownies.

Emily couldn't get her dream out of her mind. It lingered into the afternoon, preying on her while she reviewed assignments and worked on her lesson plans for the next week. Or maybe, she thought, it was Demetria who was haunting her. Emily felt she should be doing more to find her friend but she couldn't think what.

So she graded papers. Arithmetic completed, she picked up a stack of essays by the upper graders on the topic of "America, Land of Freedom". She had wanted the students to contrast life here in the United States with life under Hitler or the Imperial Japanese.

Most of the essays were a bit lackluster, but a few of the children made good points. "We have freedom of speech here in America," one child wrote, "and can worship God as we please." This was followed by "I like going to Mass on Sundays." Vinnie Mondragon had written that essay; Emily attended Mass regularly and couldn't remember ever seeing Vinnie there.

Another student wrote, "My parents were sent to boarding schools in Kansas but now we have a school right here in San Antonito. America is the land of opportunity."

Another of the fifth-grade boys, Felipe, wrote, "Anyone here can join the army and fight for our country." As Emily graded his paper, she hoped this war would be over long before Felipe would be old enough to serve. The troops were certainly fighting fiercely in the Pacific these days. She thought of her brother, sighed, and picked up another paper.

Finally, she could stand it no longer. She pushed the stack of essays to one side and set her red pencil, now sadly in need of sharpening, next to them. She went upstairs, changed into dungarees and a blouse, and headed outside, locking up the schoolhouse behind her. Emily walked briskly up the road to the center of the pueblo, through the plaza, and then towards the trail that led into the hills.

She passed Professor Bateson's house, locked and lonely. There was no sign of the anthropologist, or his dog, although she did see his old truck parked, covered in dust. Emily knew sometimes he backpacked into the wilderness, looking for archaeological sites. He had an old mule too, that he sometimes used as a pack animal, at least Demetria had told her so once. There were some sites a truck couldn't reach.

Emily left the village behind and started up the trail. By now the terrain looked more familiar. She took the left fork, the one that led to the little pond where Gilbert had said he'd seen Demetria heading, five days ago now. She had no idea what she was looking for, really, just that she needed to move and this was the last place anyone had seen Demetria.

The blister on her foot from yesterday's hike bothered her

some, but after a bit Emily managed to put it out of her mind. It was another flawless September afternoon, although she noticed some clouds building up over the Jemez Mountains. It hadn't rained in a few weeks, and the trail was dusty and dry. Emily saw the jumble of prints their party had left yesterday as they returned from the ghost town up in Bland.

The afternoon air felt hot, still, almost clammy. Emily supposed it must be the clouds; certainly the humidity didn't approach that of summers in Racine, but the air didn't seem as dry as a typical San Antonito day. From over the Jemez Mountains to the west Emily heard a faint growl of thunder, but the sun still shone brightly on this trail.

The thunder rolled away, replaced by horse hooves approaching down the trail from the mountain. Emily stood to one side to let the rider, still out of sight behind a bend, pass by.

The rider emerged. Gregorio, on Flossie. "Afternoon, Miss Schwarz," he greeted her.

"Hello, Gregorio. Were you out looking for Demetria?"

He nodded. "There's a few coyote trails up there we missed yesterday. I just thought I'd take a look. Nothing there," he said, in answer to Emily's unspoken question. "And you?"

"I just had to get out," Emily confessed with unusual candor. "I can't sit there grading papers when I don't know where she is."

"Agapita's worried. All the ladies are," Gregorio admitted.

Emily felt glad to know she wasn't alone. Of course everyone here was worried. "Well, I'm just going to walk a little bit, to clear my mind. Maybe I'll find another earring." She laughed, without mirth.

Gregorio nodded. "Go ahead, then. But that storm might roll this way. Watch the weather, Meleca."

Emily nodded, too restless and worried to take umbrage at the nickname. Gregorio tipped his battered cowboy hat to her, and he and Flossie continued down the trail towards San Antonito.

Emily reached the fork in the path and took the left-hand turn that led to the little creek and the beaver pond. The shade was a bit deeper, the cottonwood and pines a little thicker, and the air pleasantly scented. Pine needles crunched underneath her feet; the air smelled of sharp pine and dust and the pungent odor of the golden chamisa, now in flower. Emily continued until she reached the clearing and the quiet pool. Cottonwood leaves, beginning to turn yellow with the changing season, filtered the sunlight and made the space feel like a grotto, or some kind of temple, Emily thought.

She found a large sandstone boulder, covered on its north side with darker lichen, and sat down. The rock, warm from the sun, felt comforting, and Emily stayed still, enjoying the calming sensation, soaking up the strength of the earth. Her breath slowed and for a few minutes she stopped worrying and relaxed, losing herself in the setting.

A twig snapped. Emily started, the moment broken. Heart thudding, her head whipped around, her eyes seeking the source of the noise. What if it was a bear, or a mountain lion? She didn't see anything. The noise seemed to have originated from a large chamisa bush partway up the clearing. Then more branches rustled, and Emily glimpsed eyes, plus a human-shaped form, from behind the chamisa bush. And surely mountain lions didn't wear blue shirts?

"Who's there?" Emily called, hoping she sounded braver than she felt. "Come out, now!" She spoke in her teacher voice, the one she used for breaking up playground fights.

The bushes rustled and someone emerged from them. Emily wasn't sure who she thought she would see, but it certainly wasn't her third-grade student. "Gilbert! What are you doing here?"

"Playing," Gilbert whispered, not meeting her eyes.

"You're pretty far from home," Emily observed, her heart beginning to slow. She took a deep breath. "Does your mother know where you are?"

"I told her I'd be outside."

"What are you playing?"

"Army. The Japs are just over there, behind the pond. We're in the Marianas," he added, "and that's the ocean."

"The pond?"

Gilbert nodded.

"What about the salamanders?'

"Sharks," Gilbert replied. "They're sharks."

"Well, you gave me a start," Emily confessed. "And I didn't even know about the sharks."

Gilbert looked at his teacher dubiously. Finally, he smiled. "Do you want to see one?"

"That would be nice," Emily said, although she had doubts about how nice it would be, really.

"I'll show you, Miss Schwarz. There are two kinds."

"Really?"

"*P'ákuri*, water dogs. Those are the big ones. Some are really big. They're black and yellow, usually. And *beríina*, those are the little brown ones."

Gilbert moved over near the pool and started digging in the mud and turning over some dead cottonwood limbs that lay near the water. "Here's one, Miss Schwarz. Look!"

Emily came over and bent her head to look at the brownish, small salamander Gilbert held cupped in his hands. "This is one of the little ones, the *beriina*," he explained. "I'm pretending they're little tiger sharks."

Emily nodded.

"The big ones have stripes," her student continued excitedly, "and they like to live in the mud. You just find the little ones under logs." He released his prisoner and it scuttled away in the leaves. "Let's look for a big one," he continued, in that way children have of assuming no grown up could possibly be uninterested in whatever intrigued themselves. But the afternoon wasn't over yet, and she certainly hadn't found any trace of Demetria. She might as well look for salamanders.

"All right, Gilbert," she said. "Where are the big ones?"

"They like to live in the mud," Gilbert told her. "Down near the pond. You have to dig them out, sometimes. Let's look here." He moved a little closer to the water. "See Miss Schwarz, this is where they live. The big *p'akuri*."

Emily wondered if she should tell Gilbert to use the English word, but she didn't. The boy looked so excited, and animated in a way she didn't usually see in the classroom. She didn't have the heart to admonish him for using his own language. Not out here in the woods, on Sunday afternoon.

Gilbert started to dig in the dirt near the edge of the pond while Emily looked on. Mud splattered over his dungarees, and for a moment Emily wondered if Juliana would get angry about that, but she imagined Juliana was used to Gilbert coming home dirty.

Gilbert continued digging industriously, uncovering a small hole in the bank. He pointed to it. "See that, Miss Schwarz. That's his house. He's probably in there."

"Careful, Gilbert," she cautioned. "It could be a snake's house or something."

"No, I've seen him go in there. He's really big, Miss Schwarz. Don't you want to see him?"

Emily watched while Gilbert continued working, thinking he had most likely scared all the salamanders away with his excavating. "Won't they be upset?" she asked. "You're ruining their house."

The boy shrugged. "They'll make another one. It's what they do."

Suddenly she saw a glint of something shiny in the dirt. "Gilbert—"

"What, Miss Schwarz?"

"What's that? Over there, in the tunnel?"

"It's probably just a root, Miss Schwarz."

"No, Gilbert, it's not a root. Wait, I'll look."

She moved in front of the boy and picked up a stick, then poked cautiously in the hole. She dug out a little more mud, and the glinting shape became clearer. A round metal barrel. A handle.

A gun.

CHAPTER TWENTY-ONE

"**D**ON'T TOUCH THAT, Gilbert."

"It's a gun, isn't it?" The boy's eyes widened. "Let's get it out."

Emily shook her head. "No, we have to get Mr. Cruz. He's the sheriff. He'll know what to do."

She looked at the top of the bank. Someone must have buried the gun higher up, and it just happened to fall down into the salamander burrow. The ground above might have showed some signs of being disturbed, but she wasn't certain.

"Come on, Gilbert," she said, suddenly anxious. "We have to go get Gregorio. You need to stop playing right now; we need to bring the *fiscal* back here before the sun goes down."

The sun had already crested the tops of the pine trees. The clouds that had threatened rain earlier had dispersed somewhat, the remaining ones glowing faintly lavender against an increasingly orange sky. They marked the spot with Emily's bandana, tied to a stick, and started for home.

"Do you think that's the gun that shot my brother?" Gilbert asked as they hurried down the path back to the pueblo. His round face looked serious, but Emily could see some excitement flicker in the boy's brown eyes.

"I'm not sure, Gilbert. The sheriff will know what to do."

"We never did see that salamander. The gun won't hurt him, will it?"

"Gilbert, that gun is all buried in dirt. I don't think it could go off."

Gilbert smiled a little. He was an odd child, Emily thought. Sweet, but quirky.

They reached the outskirts of San Antonito, passed the few houses on the northern side, and neared the plaza. Emily was about to send Gilbert home while she looked for Gregorio, but then she thought better of it. Surely the alcalde should be told. And he might know where to find Gregorio.

The door to Atencio and Juliana's house was open, and from inside Emily could smell savory green chile stew and fresh tortillas.

Gilbert poked his head inside and was met with a string of Keres. From the sound of it, Emily guessed that Juliana was scolding him for being late to dinner. Then Atencio's wife looked up and saw Emily. The Keres stopped abruptly.

"Oh, Miss Schwarz. Hello. I didn't see you."

"I was out for a walk and saw Gilbert, so we came on home. Is your husband here? We found something. Something he should know about."

Juliana's eyes narrowed but she turned and went into the back room, saying something in Keres. After a minute she emerged, followed by the governor, who was rubbing his eyes. Emily wondered if he'd been napping, but didn't ask.

"Mr. Montoya, do you know where Gregorio is? I was out walking and met Gilbert. And we found something."

"It's a gun, Dad," Gilbert said excitedly in English. His mother admonished him in Keres but Atencio raised an eyebrow.

"Really? Where was it?"

"It was buried, Dad! In a salamander burrow!"

Atencio's other eyebrow rose. He smiled down at his son. "He likes animals, that one does," he said. "But Gregorio must be at home. I'll go get him."

"*Ch'úpe*. Eat," Juliana told Gilbert. He quickly sat down at the table and began tucking into a bowl of green chile stew and a fresh flour tortilla.

"It's dinnertime, Miss Schwarz. Sit down and eat."

It did smell scrumptious, and Emily's mouth watered. "Well, maybe just a little bit. Until the sheriff gets here."

Juliana nodded, dished up a bowl of stew, and set it on the table, motioning to Emily to sit. She did so, and took a bite. "That's delicious, Juliana," she said. The stew was spicy, but not overly so, with potatoes, corn, and tomatoes soaking up the hotness of the green chile.

"It's good in the fall, when the chile is fresh. The green ones, they don't dry as well as the red ones do."

Just then the door opened. Atencio and Gregorio walked in. Emily told them what she and Gilbert had found while the boy, excited, interrupted with his tale about the salamander burrow and the gun. Although shy at school, the boy was not so quiet here, at his home.

"Did you bring it with you?" Atencio asked.

"I wanted to, Dad, but Miss Schwarz said to leave it there."

"We marked the spot with a bandana tied to a stick," Emily added. "I didn't think we should touch it."

"Thank you," Gregorio said. He and Atencio spoke in Keres for a few minutes and then he switched to English, for her benefit, Emily supposed. "I'll go down to Cañada and give Sheriff Wilcox a call. He might want to take a look before we move anything." Gregorio glanced out the window at the darkness outside. "It's late now. I'll see if he wants to come up first thing in the morning. But I'll go down and make that call tonight. I'll just go get my truck." The alcalde nodded his agreement. "Do you want a ride home, Miss Schwarz?"

Emily agreed and a few minutes later they were in Gregorio's old truck headed south from the plaza. They reached the schoolhouse, and Gregorio pulled over. "Well, goodnight, Miss Schwarz. I'll let you know what happens."

Emily nodded, got out of the car, and went inside the school. She heard the truck heading down the road towards Cañada as she lit the kerosene lamp.

Monday morning, shortly after daybreak, Emily heard a couple of cars heading up the road to San Antonito. She glanced out the window in time to see the Bernalillo County sheriff's car as it headed towards the main part of the village. Shortly thereafter her students arrived and the school day began, precluding much else. However, thoughts of what the sheriff and his men might be finding nagged at Emily like some troublesome mosquito as she tried to concentrate on her students and their lesson. Gilbert wasn't in school, and Emily wondered about that, too. Surely his father had not let him join Gregorio and the sheriff's men as they searched for the gun. She and the boy had marked the spot, after all. There would be no reason for him to go along.

The day crawled by. Somehow word had gotten out that the sheriff was there investigating—it was impossible to keep a secret in San Antonito—and the talk Emily overheard at recess was all about cops. But none of the students asked her anything directly, and Emily said nothing to enlighten them about what had happened. It was a matter for law enforcement, and there was too much gossip about it. Emily assumed her students knew all about it already.

The sheriff had not left San Antonito by dismissal time. After her students left, Emily neatened her desk, stacking papers that needed grading in tidy piles. Then she could stand it no longer. She got her purse, put a little lipstick on, and headed for the plaza. If there had been any news, they might know at the store. Or perhaps she would just stop by Atencio's directly and see what they had found. She could always say she was checking on Gilbert, if she needed an excuse.

Sheriff Wilcox's car was parked in front of the alcalde's house, and so Emily headed that way. Juliana greeted her and invited her in. Atencio, Gregorio, and Sheriff Wilcox sat around the kitchen table, drinking coffee and eating fresh tortillas. The men stood as Emily entered the room, causing a little commotion as benches and chairs were pushed back from the table. Emily blushed, feeling awkward.

"Hello," she greeted them, refusing Juliana's offer of coffee. "I just wondered what had happened?"

"Well, we got it," Sheriff Wilcox said. "I'm taking it to the crime lab down in Albuquerque. Maybe the ballistics men there can tell if it's the gun that was used to shoot Juan. But after being buried in that dirt for a couple of weeks—well, I don't know about fingerprints. Not too likely."

Emily sighed. Fingerprints might have cleared Lorenzo.

"It's a good thing you and that young fella were out hiking and noticed that," Sheriff Wilcox continued.

"My son has sharp eyes," Atencio said.

"He was trying to show me a salamander burrow," Emily responded. "Where is Gilbert, by the way?"

"Not home from school yet, I guess," Atencio said. "He probably stopped to play along the way."

"But he wasn't in school today," Emily protested. She suddenly felt sick. "He didn't come to school."

"Well, not in the morning, Miss," Sheriff Wilcox replied. "We took him with us up the trail. The little tyke was all excited about it and wanted to come with us, and I figured it couldn't hurt. He showed us the exact spot, right where you marked it. But after that we sent him home. Even had Deputy Duran walk him down to the village.

Emily heard Juliana's gasp from the stove, where she had been cooking more tortillas. "He never came to the house," she said.

"And he never came to school, either." Emily suddenly felt faint. She wished for a chair, but there wasn't one nearby. Instead she leaned against the adobe wall a minute, her heart thudding sickly in her chest. "Where is he?" After another moment, she added, "And where's Deputy Duran? Maybe he can tell us what happened to Gilbert."

"I sent him back to Bernalillo about an hour ago, to take the gun into the crime lab in 'Burque," Sheriff Wilcox replied. "Don't worry, Mrs. Montoya, we'll find Gilbert. He probably just wanted to see what we were doing and cut back through the woods to spy on us."

Juliana did not look reassured.

"He knows all the trails, that one does," Atencio agreed, but Emily thought his eyes looked worried, his cheeks tense.

"He'll come home when he gets hungry. You know what boys are like." Sheriff Wilcox's words, meant to reassure, only brought Juliana to tears. Emily felt like crying too, but she drew a little strength from the thick adobe wall she leaned against. She steadied herself, took a breath, and spoke.

"Maybe it would be worth a call to Deputy Duran. He could tell us exactly where he left Gilbert."

"That's a fine idea," said Wilcox, his voice hearty. "I'll just drive down to Cañada and put in a call to headquarters. Then I'll come back and help you all look for that little rascal."

Juliana wiped the tears from her cheeks and eyed the brown belt that hung from a nail in the kitchen. "I'm going to whip him within an inch of his life once we find him."

Gregorio had already headed towards the door. "I'll round up some of the men. We'll start looking at the edge of the village, spread out, and search all the way back up the trail. Don't worry, Juliana. We'll find him."

"What would you like me to do?" Emily asked. "I want to help."

"Miss Schwarz, would you stay here with my wife?" Atencio asked. "I don't want her alone while we look."

"Of course. Certainly," Emily agreed.

The men left, and she and Juliana settled down to wait. They heard Sheriff Wilcox's car leave the village, and the sound of voices as the men organized the search parties. Then it grew quiet.

Juliana pulled herself together and started washing the dishes. Emily dried them. Then Juliana poured them both cups of coffee from the enamel pot on the stove. Emily put lots of evaporated milk in hers, with sugar. She sipped it gratefully, not quite sure what to say.

Eventually, Juliana spoke. "My husband knows all the trails here. And he and Gregorio are both good trackers. They'll find him."

Emily thought to herself that they hadn't found Demetria, but she didn't share that with her hostess.

After a while, they heard the sheriff's car returning. The engine stopped and a moment later a knock came at the door. Juliana opened it. Sheriff Wilcox stood on the doorstep, twisting his hat in his hands.

"My deputy said he left your son just on the north side of the village," he told Juliana. "I just thought you would like to know what he said. Now, if you'll excuse me, ladies, I'm going to find those men, and find your son. Don't worry, Mrs. Montoya."

The sheriff left. Emily and Juliana continued to sit and worry. Juliana put her daughter to bed, and Emily wished desperately that she had something to occupy herself with, to keep her mind from running in circles. Even the abandoned stacks of papers back at the schoolhouse that needed to be graded suddenly seemed attractive. But she couldn't leave Juliana.

Juliana poured more coffee, the youngest child finally dropped off, and the two women sat by the light of the kerosene lamp, not speaking, listening to the quiet snores of the sleeper.

CHAPTER TWENTY-TWO

THE KEROSENE IN the lamp had almost burned out. Emily dozed where she sat on the bench, her back slumped against the whitewashed walls. She opened her eyes, alerted by a sound outside, just in time to see Juliana set aside her embroidery—the red, green, and black designs most of the San Antonito women embroidered on the kilts the men used for their traditional dances.

"What is it?" Emily murmured, embarrassed she had fallen asleep.

"They're back," Juliana replied.

Emily nodded. She heard footsteps, and a few voices, and then the sheriff's car started up and drove away.

The door opened and Atencio and Gregorio came in. One glance told Emily the search had not been successful.

"We didn't find him," Atencio said, and then he switched to Keres, speaking to his wife. Emily wasn't sure what he was saying, but Juliana nodded, her round face solemn underneath her black bangs.

Emily looked at Gregorio. "It got too dark to see anything," he told her. "There's no moon tonight and we couldn't find any tracks, not just with lanterns and flashlights. We had to quit for now; we'll rest up a little and start again at first light."

"I'll take off, then. The students will be in school tomorrow no matter what. Or they should be. I should get on back."

Gregorio picked up the lantern. "I'll walk you down. We can't have some Meleca schoolteacher breaking her ankle out there in the middle of the night."

Emily half-heartedly protested but then gave in. She glanced at her watch. It was two AM.

They left the governor's house, and the plaza, and walked in silence down towards the schoolhouse. Emily felt glad of the little circle of light cast by the old kerosene lantern. The smell of the flame mingled with the piney scent of the canyon at night. A coyote yipped from up on the mesa, and Emily shivered. Tricksters, that's what Gregorio had told her about coyotes. She realized she still hadn't looked for that book of stories, but didn't mention it to Gregorio.

"Well, here we are," Gregorio said as they approached the schoolhouse gate. "Get some rest, Miss Schwarz. Tomorrow will be here all too soon."

Emily nodded. "Yes, my students won't care if I don't get much sleep." She unlocked the schoolhouse door. "Thank you, Gregorio. You get some sleep too."

The *fiscal* nodded and turned away. Emily heard the soft

sound of his steps as he walked back up the road, against the canvas of other night sounds—the crickets chirping and the breeze up the canyon. She watched the bobbing circle of his lantern light as it moved back to the main village, and then she went inside, locked the door behind her, and got ready for bed. School would begin in just six hours.

Of course Emily didn't sleep that night. Every time she closed her eyes, visions of Gilbert in danger filled her mind. Gilbert bitten by a rattlesnake. Gilbert with a broken ankle. Gilbert falling from some cliff to the canyon floor, where he lay dead like his brother Juan, with sightless eyes and horrible black blowflies buzzing around his body. Her eyes gritty, she finally glanced at the clock. Six-thirty. She might as well get up.

More coffee. Stronger coffee. Then school began, her pupils filing into class. Emily found herself snappish with the students, and they eventually settled down after being told to write their spelling words twenty-five times each. The room grew quiet, the scratching of pencils on paper and a few subdued sighs the only sounds inside. Outdoors, the breeze rustled the leaves of the big cottonwood on the playground, and the soft rushing noise drifted in through the open classroom windows. Emily had to fight to keep her eyelids open until the time to ring the recess bell finally arrived.

She sighed with relief as her students headed outside, the enforced quiet of the morning just a memory as the students let off energy on the monkey bars and the swing. Emily headed to the kitchen for another cup of coffee.

By the end of the day her students had writer's cramp and

Emily had graded most of their papers. She felt fairly confident the upper classes were well versed in their times tables and the younger students had gotten plenty of practice in simple addition facts.

Relieved the school day was over, Emily shooed the last of her charges out the door and headed upstairs, where she changed into dungarees and oxfords. Back downstairs, she filled her aluminum canteen with water, then left the schoolhouse and headed back up through the village, resolved to keep searching for her missing student. She stopped by Mr. Romero's store and learned that Sheriff Wilcox's men had finished their search. No one had come across Gilbert yet, but some village men were still looking for him. Emily couldn't face the Montoyas, so she kept walking, heading back up into the canyon.

As she passed the anthropologist's house, Anasazi appeared from around the corner. "Hello, boy," Emily greeted him. "Where's Professor Bateson?"

Anasazi didn't answer, of course. Emily didn't see Bateson's truck. Maybe he'd gone into town for supplies and left the dog behind. Emily headed up the trail that led to what she had begun to think of as "Gilbert's Grotto," Anasazi trotting beside her. The sheriff and the village men had finished their search here, but Emily hoped they had missed something, some clue that might lead her to the missing boy.

She and Anasazi rapidly walked up the path, now well-trodden with the footprints of the villagers, and took the turnoff to the beaver pool. The gun was gone, the salamander burrow just a pile of dirt by the pond. Emily guessed no animals would be living there now. She took her time searching the area, lingering around the chamisa bushes where Gilbert had been watching her just two days ago. Those seemed relatively undisturbed. Emily could see a depression and some broken branches; she guessed that was where Gilbert had crouched that day, watching her.

She found a weathered Dubble Bubble gum wrapper and near it, under some branches, a crumpled-up piece of notebook paper that could have fallen from Gilbert's pocket. Anasazi whined, restless.

"Just a second, boy," Emily said to the dog. She emerged from behind the chamisas and sat on the large boulder, petted the dog, and un-wadded the notebook paper. It was definitely one of Gilbert's. She recognized the dinosaur drawing. A stegosaurus about to be attacked by a pterodactyl, along with a spotted dog. Anasazi.

Confused, Emily pocketed the picture. Gilbert must have dropped it when he was playing there. She looked towards the back of the open area. Sandstone and tufa cliffs came down to meet the narrow canyon floor, where some scrubby undergrowth, mainly chamisa sage interspersed with a few junipers and small cedars, came forward to meet the canyon walls, along with jumbled piles of rocks and boulders that had fallen from the cliffs.

Emily scouted around, wondering if any trails led out of the canyon that way. Although surely Gregorio and the other San Antonito men would have known of those, and searched them. She clambered over some boulders, thinking a little height might give her some advantage. But even atop the pile of rocks she couldn't really see much else. Certainly no trails. Anasazi, waiting at the bottom of the boulders, gave a few barks. The sun had dipped below the canyon rim and the evening chill had begun to settle in.

Emily carefully picked her way down and gave Anasazi a pat. "Thanks for waiting for me, boy." Anasazi wagged his tail and Emily wished she had some kind of treat to offer him. Her family had always had yellow Labradors, and she missed having a pet. But all she had in her pockets was Gilbert's picture. A cloud blew over the sky and Emily trembled despite herself, admitting defeat. "OK, boy, let's go back."

As Emily neared the plaza, she saw the sheriff's car parked by the alcalde's house and Flossie tied up at the nearby corral. Emily headed over and knocked on the door.

"*Guw'aadzi*. Come in," Juliana called. Emily pushed the door open. Inside she saw Sheriff Wilcox and Deputy Duran, sitting at the table, drinking coffee with Atencio and Gregorio. Juliana stood at the counter, washing dishes in the enamel basin. She looked terrible, Emily thought. But of course she would. One son dead, one son missing.

"Hello, Miss Schwarz," the sheriff greeted her. "What brings you out this evening?"

She felt self-conscious, but answered anyway. "Well, I went back to that little area where Gilbert and I found the gun—I know it had been searched, but I just wanted to make sure." She saw Deputy Duran roll his eyes, when he thought she wasn't looking. "You know," she added. "I thought just maybe I'd find something else. He's my student. I feel responsible."

"I understand," Sheriff Wilcox said. "But you can't take it too much to heart. Nobody's saying it's your fault."

Exhaustion overwhelmed Emily, and her eyes teared up. She didn't speak for a moment.

Gregorio broke the silence. "And did you find anything?"

"Well, it's probably nothing, but I did find this." Emily pulled the notebook paper out of her pocket. "It was in the chamisas where Gilbert was hiding, that day we found the gun. It had fallen way down in the branches; that's probably why your men didn't spot it," she added apologetically to Sheriff Wilcox as she handed him the note.

He took it and eyed the drawing. "Duran, who searched that area?"

"Torres, I think."

"4F on account of his eyesight," Wilcox said. "Couldn't see a rattler if it was six inches from his face."

Emily shuddered.

"Pardon, ma'am. You didn't see anything else?"

"No, and that paper could have been there for a long time."

"Could have been," Wilcox agreed. "Don't worry, Mrs. Montoya," he continued. "We'll find your boy."

Juliana, who had come over to see the drawing, just gave the sheriff a long look, then nodded curtly. Atencio took the paper from Sheriff Wilcox and spread it flat on the table, carefully smoothing out the wrinkles against the hard surface of the wood. He smiled at the picture but Emily thought his brown eyes looked unutterably sad. Both Atencio and Juliana seemed to have aged decades in just a few weeks.

"May I take this for a while?" Sheriff Wilcox asked the alcalde.

Atencio nodded, methodically refolded the drawing, and handed it to Wilcox.

"You find my son," he said.

"We will," Wilcox replied, but Emily wasn't sure if he

believed his own words. She felt pretty certain Atencio and Juliana didn't.

The sheriff and Duran took their leave and headed out to their car. Inside the house, nobody said anything for a moment. Then Emily asked, "Why was the sheriff here?"

"Oh, that girl turned up."

"Consuela?"

"Yes, that little tramp," Juliana said. "She'd run off to Albuquerque like they thought. Probably whoring around down there, the Spanish *puta*."

"Somebody finally called the Sandoval County sheriff," Gregorio interjected.

Emily thought Juliana's words harsh, but remembered that neither family had been in favor of the match between Consuela and Juan. "Well, if she's willing to come in and speak with the sheriff, maybe she can clear Lorenzo."

That comment met with stony silence from Juliana. Emily continued: "They didn't find Demetria, did they?"

Gregorio shook his head. Awkwardly, Emily made her excuses and left, feeling more useless than ever.

That night she slept, regardless of lost students or missing friends. The lack of sleep and days of worry had taken their toll, and her body demanded rest.

The next school day passed more easily, but still no one brought news of Gilbert. Her students seemed agitated at recess, and Emily heard the upper grade girls whispering together when they didn't realize she could hear them. Emily didn't know whether to correct them or let the talk die down naturally, but in the end she settled on the latter. She didn't have anything to tell them; she certainly didn't know where Gilbert was. She just hoped the rumors wouldn't get out of hand.

Relieved when the school day ended, she shooed her students out the door, went into the kitchen for another cup of coffee, and then wearily headed into the classroom to tidy up after the day's lessons. She straightened the piles of paper on her desk; more things to grade, but she didn't have the heart for it right now. Worries about Gilbert crashed over her, with the distraction of the other students gone. Emily walked over to the old-fashioned wooden desk Gilbert shared with another primary grade student. The late afternoon sun shone through the large classroom window that looked out on the fenced playground with the large cottonwood tree, the leaves golden against the brilliant blue sky.

Emily decided to check Gilbert's desk. Maybe something in there would be of use. She raised the ink-stained wooden lid for a look inside.

Gilbert had jammed his papers in the desk, along with several pencils, some string, and a broken eraser. It looked like a pack rat's nest. Somewhat annoyed, Emily checked another student's desk. That one was almost as untidy. She looked in one of the girls' desks, an older fifth-grade student. That desk, at least, was neater, Clemencia's notebooks and papers stacked inside it. Emily resolved to have her students spend part of tomorrow's school day on some cleaning and straightening. She closed Clemencia's desk with a sigh and went back to Gilbert's. School had only been in session for a few weeks. How had the child managed to make such a mess?

Emily removed everything from the desk and started going through the detritus. A few chunks of chalk. Some pencil stubs, most in need of sharpening. Crayons, broken and blunted. One red pencil that looked suspiciously like the ones she used for grading papers. A broken India rubber eraser, along with a scrap of old tortilla. Emily threw that away, thankful she didn't find any mouse droppings. She would have to talk to her students about keeping food in their desks.

She turned her attention to the pile of papers. A few pages of arithmetic problems, crumpled and full of cross-outs and erasures. There were drawings of dinosaurs on the backs of the papers. Emily sighed, wondering where the boy had found the time. In one drawing, a stegosaurus gored a brontosaurus. Emily saw the red pencil had been put to good use as blood streamed from the injured plant eater. On another sheet a tyrannosaurus and a dimetrodon faced each other.

Spelling papers next. For some reason the boy reversed his letters and numbers a lot; Emily had sometimes seen it with younger children but they usually outgrew it. She looked at the list of spelling words. Borrow was spelled *dorrow*. Despite, *bespite*. She wondered what to do about that, then remembered some research they had briefly touched on in one of her teaching classes. An article by a Mr. Orton discussing reading and spelling disabilities. Maybe something in that would help Gilbert.

If he ever came home. She hoped the searchers had found him someplace today. Emily unfolded another crumpled paper. Another drawing of dinosaurs, but something was written on the bottom.

She peered at the printing: *the porfesor says he will show me binosaur dones.* Above the words, a pterodactyl attacked a tyrannosaurus. Emily studied the paper. What if Gilbert had followed Professor Bateson into the hills after the deputy had brought him back to the village? She'd have thought helping deputies recover a gun would be enough excitement for a nine-year-old boy, but young boys had an unquenchable thirst for thrills.

Maybe she could find Professor Bateson and see what he had told Gilbert about the dinosaur bones. Or "binosaur dones." Emily smiled. Some kids just couldn't keep their bs and ds straight, or ps and qs for that matter. She'd show the note to Gregorio and see what he thought about it.

She folded up the note and left the schoolhouse, locking the door behind her, and walked up to the plaza to find Gregorio. She'd have to be quick. Tonight was her ladies' class. It seemed like years, not merely a week ago, since they had made the applesauce. For tonight, Emily planned a knitting lesson. They could work on scarves as well as socks for the troops. She remembered the yarn she'd bought in Santa Fe a couple of weeks ago—that might do to get her students started. She certainly had not worked on her own intended project.

She found Gregorio, but he didn't have any news. Nothing about Gilbert, or Demetria. Gregorio didn't know if Consuela's testimony had freed Lorenzo or not. And if Lorenzo was innocent, then who had murdered Juan?

CHAPTER TWENTY-THREE

EMILY WAS STRAIGHTENING up the classroom after school on Thursday when she heard a car stop outside. Curious, she looked out the window and saw Mr. Shepherd exiting his parked Dodge. She patted her hair into what she hoped was some semblance of order, then continued fiddling with the stacks of papers on her desk, waiting. Eventually she heard the knock on the door and went to let her guest in, wondering why he had stopped by.

"Mr. Shepherd," Emily greeted him with false vivacity. "What brings you down to San Antonito?"

Shepherd smiled his slightly crooked smile. "I just had to speak with the alcalde about something."

Again? "About what?" Emily asked. "Oh, never mind," she continued, not waiting for Shepherd's answer. She figured he'd probably not be able to tell her. Emily didn't know what the man did but she knew it wasn't procurement. These days, with the war on, it was probably better not to ask. But what was his interest in San Antonito?

"Did you hear that Consuela Romero turned up in Albuquerque?"

Shepherd nodded. "Yes. Silly girl. I believe she's back home in Bernalillo now. If I were her parents, I'd lock her up and throw away the key until she turns twenty-one. What I heard was, she and some friend were hanging around the army airfield, trying to get dates with pilots."

That sounded plausible to Emily. "Where'd you hear that?"

"Sergeant O'Toole. Remember him?"

Emily nodded.

"He's based down there," Shepherd continued. "Anyway, he told me about it. Turns out one of her dates, a guy who knows O'Toole, heard the APB on the radio and alerted the city police. They called Wilcox, and that's how they found her."

"Silly girl," Emily murmured.

"I'm sure you never would have done anything like that," Shepherd said with a smile, "when you were a teenager."

"No, I most certainly would not have!" Emily laughed, and then remembered to be proper. "My mother and father would have made sure of that." Once again, she had the uncomfortable feeling Shepherd was amused by what she said.

"Is that coffee I smell?"

Really, the man was shameless, Emily thought. "Yes. I was just about to have a cup. Would you care to join me?"

"Well, thank you, ma'am. A cup of coffee would just hit the spot." Shepherd's grin widened and he followed her into the kitchen.

"I haven't spoken to Gregorio in the past couple of days," Emily said, as she poured coffee into two cups and placed one in front of Shepherd where he sat at the table. "Do you know if they convinced Consuela to talk to Sheriff Wilcox?"

"I believe she was coming in this afternoon. With her parents," Shepherd replied.

"I hope she tells the sheriff the truth."

"Well, her parents won't be in the room when she's interviewed," Shepherd replied, "and she's already in plenty of hot water for running away. I'll bet Wilcox reads her the riot act about lying to authorities. I think she'll tell the truth."

"Good." Emily took a spoon and added evaporated milk and sugar to her coffee.

"No brownies today?"

"I haven't had time to bake lately," Emily retorted. "You've heard about the missing boy? Gilbert? He's one of my students. He actually was with me when we found the gun. And there's still no sign of Demetria Gonzales, either. I helped search. There's nothing."

She sipped coffee, then continued. "I found a note yesterday, that Gilbert had written. Something about Professor Bateson and dinosaur bones. It was in his desk. I gave it to the *fiscal* last night."

"Alcalde Montoya showed me just now," Shepherd replied. "But they've already interviewed Bateson—he claims to have been up in Santa Fe the day the kid went missing. Duran says when he dropped Gilbert off on Monday, they didn't see Bateson's car. So it doesn't look like he had anything to do with it."

"People don't just vanish," Emily pointed out. "Poor

Atencio and Juliana. One son shot, the other one missing."

"Maybe someone in the pueblo has a grudge against the alcalde," Shepherd mused.

"Well, I don't know who," Emily snapped back, frustrated with the lack of information. "You'd have to ask Gregorio. Or Atencio, for that matter. If you cared enough to."

"Wait a minute—" Shepherd put his cup down and pushed his chair back from the table.

"I'm sorry. It's just that nobody has any answers. And I don't know what to do. I just feel so helpless. And my brother's in the Pacific, and the news there isn't great either, and. . . ." Emily's voice trailed off, and she feared she would start to cry.

"Well, I've heard we've taken the Solomons. So there's that, at least."

"But that's not going to find Gilbert. Or Demetria."

"No, but these days you take your good news where you can find it," Shepherd replied, and then he fell silent.

Embarrassed by her outburst, Emily didn't speak either. She stirred the remnants of her coffee and sighed. "Would you like a second cup?"

"No thank you, ma'am. But I've got an idea, and I'm not going to take no for an answer. You're spending too much time cooped up down here in this canyon. It's a pretty place, and I know you're busy with work. And you're worried about Demetria and little Gilbert. But driving yourself crazy about what you've done and haven't done isn't going to help them one bit. You're not responsible for their disappearance. Or for that kid Juan's murder, either."

But I found his body, Emily thought grimly.

Shepherd continued. "The men are looking, and if you

221

think Atencio Montoya is going to stop searching for his son, you don't know the same man that I do."

Emily nodded. She knew Juliana and her husband would never stop hunting for Gilbert.

"I'm going to come down on Saturday and pick you up. I'll be here at ten in the morning. Wear something nice. We'll go into Santa Fe, have lunch at La Fonda, maybe take in a movie or something. There's a new comedy out with Jean Arthur that's playing in town at the Paris Theater, on San Francisco Street. Just up from the Lensic. It's not quite as fancy a theater, but the movie should be funny." He paused. "I won't take no for an answer," he repeated.

Emily wanted to smile, an unexpected impulse she repressed. It certainly would be fun to go up to Santa Fe for a day. Maybe even do a little shopping, if there was time. A movie could be diverting, too. Maybe Mr. Shepherd was right; it might do her good to get away.

"Come on, Miss Schwarz, what do you say?"

Emily found herself agreeing to the date, although she wasn't sure exactly how she felt about Mr. Shepherd's high-handed tactics. She wasn't even positive that he hadn't somehow been involved in Juan's death and the disappearances of Demetria and Gilbert. But at least Consuela had turned up now. And maybe, if Shepherd were involved, he would let something slip during the day. She nearly laughed out loud, chiding herself for having an overly suspicious mind; she was being fanciful, and Mr. Shepherd was totally innocent. And she guessed it wouldn't hurt to leave San Antonito for an afternoon.

"OK, then, I'll pick you up Saturday at ten. Be ready!" With that, Mr. Shepherd took his leave. He drove off and headed up the road towards Santa Fe, leaving Emily somewhat bemused, questioning her own decision. Although the man hadn't really let her say no.

Mr. Shepherd pulled up promptly at ten on Saturday morning, and knocked at the schoolhouse door. Emily had put on a simple skirt, white blouse, and her old Pendleton jacket. She didn't own too many fancy clothes and, to tell the truth, it rankled that Shepherd had told her to "wear something nice." She figured this was nice enough for Santa Fe. However, she did put on lipstick and, at the last minute, screwed on some little silver and turquoise thunderbird earrings and the thunderbird necklace she had purchased at the Domingo trading post a year or so ago. The Indians made the necklaces from turquoise and shell, along with scrounged bits of celluloid, hard rubber from old battery casings, and even bits of broken records. They sold them primarily to tourists. The bright reds and greens of the whimsical thunderbird made Emily smile. The artist had told her that the white tail feathers came from tines of a plastic fork, while the reds and greens were from broken 78s. She looked in the mirror, gave her hair one last pat, and added her silver and turquoise bracelet. Then she felt ready to take on Santa Fe, and Mr. Shepherd.

After a quick greeting, Shepherd opened the passenger side door for her. He was wearing a white shirt, with a bolo tie and jeans, and a tweed jacket.

"Shall we get going?"

Emily nodded, and settled herself in the passenger seat.

Shepherd shut the door behind her and got into the driver's seat. He turned the car around and they headed down the dirt road that led out of the canyon and up the hill, past La Cañada.

The vista opened up before her as they drove, and Emily admitted to herself that it did feel good to get out of the canyon. The road initially led south, towards the pueblo of Cochiti and the tiny Spanish hamlets of Sile and Peña Blanca, before the highway turned left towards the La Bajada escarpment. The sun shone brightly and the views of the Sandia Mountains to the south and the Cerrillos Hills to the east were spectacular.

"The natives mined turquoise in those hills," Shepherd observed. "I see you've got yours on today."

Emily nodded. Her jewelry wasn't fancy but she enjoyed wearing it. She felt less like an outsider with it on.

"That's a nice necklace. I thought of sending one to my mother but it's not her style. It looks good on you, though."

Emily bristled a little. Was Mr. Shepherd comparing her to his mother? She didn't reply and after a moment Mr. Shepherd continued.

"Some Anglos tried mining turquoise in Cerrillos, but the market dried up by the '20s," he said. "Those mines are mostly abandoned now, like those silver mines behind San Antonito."

They started up the steep La Bajada grade and Shepherd stopped talking. Emily let him concentrate on his driving; there were plenty of switchbacks on the narrow road and she tried to concentrate on enjoying the spectacular views, despite her dislike of heights. She took a deep breath once they reached the top of the escarpment and headed up the road that led to the little village of La Cienega, and on into Santa Fe. The cottonwoods blazed yellow along the Santa Fe River, and Emily sighed at the sheer beauty of it all.

"You were right," she admitted to Shepherd as they passed through the little village of Agua Fria, "it is nice to get out of San Antonito." She admired the old San Isidro church as they drove by.

"I thought you would enjoy a change of scene. What do you want to do in Santa Fe?"

"Well, I thought you'd invited me for lunch."

"La Fonda OK?"

"La Fonda sounds lovely. And then maybe that movie you mentioned? What was it?"

"*The More the Merrier*. Jean Arthur's in it. She's pretty funny."

"Something light would be nice," Emily said. "But I feel guilty enjoying myself with all this happening."

"Well, at least you admitted you're enjoying yourself." Shepherd kept a straight face but Emily felt her lips curve upward.

They drove into Santa Fe. Shepherd found a parking spot on Don Gaspar Street, past the car dealerships and across from the De Vargas Hotel, and they strolled up to the plaza.

"Are you hungry yet?" Shepherd asked.

"I could wait a bit. Let's sit and people watch."

They found a seat on one of the cast iron benches near the Civil War Memorial in the center of the square. An obelisk, the memorial commemorated those who had died in that dreadful conflict and the wars against the "savages". Emily didn't think of her students in that way, and she wondered what Atencio and Juliana would think if they saw the inscription. People in San Antonito were warm and generous. Humorous and kind. Certainly not savage. She sighed, and Shepherd looked at her oddly, but Emily didn't share her thoughts.

Folks seemed to be enjoying themselves; the autumn day was warm and conducive to socializing. Emily saw some young girls, teenagers, she guessed, sitting on another bench. The girls smiled at some young men in army uniforms who walked by. The boys stopped to chat and Emily thought of Tom, in the Pacific. When was the last time he had been able to relax and flirt with some pretty girl? She sighed again.

"What's wrong?"

"Oh, seeing those young boys just made me think of my brother. He's someplace in the Pacific, I guess."

Shepherd nodded. "It's a nasty war. All wars are. But we're fighting for something that's worth it. There's that, at least."

"Yes, at least there's that." Emily sighed again and glanced around the Plaza. She saw a familiar figure strolling down Palace Avenue, headed towards the Art Museum. "Isn't that Professor Bateson?"

Shepherd looked over. "Could be."

"I wonder what he said about Gilbert's note." Emily reminded Mr. Shepherd about the "binosar dones." "Nobody's said anything more to me about it since I gave the note to Gregorio."

"It must not have been important. You know what kids are like."

"Probably better than you do," Emily retorted. An awkward silence fell between them for a moment.

"Well," Emily continued, "maybe I should go ask Professor Bateson."

"Oh, I don't know." Shepherd scanned his wristwatch. "We might not have time; if you go chasing Bateson down, we won't have a chance for lunch before the movie starts. It's a one-thirty matinee."

Emily hesitated. "I guess I can catch up with him sometime back in San Antonito. But it's hard to keep track of him, he's out in the back country so much."

"Do you know where he's excavating?"

Emily shrugged. "I've no idea. Someplace north of San Antonito, I guess. He talks a lot about pottery shards."

"Must be fascinating," Shepherd said dryly, and Emily smiled. "Are you ready for lunch?" he asked.

They left the plaza and walked over to La Fonda. The brightly painted designs on the glass windows of the La Plazuela dining room cheered Emily. She had felt out of sorts, thinking of her missing student. Seeing Bateson had put a damper on the day.

"How about a cocktail first?" Mr. Shepherd suggested. Emily settled on a glass of sherry and he ordered a whisky. The drinks arrived, along with some olives, and they sipped and munched in silence a few minutes until the waiter came to get their order.

Emily ordered enchiladas. She'd found she enjoyed spicy food since she'd moved to New Mexico. Shepherd ordered pork chops with Spanish rice and vegetables.

They were about halfway through their meal when Emily saw Professor Bateson enter the dining room, along with a familiar-looking man.

"Look, there's Professor Bateson again," she said to Shepherd. "He's with that same friend of his—I wonder who that is?"

"Some museum academic, I'd bet," Shepherd replied, but Emily noticed him looking sharply at the two men, who were seated in a corner of the dining room. Bateson had his back to them, but Emily noticed his friend say something and the anthropologist seemed to stiffen a moment. Had the unknown friend gestured in their direction? She wasn't certain, since his movement quickly halted when he saw Emily glancing their way.

Professor Bateson's friends weren't any concern of hers, though. Mr. Shepherd didn't seem overly worried, and ordered a piece of apricot pie for dessert, along with coffee. Emily, pleasantly full from her enchiladas, settled for coffee.

They left La Fonda and walked to the movie theatre down San Francisco Street. *The More the Merrier* proved a madcap comedy, and for a while Emily forgot all about missing students and dinosaur bones while she laughed at the depiction of the housing shortage in Washington. The crowd roared at scene where Jean Arthur, playing Connie, turned on the lights in the vestibule of her apartment house to reveal a number of men asleep on cots in the lobby.

"I've been in Washington," Shepherd whispered to her. "It's really that bad."

Emily nodded, trying to ignore the proximity of Mr. Shepherd on the seat next to her, and attempted to return her attention to the movie. As the onscreen attraction increased between Connie and Sergeant Carter, Emily found herself somewhat distracted by Shepherd. He smelled like piñon and cedar, mixed with some manly overtone she couldn't quite identify.

The film ended and they filed out onto San Francisco Street, blinking a little in the bright autumn sunshine.

"That was fun," Emily admitted as they walked back towards the car. "It's been ages since I've seen a movie. That comedy was the perfect choice."

"Things truly are that crowded in Washington," Shepherd replied. "It's extremely difficult to find a room there."

"Does your work take you to Washington often?"

"Once or twice. Not often, thank goodness."

"I've never spent time on the East Coast," Emily said. "I grew up in Racine and went to college in Chicago. That was enough city life for me. I like the space out here. You can see for miles—well, not so much down in San Antonito, it's more closed in there—but once you get out of the canyon."

"Yes. And the air is good for the lungs. Crisp. Healthy."

"That's right," Emily said, remembering. "You said your health brought you out here?"

"Yes. Thankfully, that resolved quickly; I'm fine now, have been for years. But I liked it out here, and I stayed."

"Where did you grow up?"

"Boston. One of the Boston Brahmins. My mother's folks came over on the Mayflower."

"Oh, my goodness." Emily laughed. "So did my mother's folks. We could be distant cousins."

Shepherd looked at her oddly for a minute. "Degory Priest?" he asked.

"No. Francis Eaton."

"Well, that's a relief," Shepherd said, and Emily smothered another giggle.

They had reached the car by now and Shepherd opened the passenger door for her. "Anyplace else you'd like to go?"

"No, I guess I really should be getting back. But you were right. It did me good to get away."

The engine purred to life, and they started out of town.

"Say, isn't that Professor Bateson's truck up ahead?" Emily commented as they drove along.

"You think so?" Shepherd glanced at the old Model T ahead of them.

"I guess he's heading back, too." Just then, Bateson's truck turned off of Cerrillos Road and headed left, up past the old brick penitentiary.

Shepherd signaled a left turn also.

"Where are we going?"

"I'm curious about something. Humor me," Shepherd said. He drove slowly, careful to keep a couple of blocks between his Dodge and the Model T. Emily glanced at his face; Shepherd looked serious, focused. The man who had been laughing at the comedy had vanished.

They headed east on Cordova Street and crossed Old Santa Fe Trail. The pavement changed to dirt.

What was this man doing? "Where are you taking me?" Emily demanded. "Why are you following Professor Bateson?"

"Just a hunch. Don't worry."

"I'm not worried, I just asked a question," Emily snapped back, her irritation growing. "Why are you following Professor Bateson?"

"Just keeping an eye on him."

"For whom? You're not in procurement at all, are you? Who are you working for, Mr. Shepherd?"

CHAPTER
TWENTY-FOUR

"**I** WORK FOR THE government," Shepherd replied. "But not procurement."

Shepherd didn't answer. The dirt road was rutted and up ahead Emily could see the cloud of dust Bateson's truck emitted as he drove in front of them. The dust flew back through the open windows of Shepherd's car, choking Emily and making her chest feel tight.

"Won't he see us?"

"I'm pretty far back." Shepherd took a quick turn and kept driving. Emily had no idea where they were.

"That's Sun Mountain," Shepherd said, answering her unspoken question. "The old sanitarium I stayed in when I first got out here is up that little road."

"Surely Professor Bateson isn't going to the sanitarium."

Shepherd shrugged.

"Why do you want to talk to him, anyway?" Emily persisted. "Wouldn't it have been easier to—"

A cracking sound rang out. Shepherd, his left hand still on the wheel, pulled Emily down onto the seat of the car. Another crack. Emily heard a *thud* as something hit the rear passenger-side door.

"Stay down," Shepherd hissed as he let go of her. From her cramped position, her head embarrassingly close to his legs, Emily felt him reach into his jacket. She couldn't turn to see. Her pulse drummed in her ears so loudly she could barely hear the driver's-side window rolling down. A bare second later, he fired a shot in return.

One hand still on the wheel, Shepherd kept on driving. No more shots came, and after a minute the car turned again.

"It's safe now, Miss Schwarz. You can sit up." The car pulled over to the side of the road. Emily drew a breath, then awkwardly pushed herself up to a sitting position and looked out the window. She saw a dirt road, lined with a few adobe houses.

"We're on the north side of town. Off of Camino del Monte Sol." Shepherd tucked the gun he was holding away in his jacket pocket.

"What—" Emily didn't quite know what to say. "You . . . you have a gun," she finally choked out, stating the obvious. "Why were they shooting at us? *Who* was shooting?"

Shepherd shrugged. "Probably somebody was just out hunting rabbits."

"Then why did you shoot back?" Her voice trembled despite her efforts to keep calm.

"They nearly hit us. They need to be more careful."

"That's ridiculous!" An awful thought struck her. "It wasn't Professor Bateson shooting?"

He shook his head. "The shots came from the wrong direction."

Emily took a deep breath, willing her pounding heart to return to normal. She didn't trust Mr. Shepherd; she was sure the shots had come from Bateson's truck, up ahead. But what reason did the professor have to shoot at them?

Shepherd was watching her, concerned. "Are you OK, Miss Schwarz?"

Emily nodded. She still felt shaky, but damned if she'd admit it. Mr. Shepherd got out and walked around the car, inspecting it for damage.

"Not too bad," he announced, opening the driver's door and getting back in. "One bullet hit the back passenger door."

"But, but—who was shooting at us?"

"Like I said, probably just some local out hunting rabbits. Hit us by mistake."

The runaround he was giving her made her furious. "You don't expect me to believe that, do you?"

"Well, that's what I think it must have been."

"Aren't you going to report it to the police?"

"And say what? That some local who'd had a few too many beers accidentally hit my car while we were out for a Saturday drive?"

Emily fumed. "But that's not what happened!"

Shepherd shrugged.

"You and I both know it," she continued. "And why were you following the professor?"

He side-stepped the question. "I lost him. I guess we'll have to catch up with him in San Antonito. Or I will. I apologize, Miss Schwarz. I didn't intend for you to get involved in all this."

"Involved in all what? What did you intend, Mr. Shepherd?"

He looked nonplussed. "I just thought we'd go to the matinee."

"And what about Professor Bateson? Couldn't you have spoken with him at La Fonda? Mr. Shepherd, if you think I'm going to believe that story about some drunken hunter out shooting rabbits on a Saturday afternoon, you are sadly mistaken. I know when people are lying."

"Suit yourself, Miss Schwarz." Shepherd turned the key in the ignition and they headed off again, down the sleepy road. Old adobe houses sat peacefully in the late afternoon sun. Emily saw a tabby cat jump over a fence and dart into a yard, startled by the noise of the car. She felt disoriented, almost as though she'd imagined the entire episode, but she was sure that if she looked at the back car door, she'd see a bullet hole—proof that she had not been dreaming.

Shepherd turned right, drove to the end of the street, and then turned left to go down Canyon Road, back towards the center of town. "I guess I'd better be getting you back down the hill to San Antonito," he observed, glancing up at the sun. "It's growing late."

Emily nodded, too angry and confused to speak. "That would be good," she finally managed to say through tight lips.

Shepherd drove through town and out on the road that led to the little village of Agua Fria. They didn't speak for several more miles, until they had passed La Cienega and were headed down the steep curves of La Bajada. The silence was not a comfortable one.

Eventually, Emily broke it. "Mr. Shepherd, you owe me an explanation."

"I know, Miss Schwarz, and I apologize. I can't give you one right now." He rounded another hairpin curve. "This road takes concentration."

Emily seethed, gnawing on her lower lip, and tried to focus on the amazing view before them as Shepherd guided the car down the escarpment to the plains below. The sun, low in the western sky, sent long shadows over the plains that spread out towards Albuquerque. The bulk of the Sandia Mountains to the east glowed in the late afternoon light.

Emily let out a little sigh of relief once they reached the bottom and passed the tiny Hispanic settlement of La Bajada. The road leveled out and headed west towards the pueblos of Cochiti and San Antonito, and the Jemez Mountains beyond.

"Driving should be easier now, Mr. Shepherd," Emily said, feeling like she was lecturing one of her fifth-grade boys. "I'd like that explanation, please."

Shepherd sighed. "I can't tell you much. Yes, I work for the government. You guessed it might not be procurement. I can't say. Yes, I wanted to keep my eye on Bateson, but I shouldn't have brought you into it. And yes, we were shot at. By a drunk local out hunting rabbits."

"You really expect me to take your word for that?"

"Believe it or not, that's most likely what happened," Shepherd replied. Emily didn't believe a word he said.

They reached the turnoff to San Antonito and drove across the mesa, past La Cañada, and down into the canyon. Emily shot Mr. Shepherd a hard glance. "What does all this have to do with Juan's murder, and Demetria? And Gilbert? There must be some connection, because it's all happening at once."

"I don't know, Miss Schwarz," Shepherd responded. "But I'm going to find out. That you can count on."

Shepherd pulled up at the schoolhouse and parked. He got out and opened the door for Emily. She didn't meet his eyes as she exited the car.

"Miss Schwarz," Shepherd said quietly. "My apologies for this afternoon. I intended a fun outing, lunch and a movie. That's all."

"Thank you, Mr. Shepherd," Emily replied, her voice frosty.

"I'm sorry about the rest."

"So you've already told me. And attempted to explain." Half-heartedly, Emily thought. "No apologies are necessary," she added, untruthfully. She looked at the car. There in the back passenger door was the hole the slug had left. "You'd better get that fixed," she said. "Good evening, Mr. Shepherd."

She left him standing by the Dodge, went into the schoolhouse, and locked the door behind her. After a while she heard Shepherd's car take off down the road. Emily lit the lamp and spent the rest of the evening grading essay papers in the kitchen. Perhaps her standards were a bit stricter than usual; no one received a good score.

Sunday morning Emily got up early to go to Mass. After putting on her suit jacket over her Sunday skirt and shirtwaist and donning her hat, she left the school and walked up the road into the village. The early morning service seemed poorly attended, mostly some older women and a few wiggly kids with their mothers. Emily knew most of the children present were studying in the Communion classes, taught by the priest on Wednesdays after her own classes ended. Gregorio's duties as *fiscal* included responsibility for the church, and today he actually attended Mass. Emily saw his mother there as well. She waved at Florencita, who was busy speaking with another woman and didn't see her. Emily sat down on a different bench, feeling once more like an outsider.

Most of the women had wrapped themselves in brightly patterned Pendleton shawls with long yarn fringes to combat the early morning chill. Underneath, the older women mostly wore old-fashioned calico dresses in the native style, tied with a belt woven from yarn in traditional patterns. Some of the younger women wore more modern dresses. Emily kept patterns at the schoolhouse, and the ladies enjoyed borrowing them.

The Mass began. Sun shone through the open door to the church, the thick adobe walls relinquishing a bit of their chill to the insistent warmth of the morning sun. The whitewashed walls, the dark *vigas* that spanned the ceiling, and old tin framed Victorian engravings of the Stations of the Cross hanging on the walls were very different from the Gothic-style church with its stained glass windows Emily had grown up attending in Racine, but the Latin and the ritual were the same, and after a time Emily forgot about feeling like a stranger, forgot about her annoyance with Mr. Shepherd, and even let go of some of her worries for Gilbert and Demetria as she gave herself up to the service.

During his sermon, the priest referred to the Lord helping

those in trouble, those missing, and those who had lost their way. Emily felt certain the priest meant that as a reference to Demetria, and to Gilbert. She hoped God was listening; to date the Almighty hadn't appeared overly concerned with their plight.

After Mass concluded, Emily filed out of the church with the rest of the congregation. The few men who'd attended—mostly older, perhaps dragged there by their wives—stood outside joking and laughing with Gregorio. The children, glad the tedious service had ended, greeted their teacher perfunctorily and, given nods from their mothers, ran helter-skelter off to play.

Emily made a little small talk with some of her students' mothers and told them about the upcoming ladies' class on Wednesday. Back to knitting, she thought. Socks for the troops. Turning heels. Most of the ladies should have their socks far enough along for that.

She greeted the sheriff as the crowd thinned out by the door of the church. "Hello, Gregorio. And Florencita. Good morning."

"Hello, Miss Schwarz," Florencita replied, giving Emily a broad smile. "I didn't see you in there."

"I just barely got here on time. I think you were talking to Andrew's mother when I came in."

"Oh yes. He's my godson, that one is." The old woman's eyes brightened with pride. "Does he get into much trouble at school?"

Emily thought of Andrew, a wriggly second grader. "He's energetic," She replied. "But never mean."

Florencita nodded. "That's good. Come over for coffee. I'm going to make tortillas."

Emily nodded, and Florencita headed towards the house she shared with her son, leaving Emily standing with Gregorio. Father Simon mounted his horse, ready to head down to La Cañada for the later Mass there. Gregorio spoke briefly with him and then waved as the Franciscan started down the road. Father Simon didn't look altogether comfortable on his mount, but Emily supposed the man didn't have to go too far, just a couple of miles. The horse was faster than walking.

Gregorio started talking to Atencio, so Emily left the church and started towards Florencita's. A tortilla sounded good, along with some coffee. Maybe, when Gregorio showed up, she would ask him what he knew about Mr. Shepherd. And why in heavens name Professor Bateson would be driving around the Santa Fe foothills. Maybe Gregorio had some ideas about drunken rabbit hunters, too.

Florencita welcomed Emily and her hot, fresh tortilla melted in Emily's mouth. Emily had skipped dinner the night before; she'd been far too annoyed to eat. Now she sipped coffee appreciatively and made small talk with Florencita.

"I heard Consuela showed up," Emily said.

"Yes, but now they found out that her father had a handgun. An old Colt, like the one you found, Miss Schwarz. So I think they're investigating him. That's what my son said."

That was good news for Lorenzo, but . . . "Surely someone would have seen him if he'd shown up in San Antonito with a gun in the middle of the afternoon."

"Maybe he came after dark," Florencita replied. "After Consuela got back to La Cañada. Maybe *he* shot Juan, upset about his daughter."

"But I thought he lived in Bernalillo?"

Florencita shrugged. "Maybe he came back."

Gregorio entered the house, and his mother stopped talking. "Hello, Miss Schwarz," Gregorio said. "Did you save any tortillas for me?"

"You eat too much anyway," Florencita told her son. "You're going to get fat."

Emily smiled. Gregorio was far from fat.

"Here, Miss Schwarz." Florencita put another tortilla on the plate in front of Emily. "Here's a nice, hot one for you. And here's one for you too, son."

Gregorio helped himself to coffee and took a seat at the old pine table.

Emily set her coffee cup down. "Have you seen Professor Bateson yet? Did you get a chance to ask him about Gilbert's note? And what's this about Sheriff Wilcox investigating Consuela Romero's father?"

Gregorio sipped his coffee, apparently in no rush to answer. "That's a lot of questions, Miss Schwarz."

"Well, yes." Emily waited.

Gregorio put his cup down and took another bite of his tortilla. He chewed and swallowed, then said, "Yep, Sheriff Wilcox is investigating him. Consuela spoke with the sheriff yesterday; it looks like her statement clears Lorenzo, but they haven't released him yet. I'm not sure why. And it just so happens that her father served in the last war. He had a handgun, but it's gone missing."

"Is it the one I found? What does he say about it?"

"Just that he misplaced his gun when they moved down to Bernalillo from La Cañada. But folks don't generally misplace their revolvers. He might be covering for his daughter, or else he came back and shot Juan later that night."

"What are the chances he would have buried the gun up in the canyon?"

"That doesn't make much sense, Meleca." Gregorio swallowed the last bit of his tortilla. "Not when Juan's body was found so much further down."

"So is Consuela in custody? Or her father?"

Gregorio shook his head as he reached for another tortilla. "Not yet. No proof."

"What did Professor Bateson say when you showed him Gilbert's note?"

Gregorio buttered his second tortilla and took a bite. "I didn't show him yet. He was out in the back country most of the week. He wasn't around yesterday, either. Hilario saw his truck heading up towards Santa Fe."

"Yes, he was there yesterday. I saw him at La Fonda."

"You were in Santa Fe?"

"Mr. Shepherd and I went to a movie." Emily really didn't want to explain her date with Shepherd to Gregorio, but as it turned out, she didn't need to, since he didn't seem curious about it.

"That's nice," he replied. "What did you see?"

"A comedy. With Jean Arthur. We spotted Professor Bateson earlier, eating lunch at La Fonda with some friend of his, and then we saw him again driving out of town. He turned off into the foothills." She decided not to mention following Bateson's truck up the canyon roads, and the shots fired at Shepherd's Dodge, since she wasn't yet sure what to make of all that.

"Could be some old ruins up there. There's ruins all over the place."

"So you never showed him the note about the dinosaur bones," Emily said, feeling like she did when one of her fifth graders hadn't turned in a homework assignment.

"Like I said, I haven't seen him." Gregorio put down his coffee cup, his chin jutting defiantly.

"Are there any other leads about Gilbert? Or Demetria?"

"Nothing so far."

He looked exhausted, Emily thought. Everybody was on edge these days, and she told herself she shouldn't judge too harshly. She finished her coffee, stood, and took the dirty cup over to the counter where Florencita stood washing dishes.

"Let me know what Professor Bateson says, when you do find him. Maybe he knows where Gilbert might be. He might have told the boy where he could find fossils or something, and then Gilbert went off that way and got lost."

"I sure will, Miss Schwarz. I'll get right on it." Gregorio rubbed his forehead and reached for another tortilla.

Emily left, stymied. Neither Gregorio nor Mr. Shepherd seemed overly concerned about that note. What good were men, anyway? Emily felt unaccountably glad to be independent. But what to do next? Well, she could just find Professor Bateson herself, and ask him about the note. And the gunshots. Should she have told Gregorio about that? Not that he would care. Just some crazy Melecas driving around in the foothills, he'd say. Nothing to worry about.

CHAPTER
TWENTY-FIVE

Emily's frustration grew as she walked towards the schoolhouse. Why wouldn't Gregorio talk to Professor Bateson? And why did Mr. Shepherd act so unconcerned, as though getting shot at on a Saturday afternoon was the most normal thing in the world? Emily fumed. She might as well go find Bateson herself. Surely, if he'd been up in Santa Fe yesterday afternoon, he couldn't have run off to his excavation yet.

She turned and headed towards the north end of the pueblo, where Professor Bateson's house stood. The old Model T truck sat parked near the corral, and Bateson's mule stood unconcernedly inside the fence. The professor must be at home. The mule gazed at Emily as she walked by the corral. Anasazi, lying by the front door, got up and wagged his tail as Emily drew closer.

"Hello, boy," she greeted the dog. "How's it going?"

Anasazi licked her fingers in reply as Emily bent down to pet him. She gave his ears a scratch, and Anasazi rolled over so she could pet his belly. She straightened and approached the front door. A somewhat dilapidated screen door hung against the inner wooden panel. Emily tugged the screen door back and knocked. After a moment she heard footsteps, and the door opened.

"Hello, Professor Bateson."

"Hello, Miss Schwarz. An unexpected pleasure, I must say." The professor pushed his wire-rimmed spectacles up his nose and looked curiously at Emily. She peered into the room behind him. Apparently, he had been cataloging pottery shards; Emily glimpsed some journals spread out on the table, along with a map and pieces of ancient pottery, most painted with black designs.

"Can I help you, Miss Schwarz?"

"I certainly hope so, Professor. I'm concerned about Gilbert Atencio, the boy that's gone missing."

"Oh, yes. The alcalde's son."

"Yes. I was going through some papers in his desk at school. I found a note he'd written—it said you knew where to find dinosaur bones, except Gilbert called them binosaur dones—he reverses his letters, poor thing . . ." She trailed off, embarrassed that she was babbling. She must sound like a complete fool.

"And?"

Emily swallowed and went on. "Well, I just wondered what you said to him. Where you said he should look. Maybe that's where he went. Maybe it's someplace people haven't searched yet."

"Do you have the note? Can I see it?" Professor Bateson sounded concerned.

"No, I gave it to Gregorio. He said he would ask you about it."

"I've been away a lot lately."

"I know. Mr. Shepherd and I saw you up in Santa Fe yesterday. At La Fonda, and then on our way out of town."

"Oh, was that you following me yesterday? I took a detour, and I noticed a Dodge behind me. I wanted to look for some old ruins I'd heard were in the hills on the north side of town."

"We did follow you for a while," Emily admitted. "I guess Mr. Shepherd wanted to talk to you about something. I don't know what. We were on the north side too, when we saw your car. By the way, did you hear any gunshots? Somebody took a pot shot at Mr. Shepherd's car. He thinks it was some drunks out hunting rabbits."

His eyes widened behind his spectacles. "How dreadful. I did hear something, now that you mention it. I just assumed it was a car engine backfiring. I suppose it could have been a shot. How awful for you. You're all right?"

"It was a bit more exciting than I'd have liked," Emily said with a laugh. "I thought we were just going into town to the pictures."

"How distressing," the professor said.

"I'm fine. Really. But I am concerned about my student. Can you think of anything you might have said to Gilbert that could have sent him off on a wild goose chase somewhere?"

Professor Bateson pushed his glasses up again and thought a moment. "Well, I did see the boy late one afternoon, on that little trail that leads out of the pueblo. I guess he was headed home for dinner. He had a small notebook with him. He's a shy one, but he eventually showed me some of his drawings and we got to talking. He would make a good scientific illustrator someday. His drawings are fanciful, of course, but with proper training . . ."

"Yes, but what did you tell him about fossils? Did you speak with him about that?"

"That young man is very interested in dinosaurs."

"Yes," Emily said, wishing the professor would get to the point.

"I might have showed him a few fossils I found up the trail one time. The trail that leads out of this canyon and up onto the mesa, towards the mountains. There are some bluffs there where I've happened on a few nice specimens. Near some old ruins. Wonderful petroglyphs also, very like those in Sweden, surprisingly. A European journal I have has pictures. Remarkable, really." Bateson looked at Emily. "I do hope the boy didn't wander off that way."

Emily felt let down. Her gambit hadn't paid off after all. "I imagine Gregorio and the men have searched up there. I know I went with them up that way once when they were looking for Demetria."

"Demetria?" The professor looked blank for a moment. "Oh yes, that woman who went missing a couple of weeks ago. Joe's wife, isn't she? Joe used to be my research assistant. That was very odd."

"Yes, it was. Actually, Demetria was headed over here to speak with you when she disappeared."

"Yes, you and Gregorio came and asked me about that. She never turned up?"

Emily shook her head. "They're both still missing. I'll tell Gregorio what you said about that trail, just in case he hasn't checked it yet."

"Thank you, Miss Schwarz."

"I guess they're going to release Lorenzo," Emily added.

"Oh really? I thought he shot the alcalde's older son."

"I guess not. Consuela Romero, Mr. Romero's niece, turned up, and I think her story about that Sunday will clear him. But now they're investigating her father, he had an old Colt M1917. Although I guess Consuela herself could have shot Juan. It's very hard on the Montoyas, to lose one son and have another disappear." She was babbling for sure now, sounding like an idiot, and she hadn't learned a single useful thing. "Well, I won't keep you any longer. Good afternoon, Professor."

She turned and had just gone out the door when the professor called her name. "Miss Schwarz?"

She pivoted. "Yes, Professor Bateson?"

"Why don't I take you up to the site where I saw the fossils . . . the one I mentioned to Gilbert. Maybe your sharp eyes will find something. I doubt Gregorio and the other searchers have looked there; it's a bit off the beaten track. I stumbled upon it, most fortuitously, when I was out searching for proto-Puebloan sites."

"Did you actually take Gilbert there?"

"No, but I showed him the fossils and told him where they were found. These Pueblo children know the area pretty well. So it's conceivable the lad wandered up that way."

Her disappointment had vanished. "All right," she replied. "Do you want me to get Gregorio? He might want to come along, or maybe he'd send Arturo, or Ben—"

"I don't think there's any need. Didn't you say they were helping Sheriff Wilcox with his enquiries?"

"I'm not sure about that. I don't think the sheriff would want them investigating at La Cañada, honestly."

Bateson shrugged. "Well, this is probably a wild goose chase. If you don't want to go. . . ."

"No, if there's any chance I can help find Gilbert, I'd like to try." Emily glanced down at her skirt and shoes. "I'm still dressed for Mass. What if I meet you back here in about half an hour?"

"That sounds fine, Miss Schwarz. Bring your canteen; it could be a thirsty walk."

Half an hour later Emily stood once again outside the professor's house, now properly attired for a hike in the back country.

"Which way?" she asked when Bateson appeared. He wore hiking clothes and carried a small daypack.

"It's this same back trail," Bateson said, gesturing at the pathway that led northwest, towards the back end of the canyon. "But after a while it veers off. I doubt Gregorio and the local men searched up here."

"Why not?"

"It's a very obscure track," Bateson replied over his shoulder.

Emily followed the professor as he led the way up the trail. The noonday sun shone on her back and warmed her shoulders. This part of the trail was familiar to her. Anasazi came along, at times running ahead and at other times coming back to keep Emily company, licking at her hands while she hiked. They passed the track that turned off toward what she had taken to calling "Gilbert's Grotto" and continued up the main track, the same one she had traveled with Gregorio and the San Antonito men in the search for Demetria. Was that only a couple of weeks ago? It seemed like years. And where was Demetria, anyway? What had happened to her? Emily feared the worst, that some bad accident had befallen the woman and she would never see her friend again. Why hadn't she gone with her on that day?

Emily stopped to take off her plaid jacket, tying it around her waist, and get a sip of water from her aluminum canteen. Then she and Anasazi hurried to catch up with the anthropologist striding ahead. She guessed they had gone about another mile when the professor halted suddenly. "It's just this way, Miss Schwarz," he said, when Emily reached him. "A deer track, really, but it leads to some early Pueblo sites and interesting rock formations. That's where I found the fossils I showed to Gilbert."

Emily nodded and followed Bateson onto the narrow side path, barely wide enough for a single person, which led towards the cliffs guarding the back end of San Antonito Canyon. At times the track virtually disappeared, hidden by errant chamisa bushes and the odd juniper tree, but Professor Bateson resolutely plowed ahead and Emily trudged along behind, scanning the area around her for any sign that Gilbert had passed that way. She didn't see anything.

The track gradually gained some altitude, the chamisa giving way to bare rock and rubble, until the deer trail abruptly ended at the base of a cliff that stood sentinel at the end of the canyon. Emily looked around, but saw no evidence that Gilbert, or anyone else for that matter, had been there. Just sunbaked red rocks, rearing up in front of her.

"Is this it?" she asked. "I don't see anything."

Bateson indicated a low pile of dirt and rocks, somewhat overgrown with scrub. "I've done some preliminary excavation over there. I believe it to be a proto-Puebloan site, possibly related to the site further up the Rio Grande at Frijoles Canyon. And there are some interesting petroglyphs along the cliff wall here. Come and take a look."

Emily dutifully walked over. The petroglyphs, a pale color against the darker background of the cliff, intrigued her. She saw what looked like human figures, some big-horned sheep, what could be a snake, some spirals. Surprisingly, a swastika too, the arms facing the opposite direction from the Nazi version.

"There are interesting similarities between these and certain ancient European carvings," Bateson said, launching into a lecture as she examined the designs. Emily wondered how long they had been here, and who had carved them. She turned to ask her guide, but he'd already returned to the mound. Emily didn't see anything to exclaim about there, just dirt and rocks. She ventured closer to where Professor Bateson had knelt and was digging in the dirt with his knife. Anasazi nosed around, but the professor remained oblivious. Emily thought, not for the first time, that the professor didn't pay enough attention to his dog.

"Here, come look at this, Miss Schwarz. This mound is full of shards." Bateson stood and handed her a fragment of broken pottery with black markings painted on the buff clay surface. Emily could make out what looked like some cross-hatching, lines, and spirals.

"How unusual," Emily said. Professor Bateson looked as though he could stay here for hours. The late afternoon sun beating down on the cliffs made it hot. Emily handed the shard back to him and took a drink of water from her canteen. "But where did you see the fossils? The fossils you told Gilbert about?"

"Oh, yes. Forgive me. I'm so excited about this site, but I can't expect everyone to see what I see here."

Emily waited, taking another drink from her canteen while the professor puttered a few minutes longer. "The fossils," he finally said. "We have to climb a bit to get there. You don't have any problems with heights, do you?"

Actually, she did, but she wasn't going to admit that to Bateson. He led the way, clambering up a pile of boulders and smaller fallen rocks at the foot of the cliff, then vanished into a cleft in the rocks. Emily followed and found herself in a narrow enclosure, faced on one side by the cliff, and on the other two sides by large boulders that rose perhaps twenty feet in front of the rock face.

"Watch out for snakes, they like these shady areas," the professor said. Emily scanned the ground carefully as she walked closer to where Bateson stood, but thankfully she didn't see any reptiles aside from a lizard that darted into the shadows, startling her.

"See these?" Professor Bateson indicated some depressions worn in the cliff face, spaced evenly apart. Emily thought she most likely wouldn't have noticed them on her own. "These are ancient toeholds and handholds, left by the original inhabitants of the area. The cliff dwellers. They're still perfectly serviceable."

"The fossils are up there?" Emily asked. She certainly didn't see anything from this viewpoint.

"Just a short climb. Would you like to go first, and I'll follow behind?"

The idea made her queasy. "No. I don't think I could find the handholds. You had better go first, Professor Bateson."

"It's really very easy. Just follow my lead."

Emily nodded and tried to swallow. Her mouth felt dry, despite her recent drink, and her heart thumped as she worked her way up, trying to find the hand- and toeholds in the rock, watching the professor closely and imitating him. They climbed for about fifteen to twenty feet, she estimated. Thankfully the boulders facing the cliff provided some support and might keep her from falling if she did lose her grip; she could manage, just. Her boot slipped at one point and she grabbed frantically at a ledge above, sending a hail of pebbles skipping down the cliff face.

"Everything OK, Miss Schwarz?" Bateson called from above.

"Just fine," she managed to mutter as she regained her footing, grateful for the boulder against her back as she scrabbled up the narrow chimney. "How much further?"

"You're almost there. Here, I'll give you a hand up." Bateson had already reached their destination, and he pulled her up to stand next to him on the top of the boulder. Near them, in the cliff, was a narrow recess with some stone walls built against the rock.

"It's an ancient Anasazi dwelling place, Miss Schwarz. Or

it might have been used to store maize. It's remarkably well preserved," Bateson enthused. "Here, come take a look."

He jumped across the small cleft separating the boulder from the cliff face. Emily guessed the distance was about two feet. Out to the southeast, away from the cliff and the ruins, she could see the narrow valley of the Rio Chiquito, and the pueblo, with smoke lazily drifting up from the hornos in the village.

"That's quite a view." Emily didn't want to get too close to the edge of the boulder.

"It's even better from up here. Come on." Professor Bateson reached out to help her. Emily screwed up her nerve and then jumped across.

They stood in a narrow alcove. Behind the stone wall Emily could see a broken pot, and a desiccated corncob, hundreds of years old, preserved by the dry air. On the cliff face behind the structure she saw paintings, miraculously preserved. Red ochre, white clay, and some kind of black pigment, perhaps soot? There were handprints of various sizes, even one that must have belonged to a young child. A spiral. A horned serpent.

"This is amazing," she said to Bateson. "Who lived here?"

"The Anasazi. The Old Ones. I believe the settlement down below is a bit more recent. This dates to the era, perhaps, of Mesa Verde, up north in Colorado. It's not really common to see cliff dwellings of this type so far south, although there are a few in Frijoles Canyon. Adolf Bandelier excavated there some years back. And there are some sites further south, in the Gila. Did you know Anasazi is actually a Navajo word, Miss Schwarz?"

"No, I wasn't aware of that." Though Gregorio had made a joke about it a while back, she belatedly recalled. She took a deep breath and tried to enjoy the amazing view from the little alcove in the cliff. "It looks like the people who lived here just walked off. As though they might come back at any time."

"They're long gone," Bateson replied. "But their descendants still live in San Antonito. At least that is what I believe. Some of the traditional songs reference traveling down the canyon and the Rio Grande."

"Gregorio doesn't know about this place? And the others?"

"They may know of them, but they don't come here. There seem to be some tribal prohibitions about poking around these old sites. The *caciques*, the medicine men, don't approve, from what I've been able to gather."

"Oh." Despite its fascination, the site had a sad, abandoned feel to it. Emily found herself wondering what had happened to the people who had lived there so long ago. One thought led to another. "How long have you lived here, Professor? In San Antonito?"

He shrugged. "Off and on since the mid-twenties. At first I just visited in the summers, for fieldwork, but then after I got tenure I started spending as much time here as I could. I received some new funding sources, grants and such. Now I typically teach the spring semester in Chicago and can spend the majority of the year here, excavating."

"Oh." Emily looked around. The view was certainly magnificent, the site intriguing, but she saw no sign of dinosaur fossils. "What about the fossils?" she asked. "It doesn't look like Gilbert ever came this way looking for more. Where are they?"

"All around us," Bateson said. He pulled a small geologist's hammer from his daypack and hammered at the rock face. A piece of sandstone split off from the cliff. Bateson brought it over to Emily. "Look inside," he commanded, hitting the rock again with his hammer and splitting it apart.

Emily looked. Inside she saw what looked like a fossilized snail.

"An ammonite. An underwater creature," Bateson said. "The entire state of New Mexico was once part of a large seabed. Of course, that was long before the dinosaurs roamed. Not my area of expertise, but fascinating all the same."

He pulled his knife from the sheath on his belt and used the point to flick dirt off the specimen. It was a nice knife, Emily noted, relatively new, with an elk horn handle.

CHAPTER
TWENTY-SIX

Emily swallowed, her throat suddenly dry again. She retrieved her canteen and took another sip of water. "That's an interesting knife, Professor Bateson."

"Oh, yes. I found it, actually. But it was in good working order. Finders, keepers, isn't that what they say, Miss Schwarz?"

Emily allowed as how that was probably true. "Shouldn't we be getting back?" she asked. The sun had touched the western rim of the canyon and the air was beginning to chill.

He glanced around, blinking, as if just now noticing his entire surroundings. "I suppose so, Miss Schwarz. It appears I've lost track of time again. Here, you had better go down first. If you have any trouble with the handholds, I can talk you through it.

Emily suppressed a shudder as she carefully began the

climb down, Professor Bateson pointing out each handhold to her from above. After she had descended a few feet she heard him following after her, but was afraid to look up, or down. Instead she kept her eyes, and tried to keep her mind, focused on the climb.

Out of nowhere she heard a swift rushing of air. A dark mass hurtled by her head and sharp pain surged through her right arm. A rock had fallen from above and struck her, missing her head by inches.

"Miss Schwarz, are you all right?"

Emily croaked out a yes and concentrated on maintaining her grip. Her arm throbbed but she didn't let go of the handhold. "What happened?" she called out.

"It was dreadfully careless of me. I must have knocked a rock loose."

Emily hazarded an upward glance. The cliff face looked pretty smooth to her.

"You're almost there, Miss Schwarz. Another ten feet or so to go, that's all."

Emily kept on, and finally reached the bottom. The solid ground under her feet brought her intense relief. Anasazi, who had been dozing in the shade, woke up and wandered over, sniffing at her hands. Emily examined her forearm. Blood welled from a scrape, surrounded by a red ugly swelling at the site of what would surely be a spectacular bruise. She was fortunate she hadn't lost her balance and fallen, or broken anything. She looked around for the rock that had hit her, curious, while Bateson completed his descent.

"I'm so terribly sorry, Miss Schwarz," he said, swinging the daypack off his shoulder.

"There was no real harm done, Professor." A fist-sized hunk of rubble not far from the cliff face caught her eye, and she went over and picked it up. "I think this is the rock that fell." She turned it over. On the underside, imprisoned in the stone, she saw an ammonite fossil. She quickly put the rock down. "On second thought, I doubt it. This looks like it's been here for ages." She kicked the rock, covering it in dust.

Professor Bateson walked over to her. "Here, let me see your arm." Emily gingerly extended her arm and he bent to look at it. "Nothing's broken, fortunately. It should heal up all right. You're very lucky. You could have fallen."

Emily uncapped her canteen, wet her bandana and tied it around the scrape. "It's getting late. I need to get back—school tomorrow, you know," she added with a hesitant laugh.

"Well, let's get started, then." The professor led the way down the narrow deer path that led to the route back. Emily thought the trail looked different that it had on the walk in. It always seemed that way, she guessed, going the opposite direction, but she was relieved when the track rejoined the main one and she spotted familiar landmarks as they headed towards the village.

She left Bateson and Anasazi at the professor's house, and continued through San Antonito. She thought about stopping by Gregorio's, but the twilight had just about faded, and no light shone from the windows of the home he shared with his mother. Plus, her arm was still throbbing, and school would begin early the next day. She kept on walking, past Gregorio's and through the plaza, down the road to the schoolhouse.

The next afternoon, after dismissal, Emily made her way back to village to look for Gregorio, but before she got to his house she saw him standing under the portal of Mr. Romero's shop. He and Arturo and Ben, all three men holding bottles, leaned against the mud-plastered wall of the old building in the shade cast by the long porch, chatting. About what, Emily didn't know.

Gilbert had been missing for a week now, and Emily felt sick at the thought of it. What would a little boy do out in the wilderness for a week with no food or shelter? And how could Gregorio just stand there, lackadaisical, as though nothing was wrong? Emily wondered when Gilbert would be found—or what would be found. She shivered and walked a little faster across the plaza towards the shop.

The shop door opened and Juliana exited, carrying a small paper bag. Emily smiled a greeting, but Juliana, who looked as though she'd aged decades in the last week, didn't respond. Perhaps Juliana hadn't seen her, Emily thought as she walked the final few yards up to the porch in front of the shop. The battered wooden screen door, originally painted turquoise, had long since weathered to a faded whitish blue. A metal placard on the door, also faded, advertised Royal Crown Cola. On this warm afternoon Emily, like the three men standing by the door, appreciated the cooling shade the porch roof cast over the entranceway.

"Hello, Gregorio. Arturo, Ben."

"Hello, Miss Schwarz," Gregorio replied, and took a swig of his grape soda.

"Did you get a chance to show Professor Bateson that note of Gilbert's?" Emily knew she sounded like a nag, but she didn't care.

"He left real early. Arturo, didn't you see him heading up the road towards Bland when you were coming back from Cochiti?"

Arturo took a swig of orange pop from the bottle he held, then nodded. "Early this morning."

"Gregorio, can I talk to you a moment?" Emily hoped her frustration didn't come through in her voice. Gregorio said something to Arturo and Ben in Keres, and the other two men sauntered off.

"I spoke to Professor Bateson yesterday," Emily said when they were out of earshot. "He took me to some old ruins north of here, off that main trail."

"I know the place."

"He said he'd told Gilbert about some fossils he'd seen there. I hiked up there with the professor, just to take a look. I hoped Gilbert had gone up there and maybe I'd find some clue. But . . ." Emily paused.

Gregorio's eyes narrowed. "What?"

"Well, he took me on a climb. Up on the cliff, in an alcove, are some ruins."

"Miss Schwarz, I didn't take you for a mountaineer."

"Well, I'm not, not really. And then, on the climb down, a rock fell. At least, I guess it fell. It hit my arm. I'm all right, just bruised, but . . ."

Gregorio said nothing, waiting.

"Well, I didn't see for sure. I might be mistaken, and I know it sounds crazy—"

"What?"

"I swear Professor Bateson dropped the rock—or threw it. I was below him. We were climbing down."

Gregorio looked puzzled. "It's always good to be the last person down," he said with a half smile. "That's the reason, Meleca—so there's no one above you to dislodge anything."

"No, you don't understand." Emily didn't see the humor in the situation. "It wasn't just any rock. It was the same rock he'd shown me up in the cliff house not long before. It had a fossil in it. I saw it when I got to the bottom. I picked it up, and it was the same rock. He must have thrown it at me. And there's one more thing."

"What?"

"Bateson has a knife with an elk horn handle. He said he found it."

Gregorio nodded, with a thoughtful look. Emily continued. "Juan had a knife with an elk horn handle, at least that's what Delia said. Remember, she said he went to look for it that Sunday afternoon before he left her and Lorenzo? Actually, he was meeting Consuela, wasn't he? But he did say he'd lost a knife; Delia remembers that. And it wasn't there when his body was found."

"So . . . you're saying you think Bateson tried to kill you?" Emily sighed. "I don't know. I don't know."

"But why would a Meleca anthropologist want to kill you? And what would he be doing with Juan's knife? All that guy cares about is pottery shards."

"I have no idea," Emily said slowly. "I just don't know. Maybe he killed Juan and that's when he took the knife."

"Or maybe he found it. Like I told you, that guy is always poking around places."

"Suppose he did kill Juan?"

"Why would he do that?"

"I haven't a clue, Gregorio. But where is Gilbert? And Demetria?"

"Demetria's been missing a long time." Gregorio's voice was solemn. "And Gilbert's been gone over a week now. Anything could have happened."

"By that, you mean something bad."

"Maybe."

His grim expression told her he didn't want to talk more about it, and she wasn't eager for details. "What about Consuela's father? Was the gun they found his weapon?"

"Nope. He found his gun in his shed. Misplaced during the family's move to Bernalillo last year. At least that's what he said."

"And it wasn't the gun that shot Juan?"

"Doesn't look like it," Gregorio replied. "The lab thinks the Colt you found was used for the murder."

"What about Professor Bateson? Is he a veteran?"

"I don't know if he's a veteran. I just know he's a bore. He never talks about the last war, only pot shards."

"Well, something else happened. On Saturday." Emily told Gregorio about the shots fired at Mr. Shepherd's Dodge. "Mr. Shepherd said it was drunks out shooting rabbits."

Gregorio shrugged. "Could have been. Maybe."

"But I don't think it was." Emily paused. "What do you know about Mr. Shepherd?"

"Not too much. I'd never met him until he showed up here after Juan died. He does something with the army. Procurement, he says."

Emily scoffed. "And you believe him?"

"Well, I don't know, Miss Schwarz." Gregorio's voice sounded less relaxed now. "That's what he says. Some kind of war work. Might as well call it procurement."

"And what's his interest in all of this?" Emily continued, relentless. "I don't see any factories here making army equipment for him to procure."

Gregorio shifted his weight and didn't meet her eyes. "I don't know, Miss Schwarz. But Juan worked for McKee, and they're doing some kind of government work."

"What about Arturo? And Charley? Don't they work for McKee?"

Gregorio nodded. "Yes, but they can't talk about it. That's what they say. Just that story Arturo told about Juan seeing something and getting really nervous. Arturo didn't even want to tell me that. Charley won't say anything about it all. We tried to ask him."

"Yes, that was strange," Emily agreed. "Maybe whatever Juan saw up there got him killed. Some kind of war secret, worth committing murder over."

"Maybe, Miss Schwarz." Gregorio didn't look at all convinced. "I don't know what, though. There's not much in these mountains. No bomb factories or POW camps. Just that internment camp up in Santa Fe, and McKee sure isn't working there." He took a long swig of his soda. "Besides, if it was something with McKee, then who did the killing?"

"And where is Gilbert? He's a nine-year-old boy. He certainly doesn't know any war secrets. And Demetria—how do either of them figure into this?"

"Where was Demetria headed the last time you saw her?"

"She was going to ask Professor Bateson about Lorenzo," Emily said slowly. "And Gilbert wanted to ask him about dinosaurs. Don't you see, it all leads back to him."

Gregorio sighed and put the empty soda bottle down on the bench. "Maybe. I'd better talk to Professor Bateson. I'll ask him about that knife, too."

"But not about the rock, please," Emily said, rubbing her bruised arm. "Let him think I believe that was just an accident."

Gregorio nodded, and looked intently at Emily. "OK. But lock your door when you're at home, Meleca," he said, then turned to walk towards the north end of the village.

CHAPTER TWENTY-SEVEN

EMILY SIGHED, PICKED up the empty grape Nehi bottle, and pushed the door open. She saw the proprietor standing behind the counter, arranging some tinned fruit cocktail and canned pear halves on the shelves behind him.

"Hello, Mr. Romero. Here's Gregorio's empty bottle."

The shopkeeper smiled. "*Bueno*, Señorita Schwarz. There's a deposit on those, you know. What can I help you with this afternoon?"

"Do you have today's *New Mexican*?"

"Yesterday's. The Sunday edition."

"I'll take it," Emily said. "And a tin of evaporated milk, please." She searched in her pockets for a quarter and her ration book. "Here you are," she said, putting both on the counter. "I hear your niece came back home."

265

Mr. Romero handed her the nickel change and her ration booklet. "She's *loca*, that one. She drove her parents crazy with worry. And *yo, tambien*. But these young people today . . . you should know, you teach them, you're *la maestra*."

"Oh, most of the children are hard workers," Emily replied.

"I heard the alcalde's son went missing."

The mention of Gilbert gave Emily a dreadful feeling in her stomach. "Yes. It's just terrible. You haven't heard anything, have you?"

Mr. Romero shook his head.

"Well, at least your cough seems improved."

"Osha, like I told you, Señorita Schwarz. It's good for the lungs, that *remedio*."

Emily nodded. "I'll remember that the next time I catch a cold." She took her purchases and change, and turned to leave the shop. She wanted to know if Gregorio had found Professor Bateson at home or not. And if not, what he was going to do about it. Lost in thought, she nearly bumped into Paulina, but she managed to pull up short. "Hello, Paulina."

Paulina didn't return the greeting. The woman looked tense and stressed, a furrow of worry creasing her brow. "Have you seen Charley?" Paulina demanded.

Emily shook her head. "Doesn't he work for McKee? Surely those men aren't back yet."

"No, no, he didn't go to work today. They fired him last week."

"Oh dear," Emily murmured. "Why would they do that?"

Paulina's brown eyes shifted toward a bolt of faded calico, which she examined with intensity. "He was drinking," she finally admitted. "It wasn't his fault, though. Somebody gave him whiskey. I don't know where he got it. Last week. So he went to work on Friday hung over, and they told him not to come back. He's a good boy. It's not his fault."

"I'm sorry," Emily said.

Paulina's gaze moved to the storekeeper. "Señor Romero, have you seen him? He's been gone since yesterday. He must have gotten more whiskey."

"I don't sell whiskey, Paulina. You know that."

"He must have got it down at Cañada Mercantile. Your brother's place."

Paulina's tone sounded accusatory to Emily, but the shopkeeper let it go. "Why don't you tell the *fiscal*? Or the alcalde? They can look for him," Mr. Romero suggested.

Paulina sniffed. "They're too busy looking for the alcalde's son. He's been gone a week already. They're wasting their time."

Emily reined in a flash of anger. "Gilbert's just a little boy, Paulina," she said. "I'm sure he's scared and afraid out there. But I just saw Gregorio; he was heading up towards Professor Bateson's house. Maybe he's seen Charley."

"Yes, Miss Paulina," the storekeeper added. "Go ask the *fiscal*. I haven't seen your boy. Not today, not yesterday, either."

Paulina gave a curt nod, turned, and left the shop. Emily saw her take a handkerchief from her apron pocket and rub at her eyes as she walked away.

Emily looked at Mr. Romero. "That's a shame, Charley's drinking," she said, thinking for a moment of her father back in Racine. He enjoyed his bourbon and soda in the evenings, more than one of them most nights, but he never disappeared from the house. He just sat there in his study, in a fog, until her mother started nagging.

"Well, Señorita Schwarz, I didn't sell him any whiskey. And I doubt my brother did either. He doesn't sell liquor to folks from San Antonito. He and the alcalde worked that out a long time ago."

"Well, hopefully Gregorio can find Charley and set his mother's mind at ease." Emily headed for the shop door. "Thanks again."

She left the shop and headed across the plaza. The afternoon sun shone down hotly on the brown dust. Emily saw Albertina, the mother of one of her second graders, outside their home with her two girls. Albertina frequently attended the home economics classes. Emily waved. Albertina's older daughter waved back with a smile, then returned to playing with her baby sister in front of the house. Her mother dumped a basin of soapy water at the foot of a scraggly peach tree growing by the side of the dwelling. Emily stopped to chat a moment, enjoying the shade cast by the adobe homes as the afternoon shadows began to lengthen, then she took her leave and continued on her way. She passed a few other houses, then turned down a narrow alley, really just a space between two adobe buildings, that led down to the main road. The shortcut was welcome on this warm afternoon.

The darkness of the alley contrasted with the bright sunny plaza, and it took a few steps until Emily's vision adjusted. There was a strange smell in the space—a sour, putrid smell, combined with the scent of booze. Perhaps someone had been drinking and relieved himself there instead of going to the nearest outhouse. Emily began to wish she'd taken the main road out of the plaza.

In the dimness she stumbled over something against the

side of the house on her right. She reached out a hand to steady herself on the crumbling mud plaster of the wall and looked down to see what had tripped her.

A man, his back towards her, lay slumped against the building, nearly blocking the narrow alleyway. From the smell of whiskey, Emily judged he had been drinking heavily. She wondered if it was Charley. "I'm sorry, but you really should move," she said. "Is that you, Charley? Your mother is very concerned."

The man didn't respond. Unconscious, she guessed. She reached out to shake his shoulder, and then jerked her hand back.

The body, cold and stiff, fell over towards her, the head pushed back in an unnatural spasm, the sightless eyes rolled up, whites showing. Emily grew aware of other smells beside the whiskey—urine, excrement, vomit. It took her another moment to recognize Charley.

Fighting to keep calm, she backed out of the alley. As she turned to run towards the shop, she saw Gregorio crossing the plaza with Arturo, and hurried to meet him.

"What's the matter, Miss Schwarz? I was just coming to find you. I talked to the professor. What's wrong? You look like you've seen a ghost."

"Not a ghost," Emily managed to say, her voice trembling. Her throat felt oddly tight. "Charley. Paulina was just looking for him. He's in that alley. He's dead."

Arturo looked shocked. Gregorio's eyes narrowed. "Show me."

Emily led him back to the alley entrance. By this time a few other people had gathered around, curious. Emily saw

Albertina among them, talking in low tones with another woman. Emily stood in the sun, shaking violently, feeling clammy and faint. She watched as Gregorio emerged from between the houses and sent someone for Atencio. He looked at Emily.

"You'd better sit down, Miss Schwarz." He motioned to a rough bench outside one of the houses. "They won't mind."

Atencio showed up a couple of minutes later, and more people congregated. Just then Paulina pushed her way through the crowd, her eyes wide. "Miss Schwarz, you found Charley? They're saying you found my son."

Emily couldn't say anything. She just shook her head. Other people swarmed around, talking to Paulina, who tried to rush into the narrow opening. Gregorio stopped her, his hands gentle as he spoke to her in Keres, turning her firmly around and preventing her from entering. He motioned to Albertina and some of the other women to come and help.

Paulina started wailing, *"Eh'meh! Eh'meh!"* and she fell to her knees, moaning. Each one of her cries sliced right through Emily. The women knelt by Charley's mother, supporting her and rubbing her back and arms, attempting to soothe her. Emily began to shiver again.

She heard Gregorio telling Arturo and another man to bring the stretcher from the church. Emily watched Gregorio head back into the alley, and saw him come out a few moments later with an old half-pint whiskey bottle in his hands. He sniffed at the bottle and said something to Atencio. Then Gregorio came over to where she sat. "Are you OK, Meleca?" he asked.

Emily swallowed. She couldn't get the alley stench out of

her mouth and nose. "I guess so," she replied after a moment. "What happened to him?"

"I'm not sure. He might have gotten some bad booze."

"I just saw Paulina in the store. She said Charley was drinking last week and got fired from his job."

Arturo and the other men returned with the stretcher. Emily watched as they brought the body out. It didn't look as though Charley had died a peaceful death. His neck was arched back, and in the bright sunshine Emily could see froth mixed with spittle and vomit around his mouth. Paulina tore away from her friends and rushed to the stretcher. The men set it down in front of her. She wailed uncontrollably, lying on the corpse, covering it with her tears. Finally the women were able to get her up and lead her away, and the men picked up their burden again. They spoke briefly together, and then Atencio and most of the other people there followed the sad procession down the street to Paulina's house.

"Do you need me to walk you back to the school?" Gregorio asked quietly.

She shook her head. "You must have things you need to do, with all of this. I should be all right. Maybe I could just have some water."

Gregorio nodded and went into the house behind them. He emerged a moment later with some water, in an old-fashioned pottery cup. Emily sipped for a few minutes. The water tasted of the native clay, dark and mysterious, and soothing. She started to feel a tad better.

"I'll be fine," she told Gregorio, and got up from the bench. "Thank them for the drink."

Gregorio nodded and headed off towards Paulina's house. There was nothing for Emily to do but head back home.

271

CHAPTER TWENTY-EIGHT

THEY BURIED CHARLEY in accordance with San Antonito custom. Emily knew that after a death, a wake was held that night, and the corpse interred the next day. When Gregorio stopped by later that evening to check on her, he told her that because Charley had been a young person, the burial would take place very early in the morning, just after sunrise. Emily chose not to attend. She hadn't known Charley well, and she had to teach school, of course. That couldn't be cancelled.

After the day's lessons ended, Emily once more walked up to the plaza, this time to give Paulina her condolences. She knew the ladies would have been cooking all day, feeding the neighbors who stopped by to pay their respects to the grief-stricken mother.

Emily also hoped to see Gregorio. It was unlikely, what

with all the activity surrounding the funeral, but maybe he'd have a chance to tell her what the professor had told him yesterday about the knife. The efforts to find Demetria and Gilbert seemed to have dwindled in the face of this new tragedy. She walked past Romero's store and down the narrow street that led to the house Paulina had shared with Charley. Now she would live there alone, Emily realized, as the reality of the death sank in.

The strong scents of cedar and juniper smoke, mixed with the aromas of simmering stew, wafted around to the front of the house from the backyard, where neighbor women were busy cooking large pots of posole and chile. Emily walked up to the front door and knocked.

"*Guw'aadzi*," a woman called. "Come in." Emily pushed the door open. A long table covered with a gingham-patterned oilcloth had been set up in the center of the room, with benches on either side. The benches were full of people who sat eating, there to support Paulina and honor the short life of her son.

Emily scanned the crowded room. She recognized Minguita and Albertina standing in the kitchen area. A Pendleton blanket, in faded shades of red, green, and grey, hung against one whitewashed wall, and a string of turquoise and shell beads hung from a nail on the wall opposite. Paulina sat in a chair in the corner, removed from the talk of the folks sitting at the table. Her eyes were red and she seemed to have shrunk overnight, almost like a collapsed balloon, Emily thought, as she made her way over to the bereaved woman.

"I am so very sorry," she said, reaching out and taking Paulina's hand in hers. Paulina held on tightly and burst into tears while Emily stood by, awkward, not quite knowing what to do. Minguita approached with a tin cup full of water. Paulina released Emily's hand and rubbed at her face, smearing the tears away. She tried to compose herself, and took the cup.

"I'm sorry, Miss Schwarz," she said after a sip of water. "You found him. You found my boy."

Emily nodded, close to tears herself. "I am so very, very sorry," she repeated. It seemed such a weak and paltry thing to say to someone who had just lost her only child.

"He was a good boy," Paulina said, and the tears started again.

"Come and eat, Miss Schwarz. *Ch'úpe.*" Minguita shepherded Emily towards the table. Somewhat gratefully, Emily sat down at one of the benches where a spot had opened up. She took a slice of the round, fresh-baked Pueblo oven bread and spooned some posole into her bowl. The man sitting next to her finished his meal and vacated his seat. Another man took his place.

"Hello, Miss Schwarz."

Emily looked over, a little surprised to see Gregorio helping himself to a slice of bread from the platter on the table. He'd made it here after all.

"Hello, Gregorio. How are you doing? This is very sad." Emily ate a spoonful of posole. The spicy red chile in the stew burned her tongue and she quickly took a bite of bread to soothe it.

"Yes." Gregorio went on in an undertone, his voice masked by the noise of general conversation. "We never did get a chance to speak with Charley again about what he might have seen that day, at work with Juan. Let's talk about it later, Meleca. I'll stop by." He helped himself to a stew made from garbanzo beans and beef, and then started speaking in Keres to Hilario, who sat across the table from him. Emily had no idea what they were saying.

She finished her stew and excused herself, managed to extricate herself from the bench without knocking into anyone, and carried her bowl to the kitchen area where Albertina stood washing dishes. Emily's offer to help dry them was politely refused, so she left Paulina's house and returned to the school. Restless, she killed some time by wiping down the already clean counters in the kitchen and brewing a pot of coffee. How long would it be before Gregorio showed up, and why did he want to talk with her now, when he'd been fending off her suggestions or humoring her ever since she discovered Juan's body by the Rio Chiquito?

She had just about settled down to grading some papers when she heard a knock at the door. She got up to answer it and saw Gregorio standing on the step.

"You'd better come in." Emily ushered him into the kitchen. She offered him a seat and a cup of coffee, got one for herself, and moved the pile of ungraded papers to one side.

"More arithmetic?" Gregorio raised one eyebrow. "Poor kids."

"Poor me." Emily laughed as she poured evaporated milk into her coffee and stirred it. "I'm the one that has to grade all of these. I've gotten behind, I'm afraid."

"Well, you've been busy," Gregorio said. "You haven't had time to grade papers, what with going up to Santa Fe on Saturday, and then nearly falling off a cliff on Sunday."

"And finding another dead body yesterday," Emily finished with a shudder.

Gregorio took a sip of his coffee.

"What happened to Charley?" Emily asked. "Do you think he just died from drinking?"

"He could have. Maybe he got some bad whiskey. But there was a little left in the bottle he had, and it didn't smell right to me. We sent it down to Bernalillo for testing."

"Testing for what?"

"Maybe somebody put something in the booze. His body looked like he'd had convulsions. People can have fits from drinking, but this looked different."

"But he's already buried."

"Yes."

"What if they find something at the lab?"

He didn't reply right away. "I told you we didn't get to speak to Charley about what he saw that day with Juan, when he was working for McKee," he said finally. "Suppose somebody didn't want him to tell us. Simple enough to get him drinking, and then give him some bad booze. Either way, we need to know."

"He wouldn't have noticed it tasted funny?"

"When you're drunk enough, you're not very discriminating."

Emily pushed her coffee cup away. The thought of poison put her off drinking it. "Who would do that to him? Here in San Antonito?"

"Whoever shot Juan, I guess. I don't know, Meleca. I don't know." He shrugged. "I did stop by the professor's again last night, after things settled down at Paulina's."

"And?"

"He showed me the knife. It could be Juan's, but he said he found it out in back country. I guess he could have; people lose

276

knives sometimes. His story was the same as what he told you; he said he told Gilbert about the fossils up by those old ruins, but he hasn't seen the boy."

"Where was he yesterday?"

"He claims he's found a new site, someplace off the road that goes up Bland Canyon, that he's investigating. I've never heard of much up that way, except for the old mining town. But who knows what will interest that guy."

Who knew, indeed. Emily sipped her coffee, suddenly feeling cold. The incident with the dropped—or thrown—fossil rock, the gunshots on Saturday as she and Mr. Shepherd followed Bateson's truck along the back roads, the elk horn knife . . . she was sure they all added up, but she couldn't say how. And Shepherd . . . who was he, really? She doubted he was procuring anything around here for the army. Was his real business the kind that got you shot at on a Saturday afternoon?

She glanced at Gregorio, who was finishing his coffee. If she voiced what was on her mind, he'd probably laugh at her. Then again, he'd come here to tell her about Charley and the bad whiskey, so maybe not. "I wonder what interests Mr. Shepherd," she said, feeling her way. "He keeps saying he's in procurement, but—"

Gregorio laughed. "Meleca, you ask too many questions. It's wartime. Even if he's not in procurement, do you think he'd tell you? Or me?"

Emily sighed. "No. I already asked him. He didn't say a word. Do you think he could be a spy?"

Gregorio laughed again. "What would he find to spy about here in San Antonito? No, Meleca, I think he's just hanging around because he wants to take you to the pictures."

Emily's cheeks flushed. She wasn't sure how she felt about that remark. It certainly was none of the *fiscal's* business, anyway. "Well, after Saturday, I don't think I'll be going anyplace with him again. I don't like being shot at."

"The guys serving in the Pacific are shot at every day."

"But not by drunks out shooting at rabbits," Emily snapped. "Supposedly."

Gregorio stood. "Well, I should hear something from the lab in Bernalillo in the next day or so. I'll let you know what they say."

"Thank you, Gregorio."

He left the schoolhouse, and Emily settled down with her arithmetic papers. She had, blessedly, finished the last one and was just about to head upstairs to bed when she heard another knock at the door. She remembered Gregorio's admonition for caution, but curiosity got the better of her. She peeked through the schoolroom window and saw headlights and the dark shape of a car outside. She walked down the hall and opened up.

Mr. Shepherd stood on the doorstep. "Hello, Miss Schwarz."

"Mr. Shepherd. What are you doing here? It's late."

"Sheriff Wilcox asked me to run something up to the alcalde and Gregorio."

"From the lab?" That was faster than she'd have expected, from what Gregorio had told her.

Shepherd nodded. "I heard you found the body. Again. You do tend to run into corpses, Miss Schwarz."

"It's not funny," Emily replied, her tone short. "Certainly not for Charley. Or his mother. Was the whiskey poisoned?"

Shepherd nodded. "Strychnine. Probably rat poison. Most people have some around, maybe in their sheds."

"And you stopped here to tell me that?" Emily's tone was frosty.

He shook his head. "Just to check up on you. I hope it's not too late." Shepherd glanced at his wristwatch. "I saw the light on and thought I'd take a chance. I thought you'd like to know about the strychnine."

"Wouldn't Charley have been able to taste it?"

"He'd been drinking since Thursday."

"That's what Paulina said."

"So he might not have noticed, and just kept on drinking."

"Gregorio thought so too." Emily paused. "I don't understand who would want to kill Charley. He seemed so harmless. Of course, there was that incident over in La Cañada."

Shepherd's eyes narrowed. "What was that?"

"Oh, a few weeks ago. Some boys got in a fight over a girl at the dance there. A Cañada boy was knifed, but not seriously hurt. I think Charley was involved. Ask Gregorio, he'll tell you about it all." Emily shifted her weight in the doorway.

"Well, that might be a motive."

"Maybe. You should be talking to Gregorio and not to me." She put her hand on the door, ready to shut it.

Shepherd stood his ground. "The weekend's coming up in a few days."

"And?"

"Well, I wondered if you'd like to try another little excursion."

"I don't think so."

"No shooting this time." Shepherd grinned. "We won't be near any rabbit hunters."

"Where were you thinking of going?" Emily asked, intrigued despite herself.

"Maybe a drive over to that abandoned mining town at Bland, the next canyon over. Have you ever been up there?" Emily shook her head, and Mr. Shepherd continued. "It looks like they just left yesterday, not thirty-five years ago. The guest register is still in the hotel. It's interesting. And then there's a little hike over a ridge to another abandoned mining town called Albemarle. It could be a nice little jaunt. There are some pretty views up there. Who knows what we'd find."

"I heard Professor Bateson went up to Bland recently," Emily said.

"Oh really? Who told you that?"

"Gregorio said something about it. Just what do you think you're going to find up there, Mr. Shepherd?" She thought of Demetria, and Gilbert, as soon as the words left her mouth. Could either of them be in Bland, or Albemarle—and if so, were they alive, or dead?

"I'm not sure. But we might want to take a look. And, like I said, it's a good little hike."

Her own fears, and impatience with whatever game he was playing, made her snappish. "Look, Mr. Shepherd, if you think Juan's death and these other disappearances have something to do with whatever it is you do, you should just tell us what it is."

"I can't do that. You'll just have to take it on trust."

"Why? After you got me shot at in Santa Fe? Those weren't

rabbit hunters! And what does Professor Bateson have to do with all of this?"

"I'm not sure," was all Shepherd would say. "Now, do you want to come on Saturday, or not?"

CHAPTER TWENTY-NINE

THE REST OF the week crawled by. Men from San Antonito kept up the search for Gilbert, although, since harvest season had arrived, some of their time went to harvesting the white corn and chiles that grew in the fields bordering the Rio Chiquito. The scent of green chiles and corn roasting in the hornos wafted through the air, drifting all the way down to the schoolhouse where the children let off steam during recess.

Emily couldn't sleep well. She dreamed Demetria appeared at the schoolhouse door, but when she went to greet her friend, Demetria's face turned into a skull that rolled off the steps of the schoolhouse and off down the road towards La Cañada. Another night she dreamed of Gilbert, a passenger in a car Emily drove. They sped away from a hail of bullets, Emily shouting at Gilbert to get down, but when she looked over to where he sat in the passenger seat the little boy had vanished. The nightmares and lack of sleep put Emily on edge. She lost patience with her students daily, despite her attempts not to, and the guilt she felt over that personal failure did little to improve things.

Emily told Gregorio about the planned trip to Bland—she had capitulated—and invited him to go along. On Saturday morning he arrived at the schoolhouse at 8:45, shortly before Shepherd's Dodge came down the road. Emily had made some peanut butter sandwiches, enough for all three of them, and crammed them, along with some apples and a large thermos of coffee, into her old rucksack. She was waiting on the stoop with Gregorio when the car pulled to a stop in front of the school.

Shepherd raised an eyebrow when he saw the *fiscal*. Shepherd had dressed casually today, wearing Levis, a sport shirt, and a battered old leather jacket instead of a suit. Gregorio wore his usual jeans and old shirt, with a bandana tied around his head in the traditional style.

"I thought I'd tag along," Gregorio said. "Since you're going over to Albemarle. We haven't searched over there for those two missing folks; it might be worth a look."

"Where's Professor Bateson?" Shepherd responded.

"At home. His truck's parked at his house, and the mule is there too, in the corral. He got back from some excavation or other last night. And one of his tires has gone totally flat. I noticed that this morning. Looks like there's a big rip in it. It will be hard to get that repaired, what with all the war shortages. I'm not sure what happened to it."

Emily thought she saw Shepherd almost crack a smile.

"Come on then," he said, and motioned towards the car.

Emily and Gregorio climbed into the Dodge, Emily in the front and Gregorio in the back, and Shepherd headed out of the canyon. They passed the turn to La Cañada and then took the right-hand turn up the road that eventually would get them to Bland.

"If we drive over to Bland, we can leave the car and then hike into Colle Canyon," Shepherd said. "That's where Albemarle is; it's even more of a ghost town than Bland. They blasted a road through there about forty years ago to connect the two mining areas—it cost $50,000 to construct the three-mile road. That was in 1900 dollars. Bland had three thousand folks living there. Hard to believe, now."

"You're quite the expert on this area," Emily observed. "How do you know all that?"

"Oh, I've picked up a lot of information over the years. The road up to Bland is pretty good, but we'll have to hike into Albemarle. Does that suit you both?"

They had no choice but to agree.

The road that led up to Bland was dusty and rutted. Shepherd did most of the talking. He told them that Bland had a hotel, a church, several saloons, a post office, and even a school. Now, no one lived in the town except one old woman who had grown up there during the town's heyday and refused to leave.

Bland Canyon narrowed rapidly as they drove in, the tufa rock walls towering above them. Piñon and ponderosa pines, along with some scrub, grew along the canyon floor. Emily felt hemmed in by the cliffs, claustrophobic. Gregorio didn't say too much either, and she wondered if he felt the same way.

They passed a large building and several sizeable round tubs on the right of the narrow canyon. "There's where the stamp mill was," Shepherd informed them. "They processed tons of ore here every week. Gold and silver. People said it made a horrible noise, they kept it going day and night."

"And the chemicals they used poisoned the creek," Gregorio put in from the back seat. "That's what my uncle Cipriano told me. He used to work up here some. He's gone now. He said he used to see dead animals all along the creek banks. Birds, skunks, coyotes, porcupines. Bobcats. He even saw a dead mountain lion once, and a bear cub. Died from drinking the water."

"You must know more than I do," Shepherd said. "I've just hiked around, and done a little reading. But I did hear they used cyanide and chlorine at the stamp mill. That's what poisoned the creek."

The thought of the dead bear cub struck Emily as unutterably sad. She let out a long sigh.

"That lady that lives up here, she's real nice," Gregorio said. "I met her a couple of times at the shop in La Cañada. She comes down there sometimes for groceries."

A bit before they reached the ghost town proper, Shepherd pulled the car over to one side of the increasingly narrow canyon. "Here's where the track heads off towards Albemarle. But let's look around here some first. It might be good to talk to Mrs. Jenks."

"Some of the men looked around up here for our missing folks a couple of weeks ago," Gregorio said. "But they never spoke with Mrs. Jenks."

They strolled along the narrow road that led up the canyon,

past the abandoned rooming house and other buildings. On the north end of the settlement was a house in better repair. It had been painted, at least within the past decade or so, and the roof looked intact. A screen door with some gingerbread filigree on it stood closed, but the interior door, Emily could see, was open. A rusty-tan colored dog slept on the porch, but roused and started to bark when he heard them approaching. A flowerpot with some geraniums in it provided another splash of color, and the faint scent of the geranium leaves wafted over to where Emily stood with her companions. Shepherd marched up to the screen door, despite the dog, and knocked.

"Silas! You quit that barking!" a voice called from the interior. "Who's there? I'm coming, hold on."

A few seconds later, a diminutive figure came into view. Effie Jenks wore a man's plaid shirt and dungarees, and looked to be in her sixties or thereabouts. Her tanned face was carved with wrinkles, as though she spent the majority of time outdoors. She opened the screen door, and Emily smelled cigarettes. "What do you folks want? What brings you up here?"

"Hi, Mrs. Jenks. We're just out for a hike, looking around," Shepherd said. "Thought we might head over towards Albemarle. Is it all right to leave the car here in Bland awhile?"

Mrs. Jenks nodded. "Welcome to do that. Who are you folks?"

"This is Gregorio, the *fiscal* over at San Antonito, and Miss Schwarz, who teaches school there. I'm Shepherd, just kind of along for the ride."

"I haven't seen you in quite a while, Mrs. Jenks," Gregorio put in. "Last time I think you were getting supplies at the Cañada Mercantile."

Effie's face brightened. "Oh yes, I do remember you now. Sorry about that. How've you been? How are things in San Antonito? Peaceful as ever?"

"Well, that's one reason we're here. A couple of folks have gone missing and we wanted to take a look around."

Effie sniffed. "Look all you want. Looking's free."

"You haven't noticed anything strange around here, have you? I hear Professor Bateson found some new archaeological site someplace nearby that he's all excited about. Do you know anything about that?"

Effie pulled a pack of cigarettes and a book of matches out of her shirt pocket, lit a cigarette, and took a puff.

"Any of you want a smoke? No?" She took another puff before continuing. "I've seen his old Ford a few times, down towards the stamp mill. But he hasn't come up here. If there were any ruins, I think the miners would have destroyed them fifty years ago. But look around if you want." She took another drag on her cigarette. "Why don't you just ask him about it?"

"He's kind of hard to pin down," Shepherd said.

Effie looked intently at Emily. "So you're the new teacher at the day school?"

"I've been there three years," Emily said.

"That makes you new," Effie replied. "Takes a lot longer than that to make a New Mexican out of you. Now me, I was born here. First baby born in Bland, in 1881. Left for a little while after the mines closed, and lived in Albuquerque, but after my husband died I came back up here. Still had the deed to my father's claim. No rent and I do as I please up here."

Emily smiled. "It sounds like a good life."

"Suits me just fine," Effie said, stubbing her cigarette out on the porch railing. "After you folks look around, stop back by here if you're thirsty."

They agreed they would and took their leave, heading back down the canyon. They stopped at a few places to look around, but there were no signs anyone had been there. The dust remained thick and undisturbed in the buildings, although many of them looked as though folks had walked out and just closed the door behind them, leaving bedsteads, chairs, tables, pots and pans. They poked around, but turned up nothing, and took a break back at the Dodge for some coffee from the thermos before they headed on foot up the track that led to Albemarle.

Deep ruts in the soft sandstone and pumice rock that formed the road made walking a challenge. Gregorio told them how teams of sixteen horses had pulled wagons full of equipment and ore up and down the steep grade, leaving these ruts as mementos of their efforts. "My uncle said he saw a contest once. One teamster bet another he could make it up the grade with only ten horses. Didn't work, the wagon flipped and all that ore spilled down the hillside. Had to put three of the horses down, too."

"What about the teamster?" Shepherd asked.

"Broke his leg, but they didn't shoot him."

Shepherd chuckled. "The mine only operated for a few years, right?"

"There was a bad accident," Gregorio said. "My uncle told me about it. Flooding in the main shaft. Five men from San Antonito died, drowned in the tunnel. And more from Cochiti. A few *jueros*, too. It cost too much to pump it out; they just closed it up and left it."

Emily shuddered. Winded from the climb, she didn't say anything, but kept scanning the road before her, concentrating on keeping going. She wondered how they had ever brought wagons of ore over this steep road. There didn't seem to be any place along it to look for Demetria and Gilbert, unless they had fallen into the canyon below, but Emily saw no sign of that, or anything else untoward. *Thank heavens.*

"There are some other shafts further down Colle Canyon from that main shaft, aren't there?" Shepherd asked Gregorio. "We should explore some of them." Gregorio nodded.

They reached the top and found themselves on a narrow mesa. The road cut across the mesa top, dotted with ponderosa pines and chamisa sage. Emily filled her lungs, savoring the fresh, piney scent. All three stopped to rest a moment, catch their breath, and enjoy the view.

Emily slipped off her rucksack and set it down on a large lichen encrusted boulder. Off to the southwest, she could see the open plains near the Rio Grande, with the Sandia Mountains, near Albuquerque, purple in the background. Behind them, to the north, the Jemez Mountains loomed, the round mass of Saint Peter's Dome off to their right a few miles away. Emily knew the canyons on either side of the mesa hid Bland and Albemarle, and one canyon over lay San Antonito Pueblo. But you surely couldn't see any of those places from here, just this wonderful, expansive vista.

A hawk circled above them, dark against the brilliant blue of the sky. A few clouds were starting to form over the Sandias, close to forty miles away. Emily inhaled deeply, the beauty of the day soothing her distressed spirit. Inconceivable that, somewhere in the Pacific, her brother Tim fought for his life, and it seemed equally unbelievable that in the midst of all this her friend and her pupil were still missing.

She let out a long breath.

"What is it?" Shepherd asked.

"Where do you think we should search?" she countered, not answering his question.

"Down in the canyon from the ghost town. Nobody's checked those old shafts," Shepherd replied. Gregorio nodded in agreement.

Emily sighed again. "We'd better get going, then." She picked up her rucksack and started down the trail. They quickly crossed the mesa and the trail descended, the original road partly obscured by some fallen boulders.

"That must have been some rock fall," Emily commented, picking her way over one of the big stones.

"Watch where you put your hands and where you step," Shepherd cautioned. "There might be some rattlesnakes around, soaking up the sun."

"They're not mean, Meleca, don't worry," Gregorio said, seeing her alarm. "Just let them be if you see one, and you'll be fine."

Emily took a deep breath to steady herself and scanned the rocks with vigilance, her enjoyment of the hike considerably diminished.

CHAPTER THIRTY

THE TRIO MADE their way down to the bottom. The ruins of the little ghost town of Albemarle were not as well preserved as the town of Bland. A few dilapidated wooden structures, weathered boards collapsing in on themselves like the abandoned toys of some giant child, were all that remained from the mine's heyday forty years earlier.

"You know, they actually had to blast holes in the canyon walls to build some of these shanties, the canyon is so narrow," Shepherd told them.

Gregorio nodded. "It's an out of the way place. Nobody comes here. Just coyotes. There shouldn't be any footprints to speak of."

"Just ghosts," Emily said with a nervous laugh. When Shepherd gave her a blank look, she added, "It's a ghost town, after all."

"Could be," Gregorio said. "Some of the bodies in that mine accident were never recovered. They just left them there, closed up the shaft."

Emily's smile faded. She felt foolish, embarrassed to have made that joke.

"The town never came back from that bad accident," Shepherd told her. "These mines have been abandoned a long time, longer than Bland."

"Well, let's start looking around," Gregorio said.

"Miss Schwarz and I can take the right side of the canyon, if you want to search the left," Shepherd suggested. The *fiscal* nodded, and the hunt began.

It didn't take long to inspect the ruined shacks. About eight shanties still stood in the town; the others had long ago collapsed into piles of weathered lumber. The contrast between the bright sun outside and the dark interior of the first house they entered blinded Emily at first. They saw nothing there to speak of—just an old-fashioned, rusted iron bedstead. An old tin washbasin, battered and chipped, lay discarded on the floor, and a small dust-covered iron stove stood in one corner. Worthless items, or things too heavy to cart out of the canyon when the settlement had been abandoned. They could see no sign that anyone had been in the building in the last forty years, although pungent smells made Emily suspect that some skunks had a den somewhere nearby. The next house, derelict and deserted, told the same story.

The three of them soon reconvened, hot, grimy and dusty from their explorations. Gregorio also had found nothing of importance in the houses he'd searched. "What about the shafts?" Shepherd asked him as they stood together in the sunshine.

"They're further down the canyon, most of them."

"Is there a road that comes up Colle Canyon?" Emily inquired.

Gregorio shook his head. "Nope. Just a few trails. Maybe a burro could get through, or a horse, but nothing fit for autos."

They walked southeast down the canyon, leaving the ruined village behind them. The early afternoon sun beat down on the canyon, as they walked, making the rocks and boulders shimmer in the dry heat.

"There," Shepherd said, stopping. "That looks like a shaft."

They saw a small dark opening, a hole blasted into the canyon wall. In front of the space lay a few old boards and a broken pickax handle. At least, Emily guessed that's what it was. The weathered piece of wood lay forlornly on the rocks that littered the earth outside the entrance to the mine.

"Let's take a look," Shepherd said. "Get your flashlights out."

Emily balked. "I think I might wait out here while you men look around."

"Are you getting tired, Miss Schwarz?"

"Maybe just a little. And it's hot." *And I'll bet there are snakes in there.*

"Well, just yell if you need us. Sit here in the shade, drink some water," Gregorio said, thrusting a canteen in her hand. "We won't be long."

Emily nodded and settled herself on a large sandstone boulder conveniently located under the shade of a ponderosa pine. The resinous scent of the bark relaxed her, and she lazed awhile. She could hear, distantly, the muted voices of Gregorio and Shepherd wafting out of the shaft.

Twenty minutes or so went by. The men had not returned. Emily decided to stretch her legs. She stood, and just a bit further down the trail, saw another dark opening amid the rocks at the base of the cliff. It could be another shaft.

My goodness, if they investigate every shaft, we'll be here a long time. She might as well reconnoiter. Taking her canteen and flashlight, she walked the short distance to the cliff.

The rocky approach to the abandoned shaft told Emily no stories. Dusty tailings in front of the gaping entrance to the old mining claim were littered with a few weathered wooden beams, similar to the previous site. Emily gingerly approached the mouth of the shaft and peered into the darkness. The tunnel descended at a fairly steep slope, but it looked to be walkable. Emily hesitated. Maybe it would be better to wait for Gregorio and Mr. Shepherd.

A rush of movement, seen from the corner of one eye, startled Emily. She swung around in time to spot a lizard, several inches long with a bright azure stripe down its tail, scurry across the brown earth and vanish under a rock. Emily took a deep breath. Only a lizard. The afternoon sun still baked the canyon; it was no wonder the little tyke sought some shade. He looked pretty, though, with that blue stripe.

Not quite ready to explore the mine shaft on her own, Emily picked up a stick and poked at the rock hiding the lizard, flipping the stone over. The lizard fled to the shelter of some other slabs, but Emily spied something else that drove the lizard out of her mind. Lying among the grey rocks was a splash of bright red. The stub of a red pencil, identical to the ones she used to grade her papers.

The broken-off piece lay a few feet from the opening to

the old mine. Where had it come from? It certainly hadn't fallen from the pocket of her dungarees. Abruptly, Emily remembered Gilbert's dinosaur drawings. He'd embellished them with red pencil.

Emily stuck her head into the shaft. "Gilbert? Gilbert! Are you in there?"

Nobody replied. Emily flicked her flashlight on and stepped into the mine, shining the light down the track.

"Gilbert!" Her voice rose. "Gilbert! It's Miss Schwarz!"

Only silence answered.

Emily bit her lip. He had to have been here. Or maybe still was. She doubted miners forty years back had been in the habit of using red Ticonderoga pencils.

"Gilbert!" She moved a few more feet into the shaft, shining the flashlight in front of her. After the first few feet, the height of the tunnel's rocky walls shortened and she had to stoop down. The daylight behind her, from the mouth of the mine, suddenly looked very far away.

"Gilbert! Are you there? Answer me!" He couldn't be dead. He just couldn't be. She stopped a moment, listening, and thought she heard a rock fall, farther down the shaft. And was that a muffled voice?

"Gilbert! Is that you?"

Another rock clattered against the walls of the tunnel. Another cry, louder this time, from far back in the mine. Then silence.

Emily made her way down the shaft until she came to a fork. One path went upwards a little. The other, on the left, descended. "Gilbert! Where are you?"

Emily's call was rewarded with another cry. She breathed

a sigh of relief and headed up the right-hand fork. She had to scramble over a little ledge to get there. She shone the flashlight beam down the shaft, and went from walking to nearly crawling as the tunnel narrowed. A fourth cry reached her. Her heart pounded, the sound thrumming in her ears. Could she have heard two voices?

Emboldened, flooded with fear and a hope she hardly dared admit to, Emily inched up a passage that widened into a small open gallery. Her nostrils widened as she inhaled the odors of old excrement and urine, sweat and fear, wafting over the hard dusty metallic smell of the rock tunnel. She shone her light around the tiny chamber, roughly hewn from the bedrock. And there, trussed like chickens, she saw two figures. One small, one larger. Gilbert. And Demetria.

"Over here, Emily. We're over here."

Emily recognized Demetria's cracked voice, and rushed to the corner of the gallery where her friend and her pupil were. Next to them, the flashlight picked out a couple of empty canteens lying on their sides, and an old puddle of wax where perhaps a candle had burned down. Demetria and Gilbert sat propped up against the cavern wall, their hands and feet tied with rope. Emily threw the flashlight down and fumbled in the darkness for her father's old Boy Scout pocketknife. "You're alive! Both of you! Thank God!"

"Just get us untied," Demetria whispered. "Please." She looked away from the flashlight beam, not meeting Emily's gaze. Gilbert stared at Emily, his eyes big and dark.

Emily sawed at the ropes that bound her friend's hands,

and then the ones around her ankles. Then the two women worked to set Gilbert free.

"I thought you were both dead," Emily said, and started sobbing. Gilbert cried too as the three of them collapsed into each other's arms.

After a minute, Emily got hold of herself. She wiped her eyes, retrieved her canteen, and handed it to Demetria, who gave it to Gilbert.

"Just little sips, Gilbert. Not too fast," Demetria cautioned the boy, then continued speaking to him in Keres. Still crying, Gilbert managed to drink a little, and at length his sobs quieted.

"We've got to get you both out of here. Can you walk?" Emily asked, after the two had almost emptied the canteen.

"Most likely yes," Demetria said. "Nothing's broken."

"What about you, Gilbert?"

Gilbert nodded, his face solemn.

She looked at Demetria again. "How long have you been here?"

"I don't know," Demetria said. "A long time. Then he brought Gilbert. Don't shine that light in my eyes, please. It's too bright."

"Who? Who did this?"

Demetria shivered. "Let's get out of this place. Then I'll tell you. Come on, Gilbert. We're going home."

Emily helped them both to their feet, and they started off. The trek out seemed to take forever, although paradoxically Emily thought the distance didn't seem as great as it had been when she made her way in. The journey must have seemed a lot longer to Demetria, who leaned heavily against Emily as they headed out. Once the tunnel opened up a bit, Emily picked

Gilbert up and carried him, his weight comforting against her chest. The faint glimmer of afternoon sky heartened her; it meant they'd reached the agonizing final stretch of tunnel.

As they neared the mouth of the mine shaft, Emily could hear Mr. Shepherd and Gregorio calling. "In here! We're in here," she answered.

They emerged, Demetria and Gilbert shielding their eyes from the sunlight. Emily saw Gregorio and Shepherd approaching and called out to them.

"Oh my God," Shepherd said, while Gregorio muttered something in Keres that sounded like a swear word.

The two men hurried up to them. "Cover your eyes with this," Shepherd said, offering a handkerchief to Demetria. "Just for a while. Until your eyes adjust." Demetria nodded, took the cloth, and began speaking rapidly in Keres to Gregorio, tears running down her cheeks.

Emily sat on a pile of tailings, holding Gilbert tightly in her lap. "It's OK, Gilbert, you're safe now." The boy still hadn't spoken, his eyes shut against the glare. "It's over," she repeated. "You're going home."

Shepherd fished in his pocket and finally came up with a Hershey's bar. "Are you hungry, Gilbert?" he said, unwrapping the candy and holding it out towards the boy. "Here, just eat a little."

Gilbert's eyes opened and his expression brightened. He reached for the bar and took a bite. "He left us some food," he said, after he swallowed the chocolate. "But then all the food was gone. And the water, too. I got hungry. And thirsty." He looked around and then lowered his eyes. "There wasn't any place to pee," he said softly.

Emily and Shepherd exchanged glances. "Who was that, son?" Mr. Shepherd asked. "Who brought you here?"

"The dinosaur guy," Gilbert said. "Professor Bateson."

CHAPTER THIRTY-ONE

"WHEN I WENT to see Professor Bateson that night, to ask him about Lorenzo, he refused to answer my questions," Demetria explained. "When I turned to leave, I guess he must have hit me from behind. The next thing I knew, I was tied up on the floor of his old truck."

She lifted the handkerchief from her eyes, winced, and shaded them again. "He drove up to Bland, and then marched me over here to Albemarle, to that shaft where you found me. At first he just tied my ankles, and he left me some food and water. And a candle, but that burned out pretty quick. Then, I don't know how much longer it was, he brought Gilbert." Demetria took another long drink of water from the canteen Gregorio had given her, and shifted her weight on the boulder she sat on. "How long have I been here?"

"Today's the 25th of September," Emily answered. "Over two and a half weeks since you disappeared. And Gilbert's been gone for over a week, almost two."

"We looked for you, Demetria," Gregorio said. "And for Gilbert. Miss Schwarz looked for you, too."

"I guess you didn't look in the right place," Demetria said dryly. "Until today."

"And how did the dinosaur man get ahold of you, Gilbert?" Emily asked. Gilbert still sat on her lap, but he was starting to get wiggly, which, Emily hoped, meant he was feeling better.

"Well, the sheriff and his men went and got the gun we found." Gilbert was more talkative now. "And the deputy left me at the village. I was supposed to go to school, but I saw Anasazi, and stopped to play with him. Professor Bateson said he'd give me a ride to school, but then he said he'd show me the dinosaurs first. And then he brought me here. He said the dinosaurs were in the mine, but there weren't any dinosaurs. Just Auntie Demetria. And then he tied us up and left us."

"He just left you both in the cave? Why? That makes no sense," Emily fumed.

"He didn't tell me anything," Demetria answered. "Just said he didn't want to kill a woman or child, but I think he wouldn't have minded if we starved to death in there." She shivered. "He brought us food and water once or twice but he hasn't been back in a long time."

"The man must be insane," Emily said. "Why would he do this?"

Demetria shook her head. "I don't know. I just want to go home."

"After all the kindness we've shown that man over the

years." Gregorio's voice, usually so calm, was angrier than Emily had ever heard it.

Shepherd looked grim. "We'll get to the bottom of this. I can guarantee that professor won't be troubling you folks in San Antonito again."

Emily didn't understand exactly what Shepherd meant, but her relief at finding Demetria and Gilbert alive overshadowed her questions. The two had finished the peanut butter sandwiches and apples from Emily's rucksack, and the tortilla Gregorio had brought with him. "Are you sure you can hike out of here?" Emily asked her friend.

Demetria nodded, her face grim. "I can do whatever it takes. I need to get home."

After resting a little longer, the party set out for Bland. Gregorio carried Gilbert the whole way. Their pace was slow, but determined. Emily felt vast relief when she glimpsed Shepherd's Dodge through the pine trees at the end of the Albemarle road. They piled in and drove off, leaving Bland and Albemarle behind them.

Emily went with Gregorio and Mr. Shepherd as they returned Gilbert to his family. The joy on Juliana's face warmed her heart. Atencio hugged Emily with relief and she felt tears on his cheek. Demetria went to her mother's; Gregorio insisted on it, saying she should not be alone, and escorted her over. Demetria did not argue with him. After that, Gregorio, Shepherd, and Emily stood by the Dodge.

"Mr. Shepherd, what's going on?" Emily demanded. "Why would the professor do all this?"

Shepherd looked uncomfortable. "I think Bateson could be spying for the Nazis."

"What?" The crusty professor didn't match Emily's image of a spy.

Gregorio chuckled, a breathy disbelieving sound. "He's been living here, part time at least, for years. Since before there were Nazis, just about."

Shepherd wasn't smiling. "He goes away, doesn't he? Spends part of his time at his university? Goes to academic conferences? I think the Nazis recruited him there. Part of their fifth column. I'm pretty sure he shot Juan, probably because of whatever Juan saw up in the mountains that day. And got Charley drinking, and then gave him poisoned whiskey before he could tell people what Juan had told him. We're just lucky Bateson still had a scruple or two left, and balked at killing women and children."

"And we're lucky you're nosy, Meleca," Gregorio added. "You found them in that shaft."

"You would have found them. Eventually," Emily said, but the *fiscal*'s words gave her a little thrill of pride.

"What about Bateson?" Gregorio asked Shepherd.

"Let's see if we can take him into custody now, although jurisdiction could be tricky. We can call Sheriff Wilcox, and can easily get him on kidnapping, then leave the spying charges to the army." His gaze shifted to Emily. "But you should go back to the schoolhouse, Miss Schwarz. There could be trouble."

Emily argued, but the men, implacable, refused to let her win. Eventually she had to agree, and Mr. Shepherd drove her back to the schoolhouse on his way to call the sheriff from the phone at the Cañada Mercantile. Gregorio went to round up a few San Antonito men to watch Bateson's house. They would wait to make the arrest until Wilcox arrived.

"I still can't believe it of Professor Bateson," Emily exclaimed to Mr. Shepherd as he drove the short distance down the road. "He's a bore, true, but a spy? And spying on what? I wouldn't have thought there was anything up in these mountains to be worth it."

Shepherd didn't enlighten her. They pulled up in front of the schoolhouse. "Miss Schwarz, do you want me to see you inside?"

"That's all right, Mr. Shepherd. I'll be fine. You'd better get that call in to Sheriff Wilcox."

She got out and headed for the school. Shepherd drove off. Emily unlocked the front door, breathing a sigh of relief. Gilbert was home. Demetria was safe. It was over.

Emily headed towards the kitchen, thinking maybe a cup of coffee would help her settle. She found a little in the pot, left over from breakfast. Making coffee that morning now seemed as though it had happened years ago, although just a few hours had gone by. She reheated the brew and laced her cup liberally with evaporated milk and sugar. Suppertime had passed, but Emily felt far too tired to cook. She decided to just drink her coffee and relax, maybe give a little attention to that novel she'd never finished reading. Still, questions lingered in her mind as she sipped her coffee.

Emily kept one ear peeled while she drank, listening for the sound of Sheriff Wilcox's car. Once he arrived the men could go and arrest Professor Bateson for murder and kidnapping.

But why would Bateson shoot Juan, poison Charley, and abduct Demetria and Gilbert? And if he had done all that, then surely the incident at the cliff ruins, when the fossil rock had hit her on her downward climb, was also intentional. She had been lucky. She drained her cup and let her gaze drift to the window. She found it difficult to envision the old, boring professor as a Nazi spy and a murderer. It seemed preposterous. And surely there was nothing to spy on in the Jemez Mountains.

The sound of the sheriff's car heading up towards the plaza broke the comfortable silence of the autumn night. Emily sighed with relief and took her coffee cup over to the sink, rinsed it out and got the coffee pot ready for tomorrow morning. Mass tomorrow—finally there was something to be thankful for. She was sure Atencio and Juliana felt the same way. And Demetria. And Agapita.

A noise from the schoolroom, some kind of scraping sound, made her start. On edge, she went to the schoolroom and poked her head in. One of the shades had rolled up and banged against the glass. She must have forgotten to pull it down yesterday after school ended. Emily crossed the room to the windows and adjusted the blind. Darkness had settled outside, and Emily decided to make it an early night. She'd find out what happened with Professor Bateson tomorrow, at Mass. Hopefully they already had him in custody, although she hadn't heard any cars heading back down the road to Bernalillo.

She made her way upstairs, put on her pajamas, blew out the kerosene lamp, and crawled thankfully into bed. Her muscles ached from the hiking she had done. She would sleep soundly tonight.

CHAPTER
THIRTY-TWO

EMILY COULDN'T GET air. She struggled to breathe. A heavy hand clamped down on her mouth, suffocating her with pressure. She smelled nervous sweat and couldn't cry out.

She opened her eyes. In the light of a half-moon shining through the window, a dark shape loomed over her, the hand over her mouth preventing her from screaming. She thrashed around, fighting to sit upright.

"That's it, Miss Schwarz. Take your time waking up, but don't make a sound."

Emily recognized Professor Bateson's voice. He lifted his hand from her mouth. Emily gasped for air, her lungs burning. She tried to move away but Bateson roughly grabbed her arms and held them tightly against her struggles.

"Professor, what are you doing?" Emily demanded, her breath fast and short.

"You're coming with me." The professor let go of her arms, and Emily felt the pressure of a gun against her temple. "Put some clothes on. Now."

Professor Bateson kept the gun trained on her while Emily forced dungarees on over her pajama pants and donned the shirt she'd worn yesterday.

"Boots, too, Miss Schwarz. Please." The politeness of the request almost made Emily break out in hysterical laughter. Her fingers felt like ice as she fumbled with the buttons on her blouse and the laces of her hiking shoes.

"Where are we going?"

"Just for a nice hike."

"How did you get in?"

"You left a window unlocked in the kitchen. Climbing in was easy enough. I waited most of the night outside, until after you dropped off to sleep."

"Why are you doing this?"

Bateson shrugged. "You've seen too much."

"But Demetria and Gilbert—they'll tell others it was you. They already have. There's no point—"

"Let's go now, Miss Schwarz. Down the stairs and out the back door."

Emily felt the cold iron barrel of the gun against her back. Bateson gagged her with her own bandana, the cloth filling her mouth. They descended the stairs and left the schoolhouse. Outside, the moon hung low in the west but a faint light in the eastern sky showed it was a bit before dawn.

"Hurry." Bateson led Emily behind the schoolhouse, down towards the river. The dark bulk of the cottonwood where she had found Juan's body loomed before them, and she wondered if Bateson was going to shoot her and leave her there as well. But he didn't turn that way. Instead, he headed upstream, pushing Emily before him.

September had been arid. With the lack of rain, the riverbed was largely dry sand. Just a trickle of water made its way down the canyon, leaving them plenty of room to walk.

They'll see our prints, Emily thought. *If anybody knows to look.*

"Stop," Bateson ordered. He tied Emily's hands together in front of her and held on to the other end of the rope, pulling her along behind him as he started up the streambed of the Rio Chiquito. The river ran down a little gulley. There wasn't much chance of anyone hearing them, this time of the night. Even if Emily had been able to shout. If she hadn't been gagged.

She tasted the cotton cloth filling her dry mouth and tried to breathe through her nose as she followed her captor up the riverbed. Her heart thudded, and Bateson tugged the rope so hard she nearly fell. "Keep moving," he ordered, turning around to point the gun at her again. Her stomach lurched. She complied.

They continued up the ravine. On the left-hand side of the bank, Emily saw the dark bulks of the village houses, but no lights or signs of activity. She wondered what had happened to Gregorio, Shepherd, and the other men hoping to catch Bateson. How had the professor slipped away? Were they still waiting at his house to arrest him?

"This way, now." Bateson dragged her up the bank on the right, to a small trail that ran along the arroyo. "Did you know the Navajos and many other tribes transported their captives like this?" the professor said over his shoulder in an oddly conversational tone as he pulled Emily along behind him. "It's surprisingly effective."

Emily couldn't reply, of course. She concentrated on breathing and trying to keep up as Bateson led the way up a narrow track sequestered amid the chamisa sage and juniper trees that grew on this side of the canyon. They had left the village behind, Emily figured, and then they crossed the river, just a tiny trickle here, and headed down another trail. Emily realized it was the track the professor had taken her on before, the trail that led to the cliff dwellings. Was he going to shoot her there?

They finally stopped. Bateson removed the gag, and Emily fought for breath, panic subsiding a little as her lungs filled with air.

"Where are you taking me?"

The anthropologist didn't answer, just handed her a battered canteen. Emily gratefully took a swallow.

"You know they'll find you. Whatever you're doing, this won't help." Emily tried to make believe she was lecturing one of her sixth graders, but she heard her own voice quaver.

"As I said. You've seen too much."

Emily didn't know what the man was talking about. "We found Demetria. And Gilbert. Everyone knows you kidnapped them. Killing me won't change that, it will just make things worse for you."

"This isn't about that."

"What, then?" Emily thought frantically. "You shot Juan, and poisoned Charley, didn't you? Why?"

"I had to. They'd seen too much, like you have."

"Seen what? I don't know what you're talking about."

Maybe she could convince him to let her go. He hadn't harmed Demetria, after all. Emily wrestled with her fear as she tried to reason with him. "Look, Professor Bateson, I don't know what it is you think I've seen, or know. And if I don't know, I can't tell anyone, can I?"

She knew she sounded close to begging, but she didn't care. Not really. She didn't want to die here. "I'm just a schoolteacher."

"One who speaks German."

"What's that got to do with anything? My father's parents came from Germany. I'm certainly not at all fluent. I just know a few words—"

"You know enough."

Despite her fear, Emily forced herself to think. What had she seen? Or what did Bateson think she'd seen?

"You found Juan's body," he said. "And Charley's too, from what I hear. And you found Demetria, and Gilbert. You know everything, don't you?"

Emily, mystified, didn't reply. Bateson apparently took her silence for consent. He abruptly began to move again, dragging her along. They reached the spot Emily had visited with him before, and when they got to the cliff, he untied her hands.

"Climb," he ordered. Emily felt the hard steel of the gun barrel as Bateson jammed it against her back. "Now." He shoved her closer to the cliff face. "You remember the way."

Emily wasn't at all sure that she did, but the loaded revolver proved an incentive, and some physical memory in her body recalled the handholds and toe grips. She began to climb, hoping her panicked muscles would obey. Miraculously, they did. Her heart pounded and her strength seemed almost superhuman. Emily grasped the hand- and toeholds and lifted herself up the rock ladder carved into the cliff, constantly aware of Bateson right below her, his revolver aimed at her as she climbed. The professor scaled the cliff with seemingly effortless agility, using one hand to lever himself up the rocks while he kept the gun trained on her with the other.

Finally, Emily reached the alcove in the cliff and pulled herself onto the ledge.

"Get in there." Half of him visible at the top of the cliff, Bateson motioned towards the back of the alcove with the gun. Emily complied, glad the climb was over. She looked out for a moment over the canyon, at the shapes of trees emerging in the grey light of early dawn. The view was quickly obscured as Bateson clambered up onto the ledge beside her.

"Now," the professor said, his gun still trained on her. "You're going to have a very tragic accident."

"Professor Bateson," Emily pleaded, "I don't understand. What did I see? Surely if I don't know anything, I don't need to die for it—"

"I've seen you everywhere," Bateson accused her. "In Santa Fe. At La Fonda, the day I brought you up for groceries. You weren't shopping; you were meeting up with that government agent. Spying on me. Trying to find out what I was working on. And after they burned that puppet. Then with that government man again, at La Fonda. They have you trailing me, don't they?"

"No—"

"You can't fool me. When did they recruit you?"

"Nobody recruited me for anything. I don't have the faintest idea what you're talking about!"

"You're a spy. They sent you down here to keep an eye on me, to prevent me—"

"Who? Prevent you from what? Professor, I'm not any kind of secret agent." Emily would have laughed at the thought if she hadn't been so terrified. "I'm a schoolteacher. I moved out here to get away from Racine. Who would I be spying for? Why would I be following you?"

"To stop me."

"From doing what?"

"There are things happening in the Jemez. But you know all about that."

"No, no, I don't—"

"You know what I've been doing, and who my contact is in Santa Fe. You probably sent that kid to ask me about the fossils. I'll bet you thought he could get information out of me. About my surveillance objectives." Bateson laughed. "A kid like that."

"I don't know what you're talking about. Surveillance of what? As far as I know, you're investigating early Indian ruins. I don't know about anything else." Furious that this man had endangered Gilbert, and kidnapped her, Emily forgot to appease him, and accused him instead. "But Juan knew, and Charley knew, didn't they? What was it they knew? Why did they have to die?"

"McKee Construction is working for the government. Don't pretend you don't know that perfectly well. I'm here to learn what they're working on."

"For whom? Is someone paying you? Who is it?"

Bateson remained silent.

"The Nazis," Emily said slowly. She remembered the books

in Bateson's living room. Books in German. And what Mr. Shepherd had said only the evening before. "So you're really working for the Nazis—spying against your own country. But why?"

He sounded bitter when he replied. "All the university research money's going to science these days. The war effort. Physics. Chemistry. The university cut my funding. Said it wasn't important. At a conference a few years ago in Berlin I met Ernst Schäfer. He's led expeditions for the Reich to Central Asia, Tibet most recently, in 1939. He was curious about the natives here and what connection they might have with Central Asian peoples. Both the natives here and the Tibetans and Hindus use the swastika, for example."

Emily shuddered, but Bateson didn't seem to notice. He kept talking.

"Schäfer was looking for scholars, anthropologists and archaeologists in particular. The Germans understand research; they know how important it is. They respect it. Schäfer wondered if there could be any connection between the powers of Tibetan shamans and those of the American native tribes. Himmler was curious about it, there was money."

He's insane, Emily thought. *The man is mad. And a traitor.* As Bateson continued speaking, she inched away from him on the narrow cliff. But his hands held the gun steady, trained on her.

"The Ahnenerbe, their society for the study of primeval ideas, was just planning ahead when they first recruited me. Looking towards the day the Reich would be victorious against the United States. At first I simply kept them informed on my research, and they paid me. You can't understand," Bateson said, looking directly at Emily, "how expensive funding excavations can be."

"I'm sure I don't," Emily responded in a tight tone. She had to escape. She hoped she could keep him talking long enough to pull it off.

"Since my funding got cut, the money's gotten crucial. I must continue my work, you see."

Emily didn't see. Not at all. "What about our soldiers?" she demanded. "My brother's fighting in this war. So is Demetria's husband, Joe, your old research assistant. And so many others, young boys barely in their twenties, fighting for our way of life. For freedom. The Nazis only want power. What you're doing is treason. Don't you care?"

The professor scoffed, still holding the revolver steady. "I didn't do much at first. Certainly nothing treasonous. The Germans just wanted to be kept informed of what I learned about tribal culture. Ceremonial information. The Ahnenerbe was interested. Nothing that would put your brother at risk, I assure you. But that changed about a year ago." Bateson smiled, and the gun sank a little. "The pay improved."

"All your trips to the back country—you're not looking for ruins at all, are you? What are you searching for, professor?"

Bateson bristled and raised the gun again. Emily backed closer to the alcove wall, afraid she had pushed him too far.

"There's better radio reception in the peaks. It's hard, tucked away in this little canyon. What I'm looking for is really none of your business, young lady, but there's a lot of construction happening up past the Valle Grande. On the Pajarito Plateau. A secret city, if you will, dedicated to scientific research. The fools think they can harness the power of the atom. But they won't beat the Reich."

He paused for a moment, looking at Emily and the ruins surrounding her. "And, incidentally, I have found quite a few proto-Puebloan sites. I'll explore them in more depth later on—once I'm paid for my other observations and Hitler has triumphed. I'll be rewarded, and have time to pursue my studies."

What an arrogant, selfish man he was. "That . . . secret city they're building. Is that why you shot Juan? And killed Charley, too?"

"Yes. Juan saw me up there, one day while I was reconnoitering. I was careless. So he had to go. It was too easy, really. I saw him coming back from the canyon that Sunday, and asked him to walk with me down the river. The foolish boy agreed. As for Charley, he was going to talk. The woman and the boy, too. I couldn't be sure what they knew. I left them in the mine, so nature could take its course, but then you found them. That was regrettable."

"Not for them, it wasn't," Emily snapped, her body shaking with anger.

"I hate to kill a woman," the professor continued, giving no sign he'd heard her. "Still, one does what one must. And now I feel our little conference is just about over; don't you agree, Miss Schwarz? I certainly wouldn't want to bore you."

Bateson stepped closer to her. Emily edged further into the corner between the back of the alcove and the ancient adobe wall, built by the original inhabitants of the canyon so many years ago. She didn't quite know what she was going to do, but she wouldn't give up without some kind of fight. She reached behind her. Her fingers curled around one of the rocks that formed the top course of the abandoned masonry, a large, flat one. Brick shaped. Heavy enough to do some damage, she hoped. Her heart hammered, and a buzzing filled her ears.

The professor stood with his back to the canyon, his gun aimed at her. "Now, Miss Schwarz, I'm going to have to ask you to step closer to the ledge."

Emily tightened her grip on the rock. "No," she said, her voice parched. "No." The buzzing grew louder.

She briefly shifted her eyes from the professor and saw a coiled diamondback, its tail lifted in warning. Not too big, maybe two feet long. Young. And irritated. The snake sat between her and Bateson, close to the rear wall of the alcove, where the rock started to curve towards the front of the cliff. Apparently the rattler hadn't taken kindly to having its early morning rest disturbed.

Emily inched along the masonry wall, which put her a little nearer to Bateson, but a little further from the rattler. "Don't come any closer," she said, wrenching the stone from the masonry and brandishing it in front of her. "Don't touch me."

"Miss Schwarz, cooperate. Please. I certainly don't want to shoot you," the professor replied. "That wouldn't fit my plans at all. You're going to have a tragic fall, on an ill-advised early morning climb. So foolish, to go clambering around these cliffs by yourself."

Bateson lunged towards Emily. The diamondback, startled and irate, struck hard at Bateson.

"What the devil—" Bateson reached down towards his leg. The snake struck a second time, sinking its fangs deep into Bateson's hand, and the professor staggered backwards.

Emily hurled the rock. It caught the professor's shoulder,

knocking him off balance. He lurched backward, away from the snake, away from Emily, and off the cliff. Into empty space.

The snake uncoiled and slithered across the floor of the alcove. Ignoring Emily, it disappeared through a gap in the masonry. Emily cautiously edged away from the wall. Where Bateson had loomed just seconds ago, she now saw the pale dawn sky and the pine trees that grew on the opposite side of the canyon.

She reached the rim of the cliff and peered down. The professor lay face up at the base, sprawled on some rough rocks and boulders. His head was at an odd angle, and blood ran from his ear, pooling beneath the back of his skull. His eyes gazed unseeing into the morning sky above.

Sick and shivering, Emily somehow managed the climb down. Once she reached solid ground, she gasped for air, taking big gulps, before she dared approach Bateson. She didn't need to hurry. He looked to be far past any human help.

CHAPTER
THIRTY-THREE

EMILY COVERED THE professor's face with the bandana he'd used to gag her, and then began picking her way down the track to the main trail that led to San Antonito. The sun crested the canyon walls, sending a shaft of light onto the path before her. A good omen, Emily thought as she journeyed back towards the village, but her legs and arms still trembled.

She'd hoped to find Gregorio or Shepherd at the professor's house, but all was quiet there. The men must have given up watching the house once they realized Bateson had absconded. Emily heard a whine, and Anasazi emerged from behind the house and sniffed curiously at her fingers, as though he smelled his master. Emily patted the dog on his rusty brown head. She wondered how you would tell a dog that their owner had died, but Anasazi seemed happy enough to follow Emily as she made her way into the main part of the pueblo. She saw cars parked at Atencio's house—the sheriff's car, and Shepherd's Dodge, so she headed over there.

The village looked quiet, so early in the morning. Emily saw Ben and Arturo leave their houses and walk down the road towards Cañada, going to catch the bus McKee Construction provided their workers. She wondered again what the men were building, up in the Jemez. Something important, to be working on Sunday. *A secret city*. Emily shuddered as she thought about Bateson and his spying. Spying that had cost two lives, and so nearly had cost three more, including her own.

She neared the alcalde's house. She smelled the welcome scent of coffee and heard voices inside. She knocked, but didn't wait for an answer before pushing the door open. Inside, Emily saw Gregorio, Atencio, Mr. Shepherd and Sheriff Wilcox, along with a couple of deputies, sitting at the long table drinking coffee. None of the men looked as though they had slept. A map of the pueblo and surrounding area lay open on the flowered tablecloth. The men stopped talking and stared at Emily where she stood in the doorway.

"You're up early, Meleca," Gregorio said, his voice jovial at first. He stopped, looking puzzled as he took in her disheveled appearance. "Is everything all right? What's happened?"

"Bateson's dead." Outside the door Anasazi whined, almost as though he understood her. "I need to sit down."

"Here, Miss Schwarz." Sheriff Wilcox stood up from the chair he had been sitting in. He brought the chair over and Emily collapsed onto it. Somebody handed her a cup of coffee. Black and bitter, it revived her, and she found she could begin to answer the questions that flew at her.

"He got into the schoolhouse sometime last night, and he kidnapped me. He took me back to that ruin. The one on the cliffs. He planned to kill me, but a rattlesnake bit him. He fell. He's dead. He was spying for the Nazis. He thought I was an agent, spying on him."

Emily began to tremble violently, and Juliana brought a woolen sabana and wrapped it around her. Emily hugged the wrap tightly about her shoulders, thankful for the warmth.

Sheriff Wilcox began giving orders, then left along with Gregorio and the deputies to see about retrieving the corpse. Shepherd left as well, to search Bateson's house. Emily remained, sitting at the table with Atencio and Juliana. She sipped at her second cup of coffee gratefully and finally stopped shaking. "How is Gilbert?" she asked Juliana.

"He's still asleep. I think he'll be OK. Kids are strong. He'll have lots of stories to tell his friends." Juliana smiled, and Emily saw the relief in her eyes. "Do you want to see him?"

Emily nodded and Juliana led the way to the other room in the house, where Gilbert slept heavily on an old cast iron bedstead, covered with a thick Pendleton blanket. Emily smiled, imagining the hubbub when Gilbert returned to school. He certainly would have a lot of tales to tell. Tears filled her eyes as she looked at Juliana. There so easily could have been a much less happy ending.

The women heard the front door open and shut, and footsteps across the floor. Mr. Shepherd had returned.

"What did you find?" Emily demanded.

"A shortwave radio set, for one thing," Shepherd replied. "And some codes hidden in his papers. German journals. Some strange metaphysical books. There will be a more thorough search once we get some specialists down here. For now, that place is off limits." He looked sternly at Emily and Juliana. "This is all classified. You don't know anything about it."

Emily and Juliana nodded.

"And cancel school for tomorrow. You'll have things to do, Miss Schwarz."

"I'll tell the alcalde," Juliana said. "He'll take care of that."

Gregorio and the sheriff came back a short while later, and conferred with Mr. Shepherd. Emily roused herself and helped Juliana with the dishes. Arrangements would be made to transport the professor's corpse to the Army Air Base in Albuquerque. The sheriff gave Emily a ride back to the schoolhouse, and she gratefully went inside. Despite the warmth of the morning, she made sure all the windows and doors were locked.

After a long, hot bath, in which she scrubbed and scrubbed herself, Emily wandered the schoolhouse, restless. She couldn't relax with the events of the previous night haunting her. Finally, to distract herself, she ransacked the old books in the storage room upstairs, searching for the book of Pueblo legends Gregorio had mentioned. Her quest proved successful. She found a slim volume, *Indian Tales from San Antonito and Cochiti*, by Ruth Benedict. Then, exhausted, Emily crawled into bed and slept.

The next morning, just past dawn, a black car stopped in front of the San Antonito schoolhouse. Anasazi, who had shown up at the school the afternoon before and seemed to have taken up residence on the porch, wagged his tail at Mr.

Shepherd as he came up and knocked on the door. Sergeant O'Toole and another man wearing an army uniform, who bore the insignia of a colonel, accompanied Shepherd.

"Miss Schwarz, we need to take you in for a debriefing."

They took her down to Albuquerque, to an office in a Quonset hut at the air base. Shepherd left her there with Sergeant O'Toole, who led her into a small conference room. Several other men, most in uniform, already sat around the table, waiting for her. They grilled Emily, asking her to go over, in tedious and lengthy detail, everything that had happened. Particularly all that Bateson had told her at the ruins. After some hours of questioning, the major in charge strictly cautioned her not to speak of what had transpired. Not to anyone. Emily signed papers swearing she would comply, and they released her.

She emerged into the bright September daylight, sighing, and blinking like an owl. Shepherd's Dodge was parked in front of the building. In another minute, Shepherd himself emerged from the Quonset hut. Emily wasn't sure who he'd been speaking with, or if he'd been debriefed. She guessed she couldn't ask, either.

He smiled at her. "I'm taking you to lunch, Miss Schwarz." Emily readily agreed. Now that her debriefing was completed, she felt ravenous.

They left the base, and Shepherd drove down Central Avenue to the old part of town. He brought her to La Placita, a Mexican restaurant located in a thick-walled adobe hacienda dating from the 1700s. After a lunch of enchiladas, they sat finishing *natillas* and coffee, carefully not speaking of the events of the weekend.

"Mr. Shepherd," Emily finally said, as she laid her spoon down on the linen tablecloth, "there is one thing I do have to ask you."

"I can't tell you what I do," Shepherd said. "You know that."

Emily almost laughed at his defensiveness. "I'm well aware you're in procurement. You already told me. But there's one thing you never have disclosed, Mr. Shepherd. What's your first name?"

He flushed under his tan, surprising Emily. "It can't be that bad," she said, smiling. "What is it?"

"Benjamin," he finally replied. "Benjamin Franklin Shepherd. But I go by Frank. I hate Benjamin."

"It's not so bad. It's very patriotic."

"Yes, that's what my mother thought," he replied, looking down at the table, and then he asked the waitress for the check.

They left the restaurant and headed towards the Dodge, Emily glancing at the shops on the plaza, until something in a toy shop window caught her eye. She halted suddenly. "Wait here," she commanded, and darted into the shop.

The clerk retrieved the set of brass dinosaur models from the window and boxed them up. Emily paid the bill, took the box, and left the shop. She found Shepherd waiting, bemused, seated on a bench on the grassy plaza across from the old adobe San Felipe de Neri Church.

"What was that all about?" he asked.

"Just something for Gilbert," she answered as they walked back to the car.

Shepherd drove her back to San Antonito. Anasazi, who apparently hadn't moved since Emily's departure that morning, looked up and thumped his tail in greeting as the car pulled up in front of the schoolhouse.

"It looks like you've got yourself a watchdog, Miss Schwarz," Shepherd said as he opened the car door for her.

Emily nodded. "I guess you're right."

"Probably a good idea. You never know what can happen." He paused, and gave her a long look. "I'll see you later, Emily."

Emily smiled, and went inside to put on the coffeepot as Shepherd drove away. She found some scraps for Anasazi and took them out to him, along with a pan of water. She looked up towards the plaza, and heard Flossie headed down the road. That horse's gait was unmistakable. Maybe Gregorio would like to stop in for a cup of coffee. And if not, she had plenty of papers to grade.

Author's Note

The Pueblo of San Antonito is completely fictional, a product of my imagination. There was no settlement in that tiny valley along a small tributary of the Rio Grande. The area did become a successful apple orchard after WWII until the devastating 2011 Las Conchas forest fire, and the flash floods following the fires, destroyed the orchard. The Cochiti tribe now owns the land.

The town of La Cañada did exist but now is in ruins. It was settled in the 1700s by Spanish settlers and abandoned by the mid-20th century. Peña Blanca, further down the Rio Grande, remains on the highway that runs between the town of Cochiti Lake and Santo Domingo Pueblo.

My fictional tribe speaks Keres, one of the nine indigenous languages still spoken in New Mexico. Keres is spoken by seven Native American tribes in New Mexico: Cochiti, Santo Domingo, San Felipe, Santa Ana, Zia, Acoma, and Laguna. There are several different dialects. For spelling reference I used the dictionary of Acoma Queres words available online.

During the late 1900s and early 20th century there was significant silver mining in the Jemez, but the mines closed by 1916. The ghost towns of Bland and Albemarle, connected by the Albemarle Road, stood until the horrendous Las Conchas fire burned Bland to the ground in 2011. At its height Bland possessed two banks, a newspaper, hotel, stock exchange, opera house, several saloons and stores, a school, a church, and a population of about two thousand people. Effie Jenks purchased the abandoned town in the 1940s. A Harvey girl, Effie worked in Santa Fe for many years at La Fonda and, after her retirement, lived in Bland until her death in the 1980s. Another woman, Helen Blount, who had moved to Bland with her family at age eight, also returned to Bland as an adult and lived there until her death in 2004.

The secret construction in the Jemez Mountains was, of course, Los Alamos, the secret city on Pajarito Mesa and home of the Manhattan Project. J. Robert Oppenheimer and General Groves visited the Los Alamos Ranch School, a small private boys' school on the mesa, in November of 1942 and deemed the site perfect for the army's needs. The school was closed and construction began in January of 1943. The first scientists arrived on the site in April of 1943. The McKee Construction Company handled a lot of the construction at Los Alamos, and did hire Pueblo natives for their crews although, of course, no one from San Antonito.

To my knowledge there were no Nazi spies apprehended in New Mexico during WWII but there were Soviet spies embedded in the Los Alamos community, the most notable being Klaus Fuchs, a mild-mannered young physicist who worked in Los Alamos from 1944 to 1946. In 1950 he confessed he had been spying for the Soviets for years. During his time in Los Alamos, Fuchs regularly handed secrets over to an American courier, Harry Gold, at the Castillo Street Bridge, just off the Santa Fe Plaza.

The anthropologist Ruth Benedict visited the Southwest in the late 1920s and published the 1931 volume, *Tales of the Cochiti Indians.*

ACKNOWLEDGEMENTS

This book would never have existed without Salvador Romero. You have enriched my life immeasurably. Your love, spirit, and generosity, along with that of your family and your people, continually amaze me. I have learned so much from you. Thank you for everything, honey.

My sincere thanks goes to Diane Piron-Gelman, my editor, whose keen eye and insights helped shape this book. Mateo Romero, Maya Gchachu, Robin Dunlap, Donna Lake, and Amanda McCabe read the draft manuscript and their feedback considerably strengthened my vision of San Antonito, and of Emily. Mateo in particular corrected my many misconceptions about firearms! Thanks to all of you, so much.

Thanks to Anne Hillerman, for her encouragement throughout the lengthy process of writing this book, which goes back several years ago to a discussion we had one day at Keshi. Thank you also for taking time out of your busy schedule to read the completed book and provide such a wonderful quote.

The team at E. M. Tippetts book design did their usual fabulous job of formatting, and Linda Caldwell of that crew created the deliciously ominous cover. You are all a pleasure to work with.

It is difficult, when writing about another culture, to give an accurate portrayal. The Pueblo of San Antonito is totally fictitious, and is seen through the eyes of my own mentally created Anglo school-teacher, Emily. Any errors or misrepresentations of New Mexican Pueblo culture are totally my own responsibility.

My thanks go out to everyone involved in producing, distributing, and otherwise making this book, and all books, available to readers. And my greatest appreciation goes to my readers. As I've said before, all this labor would be pointless without you.